W9-CND-301

MARGARET'S PEACE

MARGARET'S PEACE

LINDA HALL

Five Star
Unity, Maine

Five Star Christian Fiction.
Published in conjunction with Multnomah Publishers, Inc.

Cover courtesy of Multnomah Publishers, Inc.

December 1998
Standard Print Hardcover Edition.

Five Star Standard Print Christian Fiction Series.

The text of this edition is unabridged.

Set in 11 pt. Plantin by Al Chase.

Printed in the United States on permanent paper.

Library of Congress Cataloging in Publication Data

Hall, Linda, 1950–
    Margaret's peace / Linda Hall.
        p.   cm.
    ISBN 0-7862-1652-2 (hc : alk. paper)
    1. Ghosts — Maine — Fiction.   I. Title.
PS3558.A3698M37 1998b
813′.54—dc21   98-39760

Dedicated to the memory of my mother-in-law,
Eiliene Torrie Hall, 1910–1989.
A woman of peace.

The author gratefully acknowledges the support of the
New Brunswick Department of Municipalities,
Culture and Housing in the writing of this book.

PROLOGUE

DATE: SEPTEMBER 14, 1973
POLICE DEPARTMENT: BOSUNS HARBOR, MAINE
CASE NUMBER: 73-13-00568
INVESTIGATING OFFICER: DET. JONATHAN SMITH

This officer was called to #2 Coffins Reach Road at 7:04 P.M. on September 13, 1973, after a call came in from Mrs. Ruth Godwish of #3 Coffins Reach Road that her son Bradley Godwish had come upon a disturbing scene at that location. I left immediately with two other officers, Deputy Christian Rikken and Deputy Earl Kelley. When we arrived, Mrs. Ruth Godwish and her son Bradley Godwish were waiting for us outside of the house on #2 Coffins Reach Road. Bradley Godwish appeared in a state of great agitation. It seemed he could not answer our questions and his mother spoke for him. She told us that her son had gone next door to visit Norma Ann Ochs, who was alone in the house while her parents, Mitchell and Hannah Ochs, were in Bangor on a shopping trip.

According to Ruth Godwish, Bradley returned home greatly disturbed, stating that Norma Ann was sleeping on the ground and would not wake up. Mrs. Godwish then went outside to find Norma Ann lying on the ground in front of the Ochs home.

After hearing her statement, we examined the victim. A white female in her early teens, she was lying facedown at the bottom of the front porch. Deputy Kelley examined the victim. There was no pulse. From the awkward position of the limbs, it appeared the victim had fallen from a height. Next to the victim were several boards. I looked up and surmised that the victim had fallen from the third-story porch. The several slats missing from that porch seemed to match the slats lying next to the victim.

Deputy Rikken stayed with the still distraught Bradley Godwish and his mother, while Deputy Kelley and I entered the house. On the third floor of the three-story house, we examined the small porch from where the victim had presumably fallen. We took pictures and drew diagrams. We searched the entire house. There was no evidence of disturbance in any of the rooms.

After taking photographs and measurements, we proceeded outside to talk to Bradley and his mother again. Bradley appeared "slow" and his mother told us that Bradley was "mentally retarded."

After questioning the parents, who were called home from Bangor, we learned that Norma Ann often spent time on the widow's walk despite being cautioned by her father that it was unsafe. The victim's sister, Margaret Ochs (age 10), was staying with her aunt and uncle, Sylvia and Monty Ochs, at the time of the incident. We also questioned Mitchell Ochs' three brothers Leo, Monty, and Clark and wives Dolly, Sylvia, and Pat and have found nothing to indicate foul play.

The death, therefore, has been ruled accidental. At the request of the family, no autopsy was performed.

Signed,
Det. Jonathan Smith

ONE

Margaret thought she heard music, a quiet theme. A flute perhaps, or a recorder. And under it, a low tone, a drone — one note, but not discordant. Comforting, somehow; welcoming — two notes in harmony. She stood on the expansive wooden porch, weathered now by decades of neglect, and listened. But the melody had faded. In its place were only the surging sea and the cackling wind, which banged shutters and whipped her cotton coat around her bare legs.

She lifted her face to the wind and stared into it. The elements were not fearsome to her. They would be companion to her and she would heal here. In the distance, toward the point, Margaret saw a lone figure also gazing out to sea. Intent, like herself. The person, a woman, Margaret presumed, because a filmy white shawl was wrapped loosely about her, looked almost ghostlike in the fading light. Margaret looked at her for several seconds, but the woman did not move.

She fumbled in her purse for the key the realtor had given her and unlocked the front door. She entered and stood in the high-ceilinged foyer, remembering. To her right was the dark oak deacon's bench where she and her childhood friends had plunked down their buckets of crabs and rocks collected along the seafront. Above it hung the imposing gilt-edged mirror with the long crack snaking along the bottom, still there after all these years. Behind her was the wooden coat tree where all manner of jackets, sun hats, and towels were flung.

The place seemed bigger somehow than when she was a

child, and this surprised her. Normally when one returns, things are smaller, rooms are shrunken, garden patches minimal, even people more diminished. That wasn't happening now. And Margaret stood and wondered.

The house had not been rented out for the past two summers, the very peevish realtor had said when she finally located Margaret in Fredericton, New Brunswick, Canada, and what, pray tell, did Margaret plan on doing with the place now that her father had been dead and gone for more than a year? If she wanted to sell it, well, it needed work, not the least of which was a good paint job, inside and out, but it's not unmarketable, far from it; if she wanted to sell it, it was prime waterfront property and yes, Brown & Brown would be pleased to broker it for her; a number of potential buyers had already expressed interest in the old place, but she really ought to act fast, papers had to be signed, they couldn't proceed, not legally, without Margaret's signature, but faxing was okay and did Margaret want Brown & Brown to fax the papers up to Fredericton?

All of this was told to Margaret as she sat in her darkened kitchen in her home in Fredericton, a home that death had invaded and that Robin and Aislin and God had left.

"I'll come," she said quietly into the receiver.

"You'll come?"

"I'll come. I'll live there."

"You'll *live* here?"

"I'll live there."

"Well then," said the realtor.

Margaret flicked on the light switch and two bulbs in the multibulbed chandelier flickered dusky light into the hall.

She left her two suitcases by the stairs and walked into the spacious and at one time gracious living room. It was sparsely furnished now, and what furniture was there was shrouded in white drop cloths, every surface laid with a fine ashen sheen. She ran a finger along the wooden mantel, and dust smudged the air around it like smoke.

The feeling that the house had grown, was growing still, made her proceed carefully, cautiously. Almost she could hear it expanding about her, a barren tomb about to break open.

Margaret forced her mind to return to a safe time when clusters of children chased through the rooms; her friends — Valerie, Donna, Jane, Bradley, and Norma Ann — clad in bathing suits and rubber flip-flops, traipsing into the kitchen, her mother scooping out ice-cream cones and warning them not to spill a drop, not one drop, in the living room. That was the place she remembered, not this musty construction that creaked in the wind like an old woman. Perhaps coming here was a mistake, one of those impromptu, spontaneous decisions that Margaret was so famous for.

"Honey, I'm home," she called into the silence.

The edges of the room took her voice and threw it back at her, mocking her. The tall bay windows, the hardwood floors, the chandeliers, the fireplace that easily held five-foot logs made Margaret suddenly angry that her father had pronounced it "defiled," making, according to her father, further habitation of it by Ochses impossible.

She would be the first Ochs to live here for twenty-five years. But then, she wasn't really an Ochs. Not anymore. Her last name was now Collinwood. It was a softer name and it suited her better.

Margaret Collinwood, the Artist.

A Unique Show by Margaret Collinwood, Fredericton's Visual Artist Extraordinaire.

Collinwood Studio by the Sea.

No matter what happened between her and Robin, she

11

would never go back to being an Ochs. Robin had given her his name and she had no intention of giving it back.

The thing that had defiled this house was known in the family only as The Tragedy, a black vertical mark in the horizontal line that was their lives. Time was measured henceforth in terms of it.

A year after The Tragedy we did thus and such.

Three Christmases after The Tragedy, didn't we go here or there?

Hannah died, when was it? Two years after The Tragedy. Poor thing. Just couldn't cope.

After The Tragedy, her father had enlisted the agency of Brown & Brown in Bangor, Maine, to rent the house to sun-seeking, beachcombing tourists. The rent money from the summer covered upkeep during the winter. Why her father hadn't sold the place years ago was beyond anyone's guess.

Margaret walked through the dining room and entered the kitchen. The wood stove stood in the center of the north wall, just like she remembered; and to its left a range, modern when Margaret was a girl with its four burners and large capacity easy-clean oven. Now it was rickety and age-spotted. A white fridge stood beside it — the kind with a small inside freezer that holds, at most, two gray metal ice cube trays and a cardboard rectangle of ice cream. And there was the table, oak and heavy, standing firm on thick legs. This was the place where every evening she watched her older sister, face scrunched into concentration, writing in her schoolbooks, the windows behind dark with the night, the sea foaming.

There were even a few dishes in the cupboards, Margaret noted. She took one down. This heavy white crockery was not her mother's. The dishes of her childhood were a pale cream with fragile blue flowers around the rims. She put the saucer in the sink and wandered through the rest of the downstairs. The bathroom seemed to be working. The taps ran clear. The toilet flushed. A solid house it was, she thought. She would stay here. She had no illusions about "fixing the place up" — hanging calico prints at the windows, covering the love seats with chintz, and filling every corner and tabletop with country-printed bric-a-brac of the sort found in every craft store from Coffins Reach to Fredericton. No, she would let the house stay pretty much the way it was, solid and worn. It, like her, needed rest, not some hasty swathing in printed fabric.

She carried her suitcases up the stairs and stopped at the large landing, which faced the sea. This room, hallway really, would serve nicely as her studio, she thought. The light was good. She undid the latch on the window and with a few heavy shoves, managed to push it partway up. Down in front of her the ocean was dense and murky in the September half-light, the expanse of ground leading to the sea overgrown with fingers of pale grass and drifts of sand against rock.

Her mother kept a rock garden there, Margaret remembered, and would spend long hours tending wildflowers, forcing them to grow in the "right places," huddled against rocks and shells that she would gather by the apronful along the beach. But the rocks rebelled, the flowers would not be tamed. Every year her creations were destroyed by winter's tides and storms.

To her right, hidden now by the lay of the land, was the small bungalow where Bradley and his mother lived. Her friend Bradley, or rather her sister's friend Bradley was happily included in all their childish games.

She leaned her head out of the window and looked up. It was still there, directly above her: the underside of the small porch, or widow's walk as it was called in these old houses, the place where wives in long dresses and wool capes would look out at the sea for the tall sailing ships that would bring their husbands home, the place from which her sister fell to her death. Her father had forbidden them to go out there. It's dangerous, unsafe, he would proclaim. "Let me fix it first." But he never did.

Margaret had stayed off the fragile porch, but not Norma Ann. It was always her favorite place, a place for playing with Barbie dolls; and as she grew, a place for writing in her diaries and listening to her transistor radio.

Margaret forced her gaze away from the porch and looked instead far up the point to the north. The little cabin was still there, she noted, hardly larger than a boathouse and constructed of old barn boards. It was home to a bachelor named Rusty MacGregor when she was young; it looked abandoned now, an isolated shell.

The woman was still there, Margaret noticed — standing motionless near the water line, the long ends of her gossamer shawl billowing around her, becoming wet with seawater as the tide surged.

Margaret watched her. For a long time she watched the woman. How long would she stand there, still as stone? Margaret waited — five minutes, seven minutes, ten minutes — but the woman did not move. It became a grade school staring game. Who will blink first? Who will be the first to burst out giggling?

In the end, Margaret lost. It was the phone that jangled her to reality. Margaret finally located the source of the sound. Downstairs in the kitchen, on the sideboard, was the only phone in the house, a black one with a dial. Margaret answered it on the sixth ring.

"Well, hello there! I was just about to hang up thinking maybe you hadn't gotten there yet." It was the realtor from Brown & Brown. Margaret didn't even know her name —

14

Maizie or Mavis, something like that. She never gave it when she called. She was one of those people who just assumed you knew who she was.

"I just got in."

"Well, I'm glad. As you can tell, we turned on the electricity and hooked up the phone for you. The number's printed right there on the dial for you."

"Thank you."

"We also had the place cleaned up, about, oh a month or so ago, so you should find it in not too bad shape —"

"Thank you," Margaret said again.

"— top to bottom. And now that we know where to send the bill, we'll get it over to you. We tried sending it to your uncles, but they refused to pay, can you imagine? It's not like they don't have the money, none of them, but I'm happy that we were finally able to locate you."

Her uncles. Margaret had been out of touch with this side of her family for such a long, long time. Uncles, aunts, cousins, second cousins once and twice removed, cousins of cousins, nieces, nephews, nephews of nephews; the fabric of the family Ochs, interwoven like wool along the Maine coastline.

"Fine," was all she said.

"You should be aware, Margaret dear, that no matter what your uncles say, you, my dear, have clear and secure title to that house, so don't let any of them push you around or come hounding you for part of the profits from the sale. Let me know when you want to start the paperwork. I had a potential buyer walk in yesterday, right off the street, Margaret, right off the street! We really should get moving on this, summer's almost over, dear."

Dear? Margaret had never even met this woman.

"But before you list the place it might be a wise idea to get a set of dead bolt locks on both doors."

Margaret ran her fingers through her short hair. "What's wrong with the locks?"

"Oh, they're fine, Margaret dear, but they're the very same locks that have been on the place for the last thirty years, and what with summer renters and such, one can't be too careful, especially now that we're beginning to get all the riffraff, antique hunters and the like from Boston and New York coming through here all summer long."

After she hung up, Margaret sighed and went out to her car. She looked toward the point, but the woman had finally gone.

The first two things she carted in from her car were her portable CD player and her coffeemaker, which she took straight to the kitchen. She placed a Sarah McLachlan in the CD player, filled her coffeemaker with bottles of Poland spring water left over from her trip, and scooped in a generous amount of dark roast. Coffee was one of Margaret's vices. "They're going to have coffee in heaven," was her pronouncement to anyone who commented on her addiction to the bean.

Five more loads from the car and she was finished. Just in time, she thought, gazing at the rain-laden sky. There was a certain relief when she had shut and locked the front door for the last time.

A good number of the boxes she had brought with her contained art supplies. Most of her finished artwork she had left in Fredericton with her friend Joyce. The last time she had seen Joyce the two of them had sat together in Joyce's little living room on George Street, sipping red wine from slender glasses. Margaret had stood in the front window, her back to her friend. A brown paper cup from a Tim Horton's coffee shop skipped along the sidewalk in the wind.

"I have to leave, Joyce. I have to get out of here. I have to find things. I have to go."

"I think you're making a mistake. But I'll stand by you. You know I will," Joyce had said.

Now, Margaret poured fresh coffee into a white ceramic mug, crack-lined but clean enough, and drank it black while she hummed along to her CD. Then she swept the floor with an ancient but serviceable broom she found next to the back door. Her own place. This wouldn't be so bad.

Robin would like it here, she thought. He liked old houses and rocky beaches and the smell of the sea. He liked sailboats and sand castles and watching seabirds up close. Gentle, sweet, laughing Robin. He, of all people, didn't deserve what had happened.

She stopped, feeling suddenly very weary. She poured herself a second cup of coffee and sat for several minutes until the CD stopped and the world fell silent.

TWO

Her optimism was fading. The adventure of driving down the coast of Maine alone in her car, stopping when she wanted, buying chocolate bars and filling up her thermos with coffee whenever she wanted to, following her progress on a map laid out on the passenger seat — all of that was part of "the adventure." Now that she had reached her destination — a dusty, overgrown wooden-slat house that needed painting — she felt aimless and detached. The kitchen was passably clean, but she felt reluctant to move on. For several minutes she sat in the silent kitchen and drank another cup of coffee. And then another.

She forced herself to move her scrub bucket, mop, and rags into the dining room. She turned on the radio searching for voices, something with people talking to each other. Music was too mournful. All music was. She needed to be near human voices, needed to be reminded that people still talked to each other, that communication was possible. The voice she found was a deep male voice, a preacher, going on about faith as if it were a tangible thing that one kept in little boxes. She lifted the drop cloths from the furniture and shook them out the front door, then folded them and laid them on the deacon's bench.

"Have faith, don't lose it . . ." he intoned.

If he was right, if faith had to be kept and watched, if that were the case, then she had been careless. One day she had come into her bedroom to find that the little lacquered box with the mustard seed in glass on the lid was gone. She had lost her faith.

She was wiping the window ledges now with a sopping rag. Chips of paint flaked up in her rag and she had to keep rinsing it in the bucket, now a horrid mess of dirt and paint flecks.

From the window she could see only a part of the Godwish house, set back as it was. She wondered if Ruth Godwish still lived there. She would be in her sixties by now. And Bradley. Where was he? She hoped he had found happiness. She hoped he was living on his own, or maybe in a group home. But not too far from the beach. He loved the beach.

It started to rain, and swollen drops splattered against the window. Her restlessness increased. She turned off the radio preacher and remembered that she had one remaining box of CDs under the front seat of her car. Maybe there'd be something there she could listen to. She flung the foul washcloth into the bucket and pulled on her jacket and shoes and went outside. She had retrieved her CDs and was about to shut and lock her car door when she was aware of a presence behind her. She turned.

Standing there was a woman, a puckish old woman with a tiny wrinkled face who wore a rubberized yellow raincoat.

"Oh!" Margaret said, startled.

The woman's head was bare, and her gray hair was thick and long and scraggy. Her skin was leathery and deeply creviced. Her prominent ears gave her a troll-like, almost humorous appearance. She was carrying a metal bucket filled with something that looked like seaweed or green moss.

"Mrs. Godwish?" Margaret asked.

The woman peered at her though tiny marble eyes. "It's going to storm. It's going to be a bad one."

"It sure looks that way, yes."

"There've been bad ones before. Bad storms along this coast. The portents of evil." She spoke slowly and Margaret had to strain to listen over the wind.

The woman pointed at Margaret's house. "The old Ochs house."

"It's my house now," Margaret said.

"Your house? Mitchell Ochs sold it to you? He made a vow that the house would not be sold. Until . . ."

"I'm Margaret, his daughter. I lived here when I was young."

The woman moved toward her and peered at Margaret intently, up and down, as though she were examining something under a microscope. She announced, "You are Hannah. Come back from the dead. Hannah. Come back to seek vengeance. Finally."

"No, I'm Margaret, Hannah's daughter."

"But Margaret is dead."

"Margaret is not dead, Mrs. Godwish. *I'm* Margaret."

"They told me that Margaret was dead. Like Norma Ann."

Margaret smiled. "Well, you can tell them, whoever they are, that the rumors of my death have been greatly exaggerated."

Mrs. Godwish continued to stare, bucket in hand. It was raining harder now, and Margaret ran her hand back through her hair.

"I assumed that Margaret was dead too. Murdered. Just like Norma Ann."

Margaret blinked at the woman. Murdered? She recalled asking her mother once, "Is Mrs. Godwish, you know, normal?" To which her mother replied, "None of us is completely normal, sweetie, and maybe having a son like poor Bradley has put her over the edge just a bit."

The wind was picking up and a gust of it lifted the long ends of Mrs. Godwish's clumpy, tangled hair like a sheet. She peered down into the contents of her bucket.

"I should keep my herbs dry," she said.

"How is Bradley, Mrs. Godwish?"

"He is ill. I'm making him a healing tea."

"Oh, so he still lives with you?"

"Where else would he live? This is his home."

"Why don't both of you come over sometime?" Margaret offered. "It would be nice to see Bradley again."

The woman looked surprised. "That would be impossible. Bradley doesn't go out much."

"That's too bad. Maybe I could come over and visit *him*."

The woman shook her head. "Bradley doesn't see people. Not too much. Only his workshop people. It will upset him that you have returned."

"Workshop people?"

"They come for him in a bus and he goes to a workshop." The old woman looked into the sky. "I don't like this. There's evil around. Like the last time. Just like the last time. Bradley was blamed for it, you know."

"For what?"

"For the murder of Norma Ann. You know that, surely. People said he was the father."

"The father?"

"Her murderer."

"Mrs. Godwish, my sister wasn't murdered. She fell off the widow's walk and died accidentally."

The woman clucked her tongue. Without another word she turned and hobbled home across the stones and sand to the back door of her house, her yellow raincoat billowing behind her.

Margaret hugged her box of CDs and went inside her kitchen, closing and locking the door against the storm. The woman was crazy. She was as crazy as they come . . . off her rocker . . . not all there . . . a few sandwiches short of a picnic

. . . porch light on, nobody home. Remembered phrases from her childhood came back to her. Years ago she had been strange, but to talk of *murder?* Margaret forced her mind back to the time of her sister's death.

After a hurried and private graveside funeral, the family left Coffins Reach and moved into a square, squat rental house on a busy street in Bangor, and no one was allowed to talk about Norma Ann ever again. All traces of her clothing and possessions were removed. A strange pall settled over the Ochs home then. It was as if the feisty, pretty Norma Ann, the sister Margaret worshiped and adored and modeled her whole life after, had never existed. Margaret's mother took to her bed and died two years later.

At the University of Maine, Margaret met Robin Collinwood, an education student from Canada. After graduation, they married and left for Canada. Margaret was grateful to move to New Brunswick, grateful to leave her silent father, grateful to be welcomed into Robin's extended family of gentle, hardworking, God-fearing people. As the years passed, the decades gone, the memory of Norma Ann — spunky, pretty, pony-tailed, athletic — had faded.

THREE

The following morning at 6:30, Margaret rose and pulled on her sweats and went for a walk. It had been an unsettling night. After the strange conversation with her neighbor, Margaret had wandered through the house innumerable times making sure doors and windows were locked tight. All night the wind pummeled against the building, shaking the shutters and battering her dreams with undefinable horrors. Shortly after midnight she woke quite suddenly. Somewhere a child was crying, her child, its horrific sobs piercing the night.

Trembling, she sat up, turned on the bedside lamp, and hugged herself into the quilt. Several minutes later she realized it was the oil furnace groaning and shrieking. She lay back down, tentatively, body rigid. Only the furnace. That's all.

Tomorrow she'd see about getting it looked at. That and new locks. Definitely new locks. The screeching drifted in and out of her dreams as she lay on her right side, then her left, then right again. Would the night never end? She stood on the widow's walk and stared down into the puckered face of Mrs. Godwish, wrapped up in a white shawl. The old woman was offering her a bucket of tea leaves, but when Margaret reached for it, Mrs. Godwish had suddenly become Norma Ann, and the bucket of leaves a white-wrapped bundle. Over the wind Margaret could see her sister mouth the words, "Take it." Margaret took the bundle and looked down into the dead face of Aislin, damp tendrils of strawberry hair curling around her pallid skin. She screamed.

Around 4:00 A.M. the storm died and Margaret fell into a sleep, only to be awakened at 6:30 by the sun sending warm candy ribbons of light into her room. She stood for a long time at her curtainless window gazing down at the calm sea, at the seabirds lighting on it with precision and ease.

Back home in Fredericton she walked every morning. She would rise before Robin and Aislin, get the coffee going, then pull on her sneakers and leave quietly through the back door. She would walk through the city streets down to the path along the St. John River, known to locals as the Green. Sometimes she took her Walkman and listened to books on tape that she borrowed from the library. Then it was back home where Aislin would be sitting beside the kitchen window. "Mommy's home," she would squeal. And before Margaret had a chance to kick off her sneakers, Aislin would be clamoring around her legs, "Daddy made breakfast . . . I want Cheerios . . . We got you coffee and a bagel . . . Do I go to day care today?"

On this morning Margaret walked north toward the point on the gravelly beach. To her right, the Atlantic Ocean spread out with its bays, coves, and lapping fingers, its strands and rocky outcroppings. Gulls, varicolored in gray and white, swooped low and called to her, an alien visitor to this windward shore. To her right, directly opposite her, was a two-humped island, the northward hump slightly larger and higher than the southerly one, like two nesting turtles or a Bactrian camel.

She was almost opposite Rusty MacGregor's old cabin now. It did indeed look abandoned. One front window was cracked and the other was boarded up. She wondered what had happened to Rusty MacGregor and who owned this piece of prime real estate. She was surprised that Maizie/Mavis wasn't camping out on the spot, calling everyone "dear" and

24

promising to sell it by noon. She stood at the point for a moment or two and gazed across the water. A few fishing boats chugged between the island and mainland, and she wished she'd remembered binoculars.

Around the point she walked along the lee side of the reach. Up ahead was the marina. Sailboats, their sails lowered and covered with blue canvas, swung at their moorings. Tied to the wharf were a number of lobstering boats, and people walked along the wharf chatting cheerfully and carrying nets and traps. She could hear snatches of their conversation.

"Some storm last night."

"Nearly lost the rigging."

"Reckon she's past?"

"Till the winter, that is."

If she headed right across the causeway, in about a mile or so Margaret would reach the town of Coffins Reach, population eight hundred. That would be another morning's walk. Today she turned left to head back down the gravel road to her house. The mean night had left her tired.

The morning aroma of coffee greeted her as she neared the back door. Grateful that she had set her coffeepot on automatic timer the night before, she poured herself a cup and turned on the radio. Clear skies were forecast. Mentally she went over a to-do list for the day. A locksmith, a furnace repairman, the phone company to get a few more extensions put in, set up her studio, drive into Coffins Reach for a few things, and finish cleaning. Cleaning should be number one.

Midmorning, when Margaret was mopping the hardwood living-room floor, the phone rang. The pleasant-voiced caller introduced herself as her Aunt Sylvia.

"You remember your Aunt Sylvia and Uncle Monty, don't you?" the caller was saying.

"Well, of course I do. It's been such a long time. How are you?"

"Just fine, Margaret. Your Uncle Monty and I heard the news that you had moved back to that house all by yourself and we'd love to have you come to dinner tonight. We're having a few people in."

"Tonight?" Margaret's hand flew to her hair, stringing it back through her damp fingers. Dinner would mean questions. And she hadn't rehearsed any answers yet.

"I know it's short notice, but there are a whole lot of people here who would love to see you. Clark and Pat will be here. You remember your Uncle Clark and Aunt Pat? And of course there's Donna, your cousin Donna. She lives with us. Never left home. And some neighbors. Interesting people from Bosuns Harbor and Coffins Reach. Of course Leo and Dolly won't be here. They live down in Portsmouth now."

"I don't know."

"We're all looking so forward to seeing you. When Brown & Brown called, well, I just couldn't believe it! None of us could."

"Brown & Brown told you?"

"Yes, Brown & Brown. I'd like to tell you something about them, though. None of us here think you should have to pay that cleaning bill. That was always their responsibility."

"I have to admit I don't know much about the contract my father set up with them."

"Well, you should get yourself a good lawyer. That lady will rip your heart out and sell it behind your back. Monty and I were talking, and we think you should speak with someone else before you sell with them."

"I've got a lawyer friend in Fredericton. I may give her a call."

"You do that. I know Brown & Brown are going to slap you with all sorts of bills if you're not careful. They were supposed to do all the winter cleaning, furnace repairs, upkeep, the works, but half the time we've had to be right on their backs every moment to see that they got it done."

"Thanks for telling me."

"What are families for? Even long-lost families." Her aunt's voice was lilting, friendly, with a hint of laughter. "Margaret, now, if there's anything you need out at that old place, you let me know."

"Actually, there is one thing — can you recommend a good locksmith and someone who cleans furnaces? I don't know if there is someone in Coffins Reach I should use, or if I should try Bosuns Harbor, or maybe even Bangor."

"Well, I will tell you something, Margaret Ochs, you have come to the right place. Monty and his brothers own Bosuns Harbor Building Supplies. I'll give him a jingle. Knowing your uncle, he'll be out there first thing to have a look."

"Thank you."

"I'm sitting here thinking about tonight. I was thinking about giving you directions out to our place here — we've got a new place in Bosuns Harbor. But why don't I have Monty just pick you up? I'll get him to come around six-thirty. How's that sound? Maybe after he's looked at the furnace. How would that be?"

Fine, fine, Margaret said. That would be fine. She hung up. Margaret Ochs. Her aunt had called her Margaret Ochs. She was not Margaret Ochs. She had not been Margaret Ochs for a dozen years.

She glanced out of the kitchen window and thought about Robin. He had taken a leave of absence from his teaching job at Fredericton High School and was somewhere in Ottawa. That's all she knew. Hateful words had passed between them, accusing silences, and finally, he was gone. And she was alone.

But on this morning, this pleasant sunny morning, this morning when a warm breeze laced with salt and sunlight wafted through the sand grasses, she missed him. She missed his touch, his smile, his laugh. She missed the smell of him as they made love in their queen-size bed on early summer evenings with the windows wide open, the sound of people walking on the sidewalk below.

Memories clenched at her chest, suffocating her. She cradled the phone in her lap, head bent forward.

FOUR

When her mother told her that her cousin Margaret was back in town and was going to be the guest of honor at the evening's dinner party, Donna took all of her clothes, every single outfit that she owned, and threw them onto her bed. It was bad enough, these dinner parties that her mother insisted on hosting, and then worse, insisted that she help with — but now with her baby cousin Margaret coming? What should she wear? Green? No, too yuppie-environmental. Blue? Too nicety-nice, too Pollyanna at the seashore. She tried on outfit after outfit. In the full-length mirror she examined herself from all angles in a short red spandex dress. She'd kept her figure, that much you could say for her. Not like some of those women who came into the hardware store, fat and fleshy and out of shape, trailing a bunch of sticky-mouthed brats. Chubby mother ducks with their ducklings. She wondered who the husbands were who had married these cows. But occasionally she would see them: skinny-shouldered, scruffy-faced men with toothpick legs and bad teeth.

No, red wouldn't do. Not for tonight's crowd. Black. Black would be perfect. She tried on black leggings and a long, low-cut black sweater. She'd also wear her black wig and black nail polish and black high heels. Black was a good welcoming color for long-lost baby cousins.

The last time her cousin had been in Coffins Reach was when she had been ten and Donna had been thirteen. Donna remembered sitting at her upstairs window looking down at the green station wagon and behind it a U-Haul trailer. In the driver's seat her Uncle Mitch sat grim-faced and staring straight ahead. In the back seat was Margaret, pig-tailed, clutching a worn teddy bear and looking very tiny.

Downstairs her aunt and her mother had been sobbing quietly, their arms around each other. Donna didn't know where her father was. Her father and her uncles were not speaking — so what else was new? They were always arguing about something. Business usually. Clark and Pat weren't there at the good-byes either, of course. Clark, the youngest of the Ochs brothers, mostly followed his older brothers around anyway. And when the older brothers quarreled, Clark stayed away. Leo and Dolly? They had been there earlier, had even given Margaret a brand-new Barbie, but then had left.

Donna saw Margaret only a few times after that. Margaret's family never came back to Coffins Reach. She saw her when Donna and her two younger sisters and her parents climbed into the car and made the trip to Bangor, which wasn't very often. The last time she saw Margaret was the summer Donna was sixteen and Hannah had been dead for a year. At the insistence of her mother they had stopped in to visit Uncle Mitch and Margaret on their way to a cabin on Moosehead Lake. What a disaster! All her uncle did was sit in front of the TV while Margaret spent her days in her bedroom, drawing stupid pictures on construction paper. It was her own mother who bought all the groceries and made all the meals for the two days.

When Donna got bored, she'd go into Margaret's room and regale her with all of the things she was going to do after high school graduation, which was only a year away. First she was going to hitchhike across the country and land up in California. She'd work there for a few months, maybe get a bit part in the movies — people did that all the time there — and

30

then head up to Canada. By then she'd have bought a car. She had it all planned out.

By the time Donna realized it was too late for leaving, the pattern of her life was firmly established: she lived at home, she depended on her parents, she even worked at the hardware store.

Black. Yes. She smiled at herself in the full-length mirror. Black was definitely her color. She'd have to remember to wear it on her next trip to Bangor.

FIVE

True to her aunt's word, a dark blue van — imprinted along the side with "Bosuns Harbor Building Supplies, Bosuns Harbor, ME," a phone number, and a cartoon caricature of two smiling fellows carrying toolboxes, and underneath in white, "The Fixers" — pulled up a couple of hours later. Margaret stood on the small cement back porch as her Uncle Monty, smiling broadly, jumped down from the driver's side of the van, tool kit in hand. He was wearing clean blue jeans, sharply creased, and a nylon windbreaker. In the twenty-five years she'd been away, he'd put on weight and had shrunk, as if someone had placed a cement block on his head and pressed.

"Well, if it isn't little Margry! Come give your old uncle a big hug." He put his tool kit down and bear-hugged her. "You're sure looking good," he said.

She laughed. "And I suppose you're going to tell me that the last time you saw me I was this big." She stretched out her hand, palm down.

"You took the words right out of my mouth."

She remembered that wide mouth which smiled easily, that shock of thick coarse hair, gray now — black the last time she had seen him — wide forehead, and heavy eyebrows that met over the bridge of his nose.

"The hardware business must agree with you," said Margaret. "You look well."

"You're too kind. Dishonest, but kind."

After wandering around the house with her, Monty said that installing more phone extensions would be a piece of

32

cake. And yes, getting a couple of dead-bolt locks was a good idea. A very good idea. For once, he said, Brown & Brown was right on the money.

As for the furnace, he didn't know what he'd find down in the cellar, but according to the contract, Brown & Brown was supposed to be keeping ahead of those things. If major repairs were needed, Margaret should send Brown & Brown the bill. No reason she should have to pay for something like that. No reason at all. "That was their part of the bargain, little girl. They want you to pay, you tell them to come see me."

Monty whistled while he worked on the doors, and Margaret spent the next few hours cleaning and then setting up her second-floor studio. The light was perfect up here. The view from the landing was superb.

While Monty worked on the locks, Margaret made a quick trip into Coffins Reach and picked up milk, bread, toilet paper, a couple of cans of soup, some fresh produce, and a large container of chocolate chip cookie dough ice cream, realizing too late that it probably wouldn't fit in her freezer.

Monty left at 4:00, promising to return at 6:30 sharp to pick her up for dinner. He'd gotten the locks installed along with the phone extensions, but he'd be back tomorrow to look at the furnace if that was all right. Fine, said Margaret.

Margaret put on her sneakers and her beige wide-brimmed hat and headed down the overgrown path to the beach. To her right was the Godwish bungalow, a fifties-inspired square box of a house, white with red shutters, unaltered in twenty-five years. The sun was high in the sky still, but the Godwish home was shut up tight, curtains drawn. A thin plume of smoke ascended from the chimney.

She picked up a thigh bone-shaped piece of driftwood for a walking stick, a "poking stick," her mother would call it. She turned right and headed south. The first thing Margaret noticed as she rounded the curve in the reach were the number of new homes built along the water's edge — large cedar structures with angular windows and multilayered decks. Several of the turn-of-the-century homes — "wrecks," as her mother used to call them, "haunted houses," as she and her friends called them — had been extensively restored and freshly painted.

Fifteen minutes up the beach she saw children filling buckets of wet sand and overturning them. Margaret knew how to do this — she'd done this many times. Even as a child, the artist in her had spent long hours after everyone else had left, getting the castle just right: thick, secure walls of rocks and sand to keep out marauders; the moat, wide enough to thwart all enemies. Safe only within the castle walls could beauty be fashioned — the sand princess with her shell crown, the handsome prince on his driftwood horse. The story acted out.

"Hi," said a little boy around seven who wore sun-faded blue swimming trunks.

"Hi yourself," Margaret said.

"What's your name?" he asked, looking up from his bucket.

"My name's Margaret. What's yours?"

"Aaron." He paused, shaped a sand mound with both hands, and said, "Where do you live?"

Margaret pointed north. "Way up the beach. You can't see it from here. It's a big old white house."

He looked at her, his eyes wide. "You mean where the fairy lives?"

"The fairy?"

He was joined by a chubby girl with blond curls and a sand-smudged pink bathing suit. The little girl looked up at her and said, "You been in the fairy house?"

34

"I don't think so. I've been there since yesterday and I haven't seen any fairy."

"Oh," the girl said, shrugging. "Once I wanted to go there but I'm not 'lowed to go past this rock. Not without my mom."

"Well your mother is smart, then."

Another boy joined them, this one older, about ten. He turned to the two. "There's no such thing as the fairy. Don't you know?"

"Maybe I'm the fairy," said Margaret, winking at him.

The three of them stared at her, eyes wide. Then Margaret said, "That's quite a castle."

The oldest boy regarded it and said, "It's dumb!" Then he began kicking it with his bare feet, kicking, kicking, until it was a tumbledown mound of dirty brown rocks and sand and shells, despite the howling protests of the other two children.

SIX

Every spare countertop in Sylvia's spacious kitchen was laden with bowls filled with concoctions and confections. Colorful sauces simmered in little pots on the stove. Chopped-up pieces of mushrooms, green peppers, celery, and onions waited in mounds on wooden cutting boards. Donna was molding shrimp balls while her mother went on and on about Margaret and wasn't it something that Margaret was back and where had she been all these years and what had she been doing.

Now it happened that Donna knew a whole lot more about Margaret than any of her family did. Three years ago she had run into her Uncle Mitch in a Bangor bar. Wearing a short green dress and her blond wig, she was sitting at a bar stool in Bangor flirting with the bartender and waiting for the action to begin (it was only eight in the evening), when Uncle Mitch walked in. Yes, it was Mitch. No mistaking! But what a mess! He was wearing a shirt and pants that looked as if they'd been slept in and gotten sick over. He shuffled over to a booth in the back and ordered a beer. He didn't recognize her, of course. But she'd go and talk to him. Donna was never one to pass up an opportunity to get hold of useful information. One never knew when it would come in handy. She slipped into the seat across from him.

"Hello, stranger," she said.

He looked up, uncomprehending.

"You look a mess," she said.

He still said nothing, only looked down into his beer foam. He hadn't touched it, she noticed. She reached across the table and slid the mug to the side. He looked at her again.

"You have no idea who I am, do you?"

A look of complete blankness.

"Well, I know who you are, and you are a mess." She laughed.

Finally he spoke. "Who . . ." He cleared his throat. "Who are you?"

"I'm Donna, your niece. Coffins Reach? Remember? Monty's kid? The good old days? Me, Margaret, and Norma Ann, and good ole brother Monty."

A look of pain so intense crossed his face that he shut his eyes.

"Cat got your tongue?" Eyes still closed, he placed his hands palms down on the table in front of him. She reached across and gently stroked his wrist, stroking, stroking, hypnotically.

"What do you want?" His voice was low and monotone.

"I'm your long-lost niece Donna, and that's all you can say, 'What do you want?' " She paused. "I just came over to say hello. Hello."

He said nothing.

"So how's Margaret?"

"Margaret?"

"Margaret. You remember — skinny little kid, curly hair, used to draw."

"Why do you want to know?"

She placed both hands on her chest and said, "Uncle Mitch, I'm deeply hurt. I haven't seen you in lo, these many years and all you can say is 'Why do you want to know?' "

"She's fine."

"So, what's she doing? She ever get married?"

"She married a teacher. In Canada."

"Canada! Way to go, little cuz! She got any brats?"

Slowly he opened up his wallet and produced a posed picture of a little girl, sitting in a photographer's booth, pale blue dress, strawberry blond hair, curly. She turned it over. The inscription read "Aislin — age seven."

"Cute kid, grandpa," she said, slapping it down on the table like a face card in a poker game.

He nodded quietly without pleasure and placed the photo back into his wallet. She looked into his face, with its loose, sagging skin. He moved his beer in front of him, looked down into it, and said nothing. She sat making small talk and listening to his silence until he got up and shambled out of the bar. She never saw him again. The families didn't even go to Mitch's funeral two years later.

And now baby cousin Margaret was back. All grown up. Married to a teacher with a brat.

"Make those shrimp balls a bit bigger, Donna."

"Make those shrimp balls a bit bigger, Donna. Make those shrimp balls a bit bigger, Donna," she mimicked in singsong.

"Oh, Donna." Sylvia was wiping her hands on her apron.

"I should just leave," muttered Donna. "That would make everyone happy, including you."

Sylvia looked at her daughter. "Donna, are you still seeing your therapist in Bangor? Things were so much better when you were."

"Oh yeah, right. Crazy Donna, crazy like Ruth."

"Donna, that's not what I mean."

"Of course it's what you mean. You throw that in my face every chance you get. But sweet Mumsy, to answer your question, yes, I go to Bangor every Friday. You know that."

"I didn't ask if you went to Bangor, I asked if you were still seeing that therapist."

"Of course, Mumsy. I see him at the bar. I see him for dinner. We're real close, if you catch my drift."

Her mother sighed, frowned, and stirred the mushroom sauce.

SEVEN

Brown & Brown was right about one thing. By the looks of it, the Ochs family could afford a lot of things, cleaning bill notwithstanding. Monty and Sylvia's new house was an enormous, refurbished, one-hundred-year-old mansion at the top of a winding driveway in Bosuns Harbor. The exclusive part of town, presumed Margaret, because the other houses were just as imposing — stately colonial structures with wide porches and circular drives.

On the fifteen-minute drive from Coffins Reach to Bosuns Harbor, Monty had filled Margaret in on every single cousin of hers, what they were doing — computer programming, General Motors, teaching, Microsoft, medical doctor — and where they were — Omaha, Detroit, Atlanta, California, Calgary. "They've all left, every single one of them. All except Donna," he said.

Inside the front double doors of the Ochs mansion, Margaret was met with a confusing sea of faces. For a second she stood there running her hands through her hair. It was strange, this looking at the faces of barely remembered aunts and uncles, aunts and uncles who, in her memory, had stood over her, higher than her, not these small, gray people. Nervously she returned their hugs, telling everyone how good they looked.

There were tears in her Aunt Sylvia's eyes when she held Margaret at arm's length and exclaimed, "You're so like her, so beautiful, so young."

Sylvia was a tall, regal looking woman in her mid-sixties.

Her soft gray hair was tied back in a loose chignon. Behind her stood Uncle Clark, an exact replica of Monty, only half a head shorter and not so large of girth. It was as if someone had inserted Monty's features into a computer and pressed "small." Her Aunt Pat, Clark's wife, was an overgrown blowsy blond. (That couldn't be her natural color!) Her hair was badly cut and she wore a pair of pink sunglasses atop her head.

"Well, Margaret," said Pat, reaching for her and kissing the air beside her right cheek, "the years have been kind to you. And I hear you're an artist." When Margaret nodded she said, "I always remembered you as someone who colored between the lines." Pat's voice was gravelly, the kind of voice you expect on women who smoke too much. The video in Margaret's mind wound back to a much younger version of this same woman in her thirties — blond, brittle — who sunbathed, chain smoked, and read *Glamour* magazine.

"I like to paint," said Margaret, "but it looks like any serious painting will have to be done on the walls of my old house."

"*Your house,*" said Pat, shrugging and backing away. "Well, I guess it is your house now. I guess you've a right to call it that now."

Clark shook her hand and said a formal, "How do you do?"

"Fine," said Margaret, remembering that this was her least favorite uncle — the uncle who always retreated to his workshop when the throngs of children came to his house.

Donna was sitting on the couch behind the cowering group of relatives, one long leg tucked underneath her. She was making no move to rise, so after the initial greetings were over, Margaret sat down beside her. Her black hair (Black! It had been fair, Margaret was sure, when she was younger.)

was cut quite short and fit her head like a skull cap with finely gelled tendrils. Tall and long-legged, Donna always gave the impression of being lanky, all arms and legs, as if she didn't quite know what to do with her body parts when they weren't in use. At the moment her left hand rested awkwardly under her right knee and her right arm was sprawled across the back of the couch.

"Well, if it isn't the cousin," Donna finally said. "The prodigal cousin. Quick, Mommy, Daddy, kill the fatted calf."

"Hi, Donna."

"Come back to set the family straight, I'll bet. You'll have a tough go with this bunch of family." She spat out the word *family*, as if the whole idea was repugnant to her.

"So tell me, Donna, how have you been keeping?"

"I take it you want to know why I'm still at home, living with Mummy and Poppy. Am I gainfully employed or am I still sponging off Syl and Monty? Truth is yes and yes. Yes, I am gainfully employed. And yes, I'm still sponging. I've mastered the fine art of sponging."

Margaret was saved from further conversation by her Aunt Sylvia, who grabbed her by the hand and said, "Come meet the rest of the guests, Margaret."

In the dining room a dark maple table, large enough to play Ping-Pong over, was laid with china plates of shrimp, blocks of exotic cheeses, crackers, and bottles of wine. She met Dr. Roland Irons, a retired University of Maine professor. His little china plate was piled high with smoked oysters.

"Our resident mythologist," Sylvia said proudly.

Margaret extended her hand and smiled. "I guess every community needs a resident mythologist."

"Actually, I am a folklorist," he said, taking her hand.

For a few minutes the two of them chatted amiably about the University of Maine, sharing reminiscences and small

42

talk. Next she was introduced to Kevin Thomas, an accountant in Coffins Reach. "The *only* accountant in Coffins Reach," he corrected her. He was properly and conservatively suited and tied in navy. She met Bosuns Harbor neighbors Dr. Reginald Stoniard and his wife, Isabelle. Dr. Stoniard wore a badly fitting toupee, and his wife was a generously proportioned woman who had draped herself in bright-colored silk for the evening. She met Bosuns Harbor selectman or Roxanne Fisher, tall and horse-faced, who wore thick silver hoops in both ears and oversized glasses; and Lorne Maynard, bearded and rumpled. Margaret didn't quite catch what his claim to fame was. Writer, maybe? All of them said, "I've heard so much about you." She said, "All good, I hope." And they nodded.

"Are you married? I heard you were married."

Margaret found herself standing next to Donna in a corner of the dining room. Donna was holding a can of Classic Coke. Margaret had been there when Donna had asked her father for a double scotch.

"Yes, I am married," Margaret said.

"So where's hubby?"

"In Ottawa. He received a fellowship he couldn't turn down. It's to further his studies in music. He's the high school bandmaster. I thought this would be as good a time as any to come down and take care of the old place." The lies flowed so easily.

"I heard you also had a kid. Aislin." She pronounced it ayze-lin.

"It's pronounced Ash-leen. It's Irish."

"Irish! Since when did you become Irish — you of pure Anglo-Saxon stock!" Then she laughed. "Well then, since you and I are both single women on the prowl, as they say — I

43

don't believe your story about hubby, by the way — we should get together, compare notes over lunch sometime."

"Lunch would be nice," said Margaret quietly.

"We'll do lunch, as they say, in the city. We can drive into Bangor and sip Perrier under an umbrella. Then we can go down to the rec club and watch the yuppies play racquetball."

Margaret stared at her.

Sylvia called, "Donna, honey, come give me a hand here in the kitchen a minute."

"Aw, Mom, do I have to?" But she left, pouting like an adolescent, making her clumsy way into the kitchen, tottering on impossibly high heels, arms swinging awkwardly.

In the front room, Dr. Irons was in animated conversation with Roxanne. She spoke with a strong Maine accent and Dr. Irons's accent was British. From where she stood Margaret could not hear their words, but found the cadences of their speech delightful.

"Margaret," said Roxanne, noticing her for the first time and extending her hand, "Margaret, promise me you'll go out tomorrow and buy Roland's book. Such stories, such things you never thought could exist here; ghosts, spirits." She shivered in an affected way. "So fascinating. So utterly fascinating."

"What's your book about?" Margaret asked.

"It's all about the ghostly beasties on the north Maine coast."

"There are a lot of these ghostly beasties on the north Maine coast?" Margaret asked.

He told her that because Maine was settled such a long time ago, it had birthed numerous myths and legends — haunted houses, ghosts and spirits who seek revenge, secret passageways in old homes where the restless dead still wander, phantom fishing boats, ghostly sea captains. "Fascinating, simply fascinating," said Roxanne from time to time. Margaret jotted down the name of his book on a napkin, shoved it in her purse, and promised him she'd buy a copy tomorrow when she went to Bosuns Harbor.

Supper was a scrumptious lobster seafood dish served over beds of white rice. They sat around the large dining-room table spread with a white cloth and the best china. Conversation shifted from the previous night's storm and the price of lobster to the state of the summer tourist economy in Coffins Reach. Bleak, was the general consensus.

"It's the name scares people away," said Pat, holding a forkful of shrimp medley. "I don't know why they just don't change the name of the town to Sea View Point or something. Who wants to come to a beach that reminds them of a funeral?"

From across the table Roland sputtered into his drink. "Sea View Point — what an awful name. Sea View Point! Sounds like it belongs in *New Jersey* or something."

Roxanne chuckled.

Pat just shrugged.

Lorne Maynard spoke for the first time. "I think the name Coffins Reach has a certain mystical appeal."

"Just read Dr. Irons's book!" said Roxanne, who was eyeing him dreamily across the table. "It's all in there. If you ask me, I think it should be placed in every tourist packet distributed from this region. Come to think of it, I think I'll bring that up at the next town council meeting. Yes, that's just what I'll do."

Talk then drifted back to the ghosts and myths and stories. It occurred to Margaret that she could ask Dr. Irons about the fairy the children had mentioned, but by the time there was a lull in the conversation, it had moved on to something else — accountant Kevin relaying his summer sailing adventures down the coast in his Catalina 27. She'd ask about the fairy some other time.

During the meal Donna remained silent, sulky. The few times Margaret glanced at her, she looked away.

Later, over after-dinner liqueurs served in the terrarium, Sylvia sat down on the couch next to Margaret. She turned to her, her voice casual (too casual?). "Have you had any run-ins yet with that next-door neighbor of yours?"

"Next-door neighbor?"

"Ruth Godwish."

"Oh, Ruth Godwish. Yes, I met her yesterday shortly after I arrived. She was out collecting herbs or something for tea. Why do you ask?"

"Oh, I don't know." Sylvia's hands went nervously to the pins in her hair. "I thought you should know that that woman is unstable."

"She did seem a bit strange, but then she's always been a bit on the odd side."

"She's more than odd. She can be downright . . . vicious, cruel."

"Really? She didn't strike me as cruel, just strange."

"She's cruel, she's delusional. I don't know the current lie she may be telling, but if I were you I wouldn't believe a word that woman says. She has hurt this family more than you will know. But that's history, Margaret, history that does not need to be rehashed."

Margaret looked at her. Then why bring it up? "I told her I wanted to visit Bradley again."

"That poor man is totally at her beck and call. He is not the same person, Margaret, as he was when you were all children. That I can tell you. He may not even remember you. Things have changed, Margaret. You've heard the expression 'You can't go back'? That was never more true than for this

46

situation here. You can't go back, Margaret. You can't go back. Remember that."

Margaret was silent for several seconds. Across the room, Roxanne, Roland, Lorne, and Isabelle were in loud conversation about the Latin derivations of certain Anglo-Saxon words, with Lorne claiming expert status on that score. "I'm a bit of an armchair Latin buff," she could hear him say. "It's rather a hobby of mine."

Margaret turned to her aunt. "I have no intention of going back. I came here to rest and paint."

"Well, I hope you succeed in that. I truly do."

A few minutes later, when the two women rose and went back into the house, Margaret saw Donna sitting alone on a straight-backed chair, just inside, strategically positioned to hear every word of their conversation.

EIGHT

Margaret slept a bit more peacefully that night, knowing that she was safely locked behind newly dead-bolted doors, and that she and only she had keys to the place, and not all of the riffraff from Boston and New York. The next morning, as she drank her morning coffee wearing an old baggy T-shirt of Robin's, she looked absently out of the south window toward the Godwish house. She rose then, coffee cup in hand, and moved toward the window, puzzling. The path from the Godwish front door to the beach was entirely overgrown. Odd, she thought.

When she was a child the Godwish path was a well-used one, with its smooth flagstones and well-tended flower beds. It was better even than their own, and often she and Norma Ann would cut across to it to make their way down to the beach.

Now the path was barely visible. Large boulders stood in the way and a couple of heavy logs looked as if they had been purposely placed there, blocking entrance to the beach.

She decided to pay an early-morning visit to the Godwishes. Why shouldn't she, after all? Because Ruth had acted strange and her aunt had warned her that Bradley was not the same? Well, darn it all, he used to be my friend. I've every right to go over and say a neighborly hello.

Fifteen minutes later Margaret had pulled on jeans and an old Freddy Beach sweatshirt over her T-shirt, and was tentatively knocking on the Godwish back door.

No answer.

She knocked again, a little louder this time. A flicker of

curtain at the kitchen window. She knocked more loudly.

The door opened a crack and Ruth's little troll-like face peered up at her.

"Hello, Mrs. Godwish. I just thought I'd come over and visit. Maybe say hello to Bradley."

"I told you that wasn't a good idea."

"I just want to say hi, that's all."

"He's still sleeping."

"I'm sorry. It's early, I know. I saw smoke from your chimney and I thought maybe you were up. If it's nice maybe I'll come back later and Bradley and I could go for a walk on the beach." She was beginning to feel very much like a small child standing there.

"That won't be possible."

"May I come in, just for a second?" Margaret had wedged her hand between the door and the doorjamb. Ruth looked at that hand, sighed and said, "Come in."

The small, cheerless kitchen with the yellowed linoleum floor and smelling faintly of sour milk and cabbage was just as she remembered it. The curtains were drawn and the room seemed overly warm. She didn't see or hear Bradley. The door to the living room stood ajar, and Margaret could see through to a room too full of knickknacks and doilies and ticking clocks, an old person's room, a room shut in upon itself.

"Where's Bradley?"

"I told you, resting. Keep your voice down, I don't want to waken him." Ruth was pacing, nervously rubbing her square hands together. "I don't want you talking to Bradley, upsetting him."

"I don't want to upset him either."

"He's been through so much. He still sees Norma Ann in his dreams. The way she was. Every night he wakes up

49

screaming. It will just make it worse, you showing up here now."

"Mrs. Godwish, that was twenty-five years ago!"

"To Bradley it was yesterday."

"Has he gotten any help for this? Has he been to a doctor?"

"Doctors upset him."

In the doorway loomed the bulk of Bradley Godwish, a bewildered look on his face. More than two decades older, but still she would recognize him anywhere, eyes too small for that round doughboy face, wide nose. But the smile was gone, the innocent smile that was always a part of his face so many years ago. In its place she saw alarm, confusion. Time had not treated him well. He had put on an enormous amount of weight, and his face and neck were gelatinous and deeply joweled. He wore a tatty navy blue tracksuit with white piping.

"Bradley," said his mother, "please go back to your bedroom. Mama will be there in a minute. You remember what I said."

"I heard someone talking," he said, glancing uncomprehendingly at Margaret.

"Never mind, Bradley. It had nothing to do with you, now off to your room."

Margaret watched as he shrugged his shoulders, bent his head, and shuffled away.

"Bradley," Margaret called, "do you remember me?"

He looked back at her, but said nothing.

"Do you know who I am?"

Ruth was scowling, gesturing for Margaret to leave. Instead Margaret pushed past Ruth and stood square in front of the man.

"Do you know me, Bradley?"

He looked at her, something like alarm in his eyes.

"Bradley, I knew you when we were young. My name is Margaret. I used to be Margaret Ochs."

Recognition slowly dawned on that face. "Norma Ann?"

"Now look what you've done," Ruth wailed. "Bradley, dear, it's okay. Come into the living room and Mama will find you a video."

"Bradley, I'm Norma Ann's little sister. Remember the little sister who used to tag along all the time?"

He shook his head, did not look at her.

"Okay, well, that's okay, Bradley. But I just moved in next door, and I'm wondering if you will be my friend? Maybe we could go for walks," Margaret suggested. "We could walk along the beach and find rocks and shells and things. Would you like that? That used to be your favorite thing. I remember that."

A look of terror so extraordinary crossed his face that Margaret backed away. He was shaking his head vigorously. "No!" And he pressed his doughy fists into his eyes. "Can't! No! Can't! Not on the beach! Bad people!"

Margaret glanced at Ruth, who was scowling. Gently Margaret tried again. "Okay, Bradley, we don't have to go for a walk. Maybe I could come over and we could watch videos together or something."

But he hadn't heard her. He was crying now, great heaving sobs that shook his entire large frame, and when he moved his hands away from his eyes, Margaret saw fear.

Ruth led the blubbering Bradley to a recliner in the living room and tucked a beige afghan around him. "You just sit here and let Mama find you a video."

"*Robocop*?"

"Okay, *Robocop*," she said, shuffling through a wicker basket of videos beside the TV. The video inserted, the room was filled at once with the sounds of gunshots and soundtrack

51

music, masking the ticking of the clocks and hiding the audible whimperings of Bradley's terror. Margaret watched him, his mouth working, his hands trembling under the afghan, a quivering gray mound in a closed-up room.

In the kitchen Margaret said, "I'm sorry, Mrs. Godwish. I didn't mean to upset him. I just wanted to visit, to be friendly."

"My son doesn't need any friends."

"Everybody needs friends, Mrs. Godwish."

"People like Bradley don't have friends; they don't need friends."

Margaret looked at her, dumbfounded. "Mrs. Godwish." She could feel her anger rising. "Everybody needs friends. Everybody."

"Oh, and you're an expert?"

"I don't claim to be an expert in mental handicaps, but I certainly know that staying inside watching videos with the curtains drawn could not be healthy."

"The curtains are drawn because Bradley prefers it that way. He has not been on the beach for many years. That is why the drapes stay drawn and the windows stay shut. Now if you will excuse me, I have to call the handicap bus people and tell them not to come for Bradley today. He is far too anxious and upset to attend his workshop today."

"Ruth, I'm sorry, really I am."

Ruth was muttering now, but it was more to herself than to anyone within listening range. "I'm sorry too. I thought you would be different than all the rest of them. But you're not. You come in here like all the other Ochses, demanding we do things, upsetting Bradley, trying to change things, blaming him."

Margaret let herself out, shivering although the day was warm, hugging her arms around her as she picked her way back to her own house.

NINE

She brewed herself another pot of well-deserved coffee. Maybe she had been a bit too forceful. Maybe she shouldn't have barged in over there. She hadn't meant to upset Bradley, although if she were being completely honest with herself, she would have to admit to a kind of morbid curiosity. She wondered how she could make it up to Ruth and her son, or if she should even try.

Sipping on a second cup of coffee, she saw the blue van pull in. She had forgotten that her uncle was coming today to look at the furnace.

Monty eyed her quizzically when he entered. "Something the matter?"

"Oh, it's nothing, I guess. I just paid my next-door neighbors a neighborly visit that turned kind of sour."

"Strange lady," he muttered.

With Uncle Monty safely in the cellar, Margaret yelled down to him that she was heading into Bosuns Harbor for a few things and to lock the door behind him if he left before she got back.

It was foggy as she drove through Coffins Reach and onto the highway toward Bosuns Harbor. As she sped along the road, bits of ground fog followed along beside her, little wispy ghosts, rising, falling, drifting. She thought about Ruth Godwish and her talk of murder, about Bradley and his bizarre fear of the beach, about her black-clad cousin Donna, who had never followed her dream of seeing the world, about her aunt — casual, friendly, motherly, until the talk shifted to the Godwishes. Margaret had come to Maine to escape, to gather her own memories and griefs around her, to work out a way to live without Robin and Aislin, and she was already being met with ghosts from the past, wispy, rising, falling, ephemeral ghosts, following her on either side.

By the time she reached Bosuns Harbor the sun had burned the fog away. She pulled into a little strip mall she'd seen the night before and picked up a few more groceries. She opened a bank account and made the Radio Shack people happy when she walked out with two phones (one with Caller ID — she'd read somewhere that single women should always have Caller ID), a bunch of extension cords, and an answering machine.

Before heading back to Coffins Reach she decided to explore a little. Downtown she found a parking space in the gravel lot next to the wharf. From there she walked along the town's main streets. It was typical of a hundred Maine tourist towns with their gift shops of local crafts, bagel and muffin shops with designer coffees, clothing stores offering expensive hiking wear, eclectic book and record shops, and outdoor cafes specializing in iced cappuccinos and lobster rolls. She picked up a copy of Dr. Irons's book, *Ghost Stories of Downeast Maine*, at a craft shop and slipped it into her backpack. She decided to stop in at a rustic looking sidewalk cafe for soup and a sandwich. It was a cozy little log building where patrons helped themselves to fish chowder from a big black urn.

Carrying her tray of fish chowder, lobster roll, black coffee, and new book, she found a small table near the back of the cafe. The lobster roll with its huge chunks of lobster was wonderful, the coffee soothing. She watched the luncheon crowd while she ate. A group of elderly ladies in flowered cotton tops and polyester pants had pushed two tables together and were in busy conversation about the bargains at the outlet malls. A middle-aged couple, he with graying beard and ponytail, she in a long denim dress, carried backpacks to a small table behind her. Leftovers from the sixties, she presumed. She watched a young couple with four little children, the youngest just an infant, take a place at a table next to the buffet area.

She liked watching people. At least once every two weeks she and Joyce would get together for lunch, choosing a different Fredericton restaurant each time. Joyce was always a fountain of knowledge about Fredericton and its people. She would say, "You see that woman over there? Turn around slowly, pretend you're looking at the entrance, see . . . no, not that one, the one in the blue sweater. I went to high school with her, Fredericton High School. She married into money. She's done quite well for herself, wouldn't you say?"

Margaret would just laugh. "Joyce, you are such a gossip."

"I am not a gossip," she would say primly, adjusting her napkin in her lap. "I can't help it if I grew up here and know absolutely everyone in town. Oh, Margaret, that guy that just walked in? The one with the red tie, oh my goodness, it's a Mickey Mouse tie. We went to the University of New Brunswick together. I used to go out with him. Can you believe it?"

And now here she was, alone in a restaurant in Maine, miles from Fredericton and Joyce and Robin and everyone familiar. Margaret looked around at the people and wondered what Joyce would say about them.

She fetched herself another cup of coffee and pulled out Roland's book. It was a thin volume with a glossy cover, published, she noted, by a Maine publisher called Sunrise Press located in Machias, Maine. By the looks of it, Sunrise Press probably specialized in books of poetry and local color.

The dedication page had only two words: "To

Genevieve." She turned to the table of contents and read: "The Biggest Fish Story in Downeast Maine," "The Phantom Lobsterman," "The House on the Hill with a Secret to Tell," "The Sea Captain Who Never Made It Home," "Rub a Dub Dub, the Ghostly Three from a Bar Harbor Pub," "She Walks the Beach in a Long White Shawl."

She Walks the Beach in a Long White Shawl. Curious, Margaret turned to the last story and read.

TEN

The year was 1843, and Captain Gilbert Coffin had just brought his new bride, the fair and lovely Anna, youngest daughter of the duke and duchess of Wellington in England, to the shores of America. It had taken the captain five years to build for her the large three-story house located on a finger of land that now bears the name of Coffins Reach. The blue, granite foundation stones came from Maine, and marble was imported from New York and Massachusetts. Each piece of wood in the structure was carefully chosen for its grain, beauty, and strength. The captain wanted his bride to feel completely at home, and so the house was built as an exact replica of her family home in Wellington. Gilbert Coffin spared no expense for his beloved bride.

Their first few years of marriage were blissful. "She is whimsy indeed," he wrote to a friend in England. "My dear Geoffrey, you should avail yourself of the goodly institution of marriage. It is a sweet and pleasant state. My dear Anna is a great joy to me."

And Anna wrote to her sister, Charlotte, in England, "I am so happy with Gilbert. He makes missing my family less burdensome."

Captain Gilbert Coffin commanded the large sailing vessel, *The Doon*, which regularly made trading runs to India, the West Indies, and England. He brought back rugs, paintings, spices, fine china. Some of the art pieces used to decorate his home have survived and are currently on display at the Bosuns Harbor Historical Society Museum.

During one of his early trips he brought from India a large bolt of ornate woven white cloth, exceedingly delicate. It was from this cloth that Anna fashioned a shawl for herself. She was seldom seen without it after that.

These long and frequent departures, however, were what sounded the ultimate death knell to their marriage. Forced to be alone for months at a time, Anna became more and more despondent. Much of her day was spent wandering up and down the beach, wrapped in her shawl, waiting for her husband to return.

It also did not help that five years of marriage had left her childless. About this time she wrote to her sister, "It is a great grievance to me that I am barren, that I cannot give children to my good husband. I fear being alone, and would not a child keep me company on this lonely northern coast? Am I selfish? Perhaps. Perhaps that is why God is punishing me."

It was well known that Gilbert had taken many mistresses, one in every port it would seem. The most well known and documented was Helen Crayton of Northumberland, a woman older than Anna, and a woman of independent wealth. It also didn't help that she had borne him children.

Always frail, Anna's health began to deteriorate rather rapidly. "It is in my chest that the misery has settled," she wrote to her sister. "Sometimes I cough and I cannot stop. How Gilbert must hate me, for when he does come home I am sickly and become so weepy. I cling to him and beg him not to leave me. I cannot help myself. And then he pushes me away like a dog. The last time he came, he pushed me down the stairs and I lay there until I gathered my strength to arise. But I fear I am deserving of his heavy ministrations. I have not been a good wife. I have not given a son to my husband."

It was a morning in early autumn when Captain Coffin, despite the protestations of his crew, set sail in heavy seas and never returned. The night after he departed the wind raged so severely as to rip shutters off his house and fell great trees. It was reported in the newspaper that a rogue tide came nearly to the foundations of his house.

The wind blew severely for weeks as one hurricane after another raged against the coast of Maine. Captain Coffin missed his rendezvous with the East India Trading Company. He did not report to England. Anna, in her weakened condition, could not be persuaded to take to her bed. Instead she wandered along the beach watching and waiting for Gilbert to return.

He was never heard from again. It is believed that he and the entire crew of *The Doon* were lost at sea. Ten months after he left, Anna's body was found one morning washed up on the point, clothed in a dark blue dress. It is thought that in her weakened state she decided not to live anymore, so she simply walked into the cold sea and drowned. Her white shawl was never found.

Her funeral was held in the small Congregational church in the village that is now Bosuns Harbor, but as to her precise burial spot, that has never been located. Local historians, including myself, have searched throughout the graveyards along the Maine coast, but to no avail. It is presumed by some that the headstone may have been carried off by grave robbers; or by others, that it may have been overturned by the ravages of time and storm or may still be out there, entwined in the underbrush, waiting for someone to stumble across it.

But the locals believe that Anna Coffin was never buried, never permitted to rest in peace, and that is why her spirit still keeps watch along the beach. Some report seeing her on stormy nights, wrapped up in her long white shawl, wandering up and down the beaches at Coffins Reach, watching, waiting for her beloved sea captain to return to her.

ELEVEN

"What do you mean he's not here! This was his day to be here!"

Donna glowered down at the round bespectacled man who called himself director of the ceramic factory. He was rubbing his hands together, and Donna stared at the flakes of gray that fell from them like snow. He wore a clay-smudged T-shirt advertising the State of Maine Special Olympics.

"All I can say is that his mother called and said that Bradley was too anxious and upset to attend today. Those were her exact words, I think."

"That little rotten scummy woman who calls herself his mother," she was muttering. The director, whose name was Arnie, just sighed.

"If you'll excuse me, Donna, I have work to do." And he walked away from her.

He didn't like her, that much she knew. Not that she cared. No matter how many times she came to see Bradley, Arnie was always the same, voice barely pleasant, complaining when she would take Bradley out early for a drive, scowling at her through smeary glasses.

She called over to him loudly, "Did she say if he was sick?"

The moon faces around the table stared up at her. One toothless woman was humming tunelessly as she rolled a long piece of clay, rolling, rolling, making snakes out of clay. Donna had to get out of this place.

"No, just that he was anxious and upset."

"I'd be anxious and upset, too, if I had to live with that Nazi!" she said.

Then she turned on her heel and walked out into the sunshine. She got in her car and headed north. I should just drive away, she muttered. Just get as far away from Sylvia and Monty as I can, as far away from Coffins Reach and Bosuns Harbor as I can. I should go to California. I should go to Mexico. Canada. Run away to Canada like Margaret.

As she turned onto the highway her head began to throb. What she didn't need now was a migraine. "I don't need this!" she shouted at a passing car. She turned on the radio loud, hoping it would stifle the thoughts that were demanding entrance. She pounded the steering wheel with the palm of her hand. Bradley was the reason she had never left. Sometimes she thought of taking Bradley with her. She would take care of him. She could. Better than that witch with her magic herbs who called herself his mother. She would take care of him the way no one took care of her.

All those years of one therapist after another, those nurses who tried to look so concerned when they held her hand while she screamed. She knew very well that when their shifts were over they breathed sighs of relief, dropped their nursy whites, and headed out to their very normal homes.

Bradley was the one constant.

TWELVE

Her coffee grew cold in her mug as Margaret turned back to the beginning of the story and read every sentence again, word for word, slower this time. The family with the four little children, the denimed couple who leaned toward each other over their herbal tea, the old ladies who giggled in their polyester, these were not a part of reality. Her reality was spinning. Unconsciously she clung to the table edge for support. Had *she* seen the ghost of Anna Coffin? But no! The whole idea was ludicrous! The woman she had seen was real. And could *hers* be the house that Gilbert Coffin had built? Had Anna Coffin lived in *her* house? Why had she never heard this story before?

She read through the story a third time. At the end of this reading she felt not fear, but a strange and curious connection, a kinship almost with Anna.

Anna had grieved because she had no children. For many years Margaret had known that kind of longing. She and Robin had been to every fertility clinic from Fredericton to Boston. And then just as they were about to give up, Margaret was pregnant. *Low sperm count, low but not nonexistent — one of those little buggers got through,* said the doctor, all smiles. Aislin, the child they had prayed for, planned for, and hoped for, was born. *An answer to prayer! God is so good!*

The church ladies gave her a baby shower in the fellowship room. They ate cheesecake and oohed and ahhed over pink dresses, terrycloth sleepers, and fuzzy teddy bears. Robin brought her flowers every day for a month, and Joyce got her a subscription to a parenting magazine. Life was good then;

hectic but satisfying, busy but fulfilling.

And then Aislin was taken away.

Margaret could still see the road, shimmering under the streetlights as she and Robin sped through the rain to the hospital while she held the motionless child in her arms.

But Aislin had already died. *Meningitis,* the doctor told them later in a tired voice. *We did everything we could.* Robin and Margaret clung to each other as the white dawn lifted slowly over Fredericton and the sun blazed down, showering the city with light. How dare the sun rise on a day like today! How dare it!

She pushed her chair away from the cafe table, a rough creaking sound on the hardwood. Memories rose in her like a nausea that made her choke. The denimed woman looked over at her. The toddler grinned up at her. Margaret gathered up her book and her backpack and headed outside into the afternoon.

At the corner she found a public phone, but the phone book had been torn off its hinges. Why can't people leave things the way they find them? Why does everything have to be ruined? Back in the cafe she asked the proprietor if he had a phone book she could borrow. He looked at her strangely, at her demanding manner, at the way she swallowed and ran her fingers through her hair.

"You okay?" he asked.

"I need a number," she mumbled.

She flipped open the book that he handed to her. There it was, Roland Irons, an address on Shore Line Drive in Bosuns Harbor and a phone number. When the proprietor turned to stir the chowder, Margaret ripped the page out of the book and shoved it into her backpack.

At the corner booth she inserted a coin and tried Roland's number.

The clipped, friendly British voice told her that he was sorry he was unable to come to the phone, but would she please leave a message.

She did.

THIRTEEN

Clark Ochs was tired of the hardware store, tired of playing what his wife constantly referred to as "second fiddle" to his big brother, who called the shots on just about everything. He was tired of Pat constantly harping about the amount of money they didn't have in comparison with Sylvia and Monty and, of course, Leo and Dolly down in Portsmouth with their mansion and forty-foot yacht.

And right now, here today, this was the last straw. Here he was in the warehouse, helping building contractor Will Stam load his pickup with plywood, and then Will gets back in his pickup and is sitting there drinking coffee out of a paper Dunkin' Donuts cup saying he's going to wait for Monty to get back from wherever it is Monty has gone to. Says he can't leave, 'cause he's sure Monty will give him more than a 10 percent discount. Fact is, Monty won't. As much as Clark points this out, Will just sits there, smiles, drinks his coffee, and says he's in no hurry. "I'll just wait for Monty," he says.

Fuming, Clark left the warehouse and walked across the lot and back into the hardware store. Let him wait. Maybe Monty'll stay out all day. Serve him right to sit there in his truck all day. In the coffee room Clark grabbed a Coke from the fridge, flipped the top open, and sat down heavily on the sofa.

And then there was his wife constantly nattering at him, telling him that he didn't have the guts to stand up to his brother in anything. On that score she was probably right. This was just a job to Clark and he didn't pretend otherwise.

When you thought about it, it really stank to high heaven. Years ago he was a part of the partnership their father had set up. Years ago it was him and Mitch and Monty and Leo. And now look at them — Mitch dead, and Monty and Leo *hiring* Clark, if you please. They always told him they'd bought him out for his own good. And at that time he believed them. At that time he felt destined for better things. And then when the deal was complete they took every chance they got to ridicule him.

And why did Leo come home so infrequently? He was half owner, along with Monty, but living high on the hog down in New Hampshire. And when he *did* drive north it was him and Monty closing the office door behind them and talking about who-knows-what. Cooking up stuff and leaving Clark out, no doubt.

And now his niece Margaret was back, Mitch and Hannah's girl. Funny how he hadn't thought about that part of their lives for so long — that time with Norma Ann. He'd had his doubts about that whole story right from the beginning, let me tell you, but did anyone want to hear his side? No, the cops wrote down "accidental death" in their books and that was the end of it. A few years after she had died, he tried calling that Detective Jonathan Smith, the one who had headed up the investigation, the one who'd talked to them all, only to discover that he had died in a car accident. High-speed chase. A little fishy, don't you think?

Clark heard Monty's voice. He threw the empty pop can into the garbage and stood up. Monty was in the coffee room now, arm around Will Stam, smiling and saying loud enough for everyone in the entire store to hear, "Don't you know my best customers always get 15 percent?"

Clark scowled. Just yesterday he'd been there, right there, when Monty had changed the discount policy from 15 to 10

66

percent for bulk buyers. "We just can't afford to give any more discounts, what with the price of lumber going up and all."

Will cast him a triumphant look. Clark clenched his fists, got up, and walked out of the store. Didn't even stop to say good-bye.

FOURTEEN

She would go over there. Maybe it was just a case of Dr. Irons not answering his phone. People did that sometimes. At a corner convenience store Margaret asked a skinny girl behind the counter where Shore Line Drive in Bosuns Harbor was.

"Down someplace by the water, I think."

"Do you have a map or anything?"

"A map?"

Margaret shifted from foot to foot. "Yeah, a map. A folded piece of paper? Lines on it that stand for streets? Helps people find where they're going?"

The girl called in a loud voice, "Gus, do we got any maps?"

A thick-limbed young man moved toward her, squinting.

Margaret said, "Actually, what I want to know is where Shore Line Drive is."

He pointed. "Oh, that's easy to find. You head out here, hang a right, then a left on Bryce. You'll come to Route One then. Then you go left on O'Glennis. You'll run right into Shore Line Drive. It runs along the waterfront. You go along the waterfront and eventually you'll hit Shore Line Drive."

"Thanks."

The sun was high in the sky when she took a right, a left on Bryce and then onto Shore Line Drive. She smoothed the page from the telephone book onto the passenger seat. Number 14 Shore Line Drive was a narrow, three-story, well-kept white house. A long driveway led down to it. No one answered her knock at the back door.

She walked around to the front of the house on a walkway of white pebbles. She stood for a moment, admiring the view from here. Dr. Irons's house was set farther back from the shoreline than hers was, and the front of his house offered an unobstructed view of the Atlantic, the horizon not dotted with islands. Far out to sea a two-masted sailboat surged northward through the waves.

Like most of the homes along the waterfront it featured a large porch on the waterfront side. She took the steps two at a time and rang the bell. No answer.

She peered through partly opened curtains. The interior was a study in woods; dark wood on the floor, lighter wooden walls, floor to ceiling bookshelves along the back wall. Framed prints, of the type found in upscale art galleries, were hung here and there on the available wall space. It seemed that Dr. Irons had eschewed the popular New England colonial style for something quite different. Margaret called out several times before she fumbled in her bag for a pen and wrote a hurried note on the back of a deposit slip from her checkbook and then slid it into the side of the front door.

The phone was ringing when she pulled in to her own driveway. She raced to answer it.

"Hello, Margaret."

"Andre!" said Margaret. Andre was her agent. Well, that was stretching it a bit. Actually, he was the curator of one of Fredericton's smaller art galleries. He called himself "agent" to all of the artists who had ever shown their works in his gallery. He was also her friend.

"Don't sound so disappointed, Margaret."

"I'm not disappointed."

"You were expecting maybe a certain high school music teacher?"

"No. More like a professor of folklore."

"Margaret, what I want to know is when you are coming home. I've had a number of people already in here asking about you, wondering when they are going to see another Margaret Collinwood hanging on my walls. People love your work, Margaret."

"Yeah, right," she said. "Andre, you know I have some personal problems I'm trying to work through."

"The whole world is trying to work through personal problems, Margaret. You have too much talent to lose. Tell me something, how long has it been since you picked up a paintbrush?"

"Just the other day when I was arranging my new studio. I moved my paintbrushes from a cardboard box to the table."

"Always the funny girl, Margaret. I will be quite blunt. Aislin died more than a year ago. You and Robin have been separated for what? Three months? When are you going to get yourself pulled together?"

"My plan is to do that here. And, just curious, how did you get my number?"

"Your husband gave it to me."

"What?"

"I saw him in Fredericton the other day."

"Robin was in Fredericton?"

"Yes, he was . . . is, as a matter of fact."

"But how did he get my number here?"

"I have no idea of that, Margaret. Why don't you come home? My advice remains the same: come home. Robin needs you."

"That's debatable."

"No, it's true."

"I'm tired of this conversation. Can I go now?"

"No, just one more thing. You are in danger of losing

more than your talent, Margaret, you are in danger of losing yourself."

Later after she hung up, Margaret meandered aimlessly from room to room in the big house. No matter where you go to escape, you always end up taking yourself with you. Although she wasn't thirsty and really didn't feel like it, she brewed a pot of coffee and sat in the dark and quiet beside the bay window and drank cup after black cup until the sea faded into darkness in front of her.

FIFTEEN

That night Margaret had her first Anna Coffin dream. In her dream Anna was standing knee-deep in the swirling tide. Even though she looked out to sea, Margaret could see her face clearly. It was a young face, very pale, very white, with large blue eyes and a thin straight mouth. Anna Coffin held a baby wrapped in a white shawl. Instinctively, Margaret knew the baby was dead.

Anna was singing softly, and in the night her song sounded like a flute, high and mournful. Then she laid the bundle gently down into the sea. For several seconds Anna watched the child disappear under the foam while the burial song continued.

Margaret woke suddenly. A whisper? A song! Robin singing! Clearly she could hear him. But when she sat up it was gone. Dream remnants, she thought, the last vestiges of sleep that end in song.

She thought of Robin then, Robin who was always singing. He hummed while he dressed for work, sang loudly in the shower, sang in the kitchen while he poured milk over his cornflakes. It used to surprise her that he could be so uninhibited as to sing loud, profound songs, all verses, with the windows open.

He sang in the church choir, often taking the difficult tenor solos in the Christmas cantata. For a couple of seasons he was a member of the Bel Canto Singers in Fredericton. He had also been in a few city music productions, *Brigadoon* and *My Fair Lady*, to name just a couple. If he were here he would be singing to her now, making up songs, eventually going into his Pavarotti imitation. It was a game they played. She would laugh and yell "bravo!" He would embrace her then, swing her around in a dance to his song until they collapsed on the bed.

But Robin wasn't here now, and the song was gone, the tattered and frayed edges of it dissolved into the morning. She rose from her bed, pulled off the quilt, and wrapped it tightly around her shoulders as she stood by the window. The sea was quiet in the morning sun, fingers of it gently lapping against the gravel beach.

Downstairs she pulled on sneakers and a sweatshirt. A walk. She'd go for a walk. She walked south, past the God-wish house, past the place where the children told her about the fairy. She'd talk to Dr. Irons today. She'd find out all about this so-called Anna Coffin, this so-called ghost, this fairy.

In the distance a lean-muscled jogger was making his way toward her in navy jogging shorts, tank top, and a wide-brimmed beige safari hat. A little closer and she recognized him.

"Dr. Irons! Good morning," she called cheerfully, waving.

He slowed down and said, "Well, hello there! I got your note and your phone message," he said. "It sounded rather urgent. Although I can't imagine why someone needs to see a folklorist on an emergency basis." He smiled.

She shaded her eyes with her hands. "I bought a copy of your book yesterday. When you have a minute I have a question about it."

"How about when I finish my run? That may be as good a time as any."

"Come to my house then. I'll put on a pot of coffee and I'll even treat you to my special cheddar and green pepper scrambled eggs."

"Now, there's an offer this lonely old soul can't refuse. I'll be there in short order."

"I live just back up the shoreline, the big white house. Needs paint."

"I know where you live," he called, already running away from her, his legs and shoulder muscles sinewy and tan.

SIXTEEN

At Dunkin' Donuts, Clark muttered to himself as he sat alone drinking a large coffee, double cream, and scanning through the morning edition of the *Bangor Daily News*. He grumbled at the booth of teenagers at the table behind him. This was supposed to be a no-smoking section, and there they were lighting up. He could smell it.

Finally Clark could stand it no longer. He turned and pointed. "Hey, can't you read the sign?"

"Smoking section's filled up, gramps," was the reply.

Clark growled and turned back to his bran muffin and newspaper.

What was the matter with him this morning? He had griped at Pat, had grumped at the old cat, who had looked up at him and meowed loudly.

"What's your problem?" Pat had said, tying her belt around her housecoat as she made her way into the kitchen.

"Nothing!"

But deep down he knew, or at least he thought he knew. It was seeing Margaret again after all these years, reminding him of a whole part of his life that had been stolen. He broke off a piece of bran muffin. Nothing had been the same after Norma Ann's death. That one event had changed everything. A few weeks after her death Mitch moved away and Monty and Leo came to him and bought him out.

He tried to remember back to that time, wishing he had been more observant. But during those days he spent most of his time out in his workshop, carving miniature soldiers. His goal was to have a battalion of troops from every war, all carved in miniature. He would open a studio where he would teach carving. Eventually he would have a museum with tableaus laid out from every war. Tourists to Maine would come and see it, and groups of school children would file through, their teachers talking about the importance of various battles. Pat called his artistic endeavors foolishness, but he continued, thinking himself destined for artistic greatness.

His dream had died a long and painful death through the years. Oh, the workshop was still out there. But now it was a storage shed, where Monty piled boxes and equipment and lumber for the store. It wasn't even his anymore.

On the day that changed everything, the day that Norma Ann had died, he was out in his workshop, putting the finishing touches on his highland regiment pipe band that he planned to exhibit at the state fair.

But on that day was there a kind of electricity in the air? Or had the years put a spin on his memories? He remembered his wife that day, cupping her hand over the phone in whispers and frowning at him when he came inside for a glass of iced tea.

In those days Pat was a looker, that much was for sure, and she had the tight shorts and low-cut sweaters to prove it. He wasn't blind then to the overtures of Monty toward her and her to him. The two had dated briefly before Monty married Sylvia. Clark suspected there may have been something going on between Monty and Pat even after he and Pat were married, but in typical Clark fashion, he never said anything, just painted dark eyes on more tiny fighting men.

A whole lot of time had passed since then. There were a lot of things he should have paid attention to. His head hurt for the remembering of them. He fingered the edges of the paper muffin cup.

For some reason he'd kept tabs on all three officers who'd come out to Mitch and Hannah's then. Jonathan Smith was dead. Earl Kelley was a police officer in D.C., and Chris Rikken had resigned from the police force and was working as a private investigator in Belfast, Maine.

And now Margaret showing up all of a sudden. Clark wasn't the type to believe in omens. Clark wasn't the type to believe in anything. But why did his hands suddenly feel so cold?

SEVENTEEN

Later that morning Margaret and Dr. Irons were seated at her kitchen table, which she had pulled into the center of the room and covered with a white cloth. Dishing helpings of eggs and toast onto two plates, she said, "You're lucky I went shopping yesterday."

"I can see that."

"One thing I've got to do is get myself some decent pots and pans; look at this frying pan. We could get lead poisoning or something."

"What would you need new pots for? I'd gotten the impression from Sylvia that you were just here until the house sold."

She looked at him. "I'm not sure. I haven't made any plans."

"So your house isn't for sale?"

"I haven't come to a decision yet."

"I'm sorry. I don't mean to pry."

She smiled. "No, I came here because I need time to think."

"This is a good place to think, the Maine coast is. Many thousands of thoughts have been thought here."

"My thoughts will just add to them," she said. "The air will be dense with thoughts."

"How poetic."

"Just curious, how well do you know my aunt and uncle?"

He laughed and knifed some scrambled eggs onto the back of his fork, British style. "Not well. Bosuns Harbor is a small place. People know each other but not well. I often get invited to parties, don't ask me why."

"I think it's your British accent."

"Oh, I don't think so."

"Well, then how about your book? That person, that Roxanne seemed quite taken by it."

He laughed again, a hearty sound.

She looked at him. "Can I talk to you about Anna Coffin?"

He leaned back. "She walks the beach in a long white shawl."

"That's the one."

"What would you like to know about her?"

"Is this — was this — her house?"

"This house. This precise house was hers. Yes."

She surveyed the kitchen, with its faded flowered papered walls, its rough, discolored floorboards, the wood stove rusted in places, the glass-fronted cupboards, the high ceilings and ornate moldings. She said, "I can't believe I never knew this before. All those years and I never knew why this place was called Coffins Reach. I never knew who built this house. I grew up in this house until I was ten, and I never knew this story."

"Your parents may have known that this house had historical significance" — he leaned forward, his elbows on the table — "but they may not have known it was haunted."

"*Haunted?*" Her eyes were wide.

He winked at her. "Oh, I'm just teasing. I would say that the ghost related to your house seems to confine her activities to the *outside* of the place." He smiled. "But I don't for one minute believe that any of these places I write about are truly haunted. There's a lot to the power of suggestion. And I think it's odd, don't you, that no one saw this ghost until *after* my book came out two years ago? There were some sightings of the ghost in the late 1800s. Then nothing until two years ago. For me it's all in fun, and if I can do something to aid the ailing tourist industry, well, then I'll do my part."

"This house . . ." said Margaret, looking around her.

"This house. If I could be so bold, I would love a tour of this place. I was never allowed a tour through this house. I desperately wanted to when I was researching the life of Anna Coffin, but I was denied permission."

"By whom?"

"The realtors who manage this place."

"Brown & Brown."

"I think that's the name, yes."

She rose, pushing herself away from the table, "Well, this is *my* house now and I'd be *happy* to show you through. But I have to warn you, I haven't even gone through the whole of it yet. The cellar's too damp and the attic . . ."

He raised his eyebrows.

"Where do you want to start?"

"Actually, the outside, the foundation stones. I wasn't even allowed on the property."

"Follow me, we'll go through the front door."

As they strode down the front hall, Margaret was full of questions. "What about the story you wrote? What about her tombstone and the white shawl? Are they really missing?"

"That may not be as mysterious as it sounds. The record of where she was buried may have been lost. As for the shawl, it was probably stolen. It was made from some very exquisite cloth. Look at this banister," he said, stroking it. "Solid walnut, a beauty."

"I think it needs some buffing up or something. I'll have to find out what to do. I've been meaning to ask my Uncle Monty. In his line of work I figure he should know."

"One would hope."

Out on the front porch Margaret asked him, "Is this ghost ever called a fairy?"

He brightened. "Yes, as a matter of fact it is. When the local paper reviewed the book they referred to Anna Coffin as a 'fairy.' The name has stuck in some quarters."

"You must have done a lot of research."

"Not enough, it appears. When I wrote the book I didn't know about the music."

Margaret hoped her sharp intake of breath was inaudible. "Music?"

"After the book came out I came upon some letters of Anna's which mention her love for the flute. She used to take it down to the beach and play for hours. She could have sat just down there." He pointed toward the rock-lined shore. "It made her feel less lonely, and she thought that by playing it she could lure Gilbert home. Apparently it was Gilbert who brought the flute to her. I think it was from India."

"What a scumbag!"

"Who?"

"Gilbert. All men."

He laughed. "Delightful story, isn't it?"

They walked around the south side of the house, and Roland knelt to examine the stones. Ruth Godwish was there, hunched over and poking at the ground with a long stick. Although they couldn't have been more than ten feet away, and talking loudly, she did not look up at them.

Back in the kitchen door, Margaret asked suddenly, "Who's Genevieve?"

"My wife. She's gone now. Five years gone. Cancer."

"I'm sorry."

"She was quite a lady. She was the real writer in the family. I only dabble." He was walking toward the cellar door. "May I?" he asked.

81

"I have to warn you, I have yet to go down there. I even keep it locked."

"I can see that."

She pulled back the flimsy bolt and they descended down a stone staircase. A lone lightbulb hanging from the ceiling did not illuminate the place much. Part of the cellar had a dirt floor. The part that was made of concrete held a fairly modern furnace. Along the walls of the cellar were wooden boxes. She supposed that at one time they would have contained firewood or maybe even coal. There were also stacks of graying boards. A cupboard stood against one wall, the door crookedly open. "The canning cupboard," said Margaret. "I remember I hated being the one who had to come down here for jams or preserves. This place still gives me the shivers."

"A perfect root cellar," Roland said.

"It's damp down here."

"Dirt floor. My wife would like this — perfect place to bury the bodies."

"Your wife?" And then something clicked in Margaret's mind. She stared at him. "Genevieve Irons, the mystery writer? She was your wife?"

He nodded.

"I love her books! I've read every single one of them, especially the Detective Partridge series."

"That was her favorite series as well. I think in some ways she became the alter ego of Melissa Partridge."

"Melissa's so wonderful! Did you live here then, when she wrote those books?"

"We did, yes. Fifteen years we've been in our place on the beach here. Before that it was England. As you know, I came over here to teach at the university."

"If I had known that Genevieve Irons was living here, I would have come down and gotten her to autograph all of my books. I own most of them."

"Genevieve said she found the rugged Maine coastline conducive to writing. Especially mysteries."

They talked while they walked, leaving the cellar and climbing the steps to the main floor, where Roland admired the fireplace, the high-beamed ceilings, the bay window in the living room, the spacious dining room.

"It's not as clean as it could be," Margaret said.

"It looks marvelous."

They continued up the stairs to the second floor.

"The landing!" said Roland. "What a wonderful place to set up a studio. You paint?"

"I dabble."

"I'm sure you're being quite modest."

The second floor had four very large rooms plus a bathroom. The master bedroom faced the sea and had tall windows neatly divided into four panes. There was a fireplace in the master bedroom, but Margaret never remembered anyone lighting a fire in there.

"This would have been Anna's room," Roland said.

"It was my parents' room. I'm using it now. I always liked this view. When I was a little girl I used to come in here and sit at this window seat for hours."

They toured through the other three rooms, only sparsely furnished with blanketless beds and empty wooden bureaus with drawers that stuck.

Her sister's room faced south and her childhood room faced north. But this stark, empty place with the dull wood floors bore no resemblance to the place where she had lived for ten years. She used to line up all her stuffed animals along the wide window ledge, and then sitting in the midst of her large family of comfortable, soft dolls, she would look out at the point. The single bed was still there, with its bare mattress, but that was all. Her stuffed animals were gone, along with all the notebooks filled with her drawings.

The room that ran along the back of the house was her mother's sewing room. It was a large room, and along with the sewing machine, there was a day bed in there with two dolls, her mother's dolls. Her mother's dolls were not for playing with, but for looking at. They would sit there, porcelain-faced, dressed in ornate dresses from the nineteenth century.

The room now was completely empty. No furniture, just dingy floors and walls that were water-stained, cracked, and in need of paint.

"This house needs a lot of work," she moaned.

"But it's such a fine house, such a specimen."

Back out on the landing, Roland said, "Shall we venture upstairs?" A locked door led to the third floor.

"I haven't been up there yet. I keep it locked. Like the basement."

When she was a child, the third-floor dormer was a large open room. The back half contained stacked trunks, boxes, and wardrobes filled with musty suits of her grandfather's and flimsy, flowered dresses of her grandmother's. As children they would drape themselves in these clothes and play for hours.

The third floor was also the place for slumber parties, where groups of giggling girls chatted until morning, with sleeping bags end to end, a record player, bags of chips.

Margaret slid the bolt back and opened the door. The steps up were steep, the hallway narrow. Roland ascended cheerfully, a spring to his step, a child exploring, while Margaret followed more slowly, a curious fear leadening her steps.

The top floor was lit only by the sun, which filtered

through smudgy windows casting elongated shadows on the walls. The ornate wooden wardrobe was still there, standing askew on crooked legs. The trunks and boxes were gone.

"Oh my," said Roland, delighted. "Look at the wood-work, the intricate wainscoting, even up here."

Margaret stood for several seconds watching him before she moved tentatively toward the door that led to the widow's walk. It was shut and nailed closed. A couple of two-by-fours crossed it and were nailed into the wood of the frame. On either side of the door were long narrow windows. She looked through one of them to the small porch. Some attempt to fix it had been made, she saw.

"The cupola," said Roland, walking toward her.

Margaret nodded.

"There was a death up here, wasn't there?"

"My sister."

"That must have been some time ago."

"Nearly twenty-five years."

Roland nodded.

Margaret said quietly, "She fell from this porch when she was thirteen."

"That would explain your reluctance to come up here."

She looked around her. She should do something with this place, have that porch removed, have that door walled over, keep the lock to the third floor securely bolted. Never come up here again.

EIGHTEEN

The only time Donna felt completely safe was on her weekly trips to Bangor. Every Friday she went. Every Friday she would pack up her shoulder bag, climb into her car, and head out, ostensibly to see her shrink, but what her parents didn't know wouldn't hurt them.

During those first trips, her parents drove her. That was before she could drive, when her eyes wouldn't focus on the road and her mind wouldn't focus on the thinking of it. But that was a long time ago. When she was able to drive again, she insisted on going alone.

"But Donna, dear," said her mother, "we're only thinking of your safety. Your father and I don't mind accompanying you."

It was when she looked at the two of them, her mother sitting stiffly, knees together, looking concerned, and her father in his easy chair regarding her with an uneasy smile, that she told the first of her lies.

"My doctor says it's good for me to drive alone. In fact, that's what he's recommending, now that I've got my license back. That's what he said."

"Well," said Sylvia doubtfully, "if it's recommended by your therapist."

Donna brightened. After that the lies came easy. Now, nearly twenty years later she still went to Bangor each Friday, and became another self there, changing into different outfits that she packed in her shoulder bag. She no longer saw a therapist of any kind. It was Bangor on Fridays and Bosuns Harbor and Coffins Reach the rest of the week. Although she threatened, the thought of actually getting into her car and driving to Canada or out west brought back all the fear and pain. Her therapist (when she was still seeing him) told her that she had a kind of agoraphobia. Terrified to leave that which is familiar. Bosuns Harbor was familiar. Coffins Reach was familiar. The rest of the world was not. She had two sisters who lived in California. They had left and had never come back. Maybe they were as afraid to come back as she was to leave.

It wasn't Friday today, so Donna was in the hardware store showing paint samples to Mrs. Florid, complying with her never-ending quest to change the colors of her walls.

"You have such a flair for color, Donna, what color do you think goes with this dish pattern? Here, I brought a teacup along."

Outwardly Donna smiled, remained pleasant. She really did have a flair for color, that much was true.

"I would say the periwinkle blue. That's a lovely pattern." She kept the sarcasm out of her voice.

"Isn't it, though? I picked this set up in Bar Harbor. Have you been there recently? There's a lovely little china shop there. A new one on the waterfront."

Donna shook her head. "Not recently." She smiled as she mixed the paints.

"I hear a relative of yours has moved into the old Ochs place, the one in Coffins Reach, the house next to that backward boy and his mother," Mrs. Florid said.

Donna's smile froze. She felt hot, faint, like she needed to sit down. She said, "It appears so, yes. She's a cousin of mine." And don't call him "backward," she wanted to add.

"Well, that's something, isn't it. It's nice to be reunited

with family, that's what I always say. One can't have too much family. I do think I like this blue. Donna, you're so clever with colors."

NINETEEN

Two evenings later Margaret sat at the master bedroom window and wished she had a television. Back in Fredericton she seldom watched it. She usually sat on the couch and read, mysteries mainly, while Robin watched PBS movies with Aislin on his lap. But here, in this voiceless place, where ghosts wandered in and out of her thinking, Margaret would leave a TV on at all times, just for the company. Daytime wasn't too bad. Evenings were the worst. During the day she could make pots of coffee, listen to her CDs, and scrub the house. There was always something to do in this old house. When she finished one task, another one loomed; windows to scrub, floors to mop, cupboards to clean out, trash to bag and get rid of. She also spent a lot of time getting her studio just the way she wanted it, with the easel facing the correct angle so that it caught the lights of the eastern sun. She organized her paints, lining them up first alphabetically and then according to color, starting with the darkest on the left and fading across the table to the lightest, and then changing, putting the palest first.

Daytime radio was decidedly different, more upbeat, more cheerful, than the nighttime FM voices. During the daytime she also could listen to children at play, yelling to each other as they chased across the beach, mothers calling that lunches were ready, joggers pounding along the path by the shoreline, beachcombers chatting, waving to her as she carried flat stones up from the beach for her path.

She remembered reading once that the group of people who watched the most TV were middle-aged single women.

She remembered scoffing at that statistic. Now she understood.

In the evening, she would faithfully and methodically shut herself in, double locking the outside doors, checking each window and then carefully bolting the doors to the third floor and to the basement.

As she stood on her front porch, a lone jogger cut a winding path through the rocks and sand down in front of her. She watched him. It wasn't Roland, but someone much younger, in his twenties. His upper arms and thighs were sheened with sweat and he was clad only in silk shorts even though it was September, even though the evenings were getting cool.

Her phone rang. She went inside and shut the door.

"Hello, Margaret."

"Robin," she said.

A pause.

A longer pause. Margaret waited.

"I called . . ." He cleared his throat. "I called to see if you were all right."

"I'm fine."

"I would like us to talk, Margaret."

"Why?"

"We could start over, maybe we could."

"I heard you came home finally. That was nice of you."

He cleared his throat. "I was wrong to leave."

"Yes."

"I want you to come home."

"Oh really?"

There was silence. Then, "Don't be like that, Margaret."

She could picture him on the other end of the line, holding the phone in both hands, thin strands of auburn hair falling across his forehead, shoulders bent forward. She wondered where he was calling from. The house? Their house? Which phone was he using? Did he notice that she had packed up all her clothes, all her paints, even most of the kitchen dishes? And the coffeepot?

"Good-bye, Robin."

She hung up. The call left her unnerved and panicky. She looked at her watch; it was only just after eight o'clock, still too early to go to bed.

On a whim she dialed Roland's number. When he answered she said, "I wonder if one lonely old soul would like to go out for coffee with another lonely old soul?"

"I'd be delighted. Where to?"

"How about you choose."

"I know the perfect spot," he said.

He suggested a place called Wellingtons Bake Shop on Harbor Road, "just behind the post office, you can't miss it." But when Margaret pulled her car up to the front of a well-weathered house with the words "Wellingtons Bake Shop" barely visible in the bleached wood above the door, she had her doubts.

It was an old house, much like her own, with a sagging front porch badly in need of paint. She headed to the front door and Roland came out to greet her.

"This is the place?" she asked.

"This is the place. The building's not much but the coffee's the best in town, and if your cholesterol levels need a boost, they serve a scrumptious array of baked goods."

She followed him down a narrow hall lined with log shelves, which held jars of oddly shaped pastas, and green and amber sprigs immersed in bottles of exotic wine vinegars. The brief hall opened out into one room that held small, mismatched wooden tables and chairs. There were a number of people in the room already, gabbing back and forth as if this were a family supper rather than a public restaurant. Margaret recognized Lorne Maynard leaning against the wall on the back rungs of his chair. He raised a hand in salute. She also saw Dr. Stoniard, who sat on a wooden chair, leaning forward, thighs spread, feet flat on the floor. Along one wall was a counter with metal coffee thermoses and plates and baskets of muffins, squares, cookies, and scones.

Roland had retrieved two mugs. "There's Irish Cream, French Vanilla, Amaretto Almond . . ."

"Any good old-fashioned regular?"

"Ah, a purist, are we?"

She took her coffee black and followed him to the only available table, a small round one with wobbly legs. He also grabbed a couple of chocolate-covered somethings and placed one down in front of her on a napkin. Several people had already greeted Roland and introduced themselves to Margaret.

"This your hangout?" Margaret asked.

He chuckled and leaned toward her, his voice low, a twinkle in his eye. "Wellingtons attracts a certain, shall we say, eclectic crowd."

Margaret grinned. "And you fit right in."

He leaned back. "Well, of course."

Margaret enjoyed the casual banter of Wellingtons's patrons. This was just what she needed. For a moment or two she could forget about Robin, forget that he was in Fredericton, forget that he had her telephone number. So much for anonymity.

Roland introduced Margaret to Stu, who wore his shaggy gray hair in a ponytail. His wife Vivian sat next to him, half-glasses perched on the end of her nose. She also met a retired lawyer, an unemployed teacher, and a couple of local politicians. All were dressed casually, nattily, in denim coveralls or cotton trousers, boots and khaki jackets.

"So Margaret, what do you do?" Stu asked.

"I'm an artist by profession."

"Wonderful!" Vivian said.

"She lives in the old Ochs house on Coffins Reach," Lorne Maynard said.

"The old Ochs house?" Vivian looked up at her over the tops of her glasses. "That place has quite a history."

Margaret nodded.

"The famous haunted house," said Dr. Stoniard. "Our own Roland made that place famous."

Roland chuckled again.

"The ghost of Anna Coffin," said someone else.

"This coffee shop is named after the birthplace of Anna — Wellingtons," said another.

"Now, there's a subject for you," said the paunchy bearded man who Margaret remembered someone called Howard. "Paint a picture of our own Anna Coffin. Illustrations for Roland's books." He turned to the others. "Don't you think that's a good idea?"

"We have the portrait," Vivian said. "I believe there's only the one."

"I've seen the portrait," said Lorne. "But don't you think there are definitely more moods to the girl than the painting portrays?"

As Margaret listened to the back-and-forth chatter, a gem of an idea was being spawned in her mind.

TWENTY

Chris Rikken decided to take the case. Maybe it was the fact that he had nothing better to do now or maybe it was that the whole thing intrigued him, but as he sat in the cabin of his thirty-three-foot Mirage sailboat sucking on a juicebox, he decided to call Clark Ochs. He rose and headed out into the bright sun of the cockpit. This boat was his home, had been ever since Ginny left with the girls and he'd quit the police force. In another month, maybe earlier, it would be time to set sail for southern ports. He shaded his eyes. It would be another fine day. He thought about taking the boat out around the bay, maybe sail up past the point. There wouldn't be too many warm days left. Just a short sail. But he needed to give the cabin a thorough cleaning, he had laundry to do, and he needed to get started sanding and polishing the teak boat rails.

But first he'd call Clark Ochs. Anything to do with the Ochs family fascinated him. He had been a young deputy recruit, barely nineteen years old, when that Ochs girl had fallen to her death in Coffins Reach. He had to shake his head over that one — the way the Ochs family controlled the entire case, what went into the police report, and what was kept out. And Jon Smith, the investigating officer, just kowtowing to the Ochs brothers left and right.

Chris sucked up the last bit of juice from the box and threw it into his garbage pail. He fingered his rigging a bit; he could use a new main sheet. That was another reason to take the case. The money would come in handy. And anyway, the case seemed pretty straight-forward. Two maybe three weeks at the outside, and he could leave with a little bit more money in his bank account.

He waved to a returning lobster boat. He knew the lobstermen well. Often they would share a cup of coffee or a game of cards, the only difference being that once the card game was finished and the coffee consumed, the fishermen went ashore and drove home to their wives and children while he bedded down in his V-berth.

Yesterday the youngest of the Ochs brothers had called him around lunch, asked could he please meet with Chris that evening. Chris never allowed clients on his boat. His office became whatever coffee shop or restaurant the client chose to meet him in. In this case it was the Bulldog Cafe at 9:30. Chris arrived at the Bulldog fifteen minutes past the scheduled meeting time. He always did that. Keep the clients waiting. Then when you finally arrive, they're nervous and upset and then you have the upper hand.

Clark Ochs was sipping on a Coke when Chris arrived. He knew Clark was in his late fifties, but he appeared much older, crusty and sour looking. His hair was gray-brown and combed across the top of this head in an attempt to mask a balding pate. Got news for you, Chris wanted to tell him, it's not working.

"It's my brothers," said the man when Chris sat down.

"Yeah?"

"They're planning something against me. I want you to find out what it is."

Sounds to me like you need a shrink, Chris thought. A waitress came and took his order. A ginger ale, lots of ice. He used to drink. Not any more. It cost him his wife, his career, his kids.

"This Margaret coming back, it's like an omen."

"Whoa!" said Chris, a hand raised. "Back up. Start way

95

back at the beginning. Who's Margaret?"

Clark started back on the day when the girl had died and her family had moved away. Chris kept nodding and urging him to continue, while he wrote notes in the little spiral book he always carried. A lot of PIs didn't use notebooks, relying instead on their memories, but his years in the force had trained him. Some habits die hard.

"It's a conspiracy, it always has been," said Clark, leaning forward. "That was the beginning of it, the girl dying. All of a sudden Mitch moves away, and then, this strange thing happens. Monty comes to me and offers me money if I move away too, if Pat and I moved away. We had two kids at the time. Little kids, so I think to myself I could never uproot them from school. And not Pat, either. So I didn't go."

"Why did he offer you money? Under what pretext?"

"Under the pretext that they, Leo and Monty, were going to buy out my portion of the partnership. Leo's giving me this song and dance that I don't hold enough shares anyway, that it was him and Monty and our father who built the hardware business. They got a chain of them, you know. He comes to me offering me a bunch of money if I move away. Why, I say, and he says it would be easier for me to start over fresh someplace. Then he changes his tune, says I can stay but they buy out my shares. They had all these good reasons, and like a fool I signed. Pat said I shouldn't take it, that I should fight it in the courts."

"Did you? Did you get a lawyer?"

"Nah. I should've. I really should've."

"Yes, you should have."

"But that's water under the bridge now. I don't take the money, and so then I don't have a job, then Monty hires me like he's being the generous big brother."

Chris blinked at him. "But what was the reason for wanting to buy you out? Did you ever find that out?"

"They wanted my share of the holdings I guess. More money for themselves is my guess. That's all I can figure out. Thing is I can't figure it out. That's where you come in. I'm thinking, I've always had this thought that there was more to it than just wanting to buy out my shares. Because this all happens right after my niece dies. Mitch takes his money and runs, moves to Bangor. I should have done the same thing."

Chris looked at him across the table. "And you want me to dredge up anything I can find about Monty and Leo and that business deal of twenty-five years ago."

"Right."

Chris closed his notebook. "I'll let you know."

"You'll let me know?"

"Yeah. Tomorrow at the latest."

Clark seemed surprised. "Can't you make a decision now?"

"I don't usually do these revenge things. Too risky."

"It's not revenge. I just want to find out."

"I'll let you know." Chris rose.

He left the bill for Clark to pay.

But this morning as he peeled an orange sitting in the full sun in his cockpit, he made a decision. He'd take the case.

TWENTY-ONE

When Margaret was absorbed in a project, be it a painting, a drawing, or even the doodlings of an idea, everything else in her life settled almost effortlessly into a comfortable rhythm. She would spend every moment she could at the canvas. This oddly left her not depleted, but energized for her role as wife, mother, friend. The evening meal became the time when she would listen with interest to Robin's day at school, laugh at some antic or other of Aislin's. But the following morning when Robin dropped Aislin at day care, Margaret would go into her studio and find herself.

She would enter into the canvas as she laid color on color. She would be there — standing next to the barns she drew, running through the fields, exploring the insides of the old homes. She rode the waves and felt the spray, she wept with the faces of sadness that came from her brush, she heard the cry of the gull, smelled the apple blossoms.

During these project times she would sometimes waken in the middle of the night fully rested and get up and go into her studio. Just a quick touch here, a bit there, she would tell herself as she dabbed on a point of paint. "I just thought of something I had to do," she would tell Robin should he wander in, squinting and tousle-haired and wondering what in the world she was doing up in the middle of the night.

It was during these times that she would stop in odd places, a grocery store perhaps, and note the diamond patterns of light on the newly sprayed vegetable bins. She'd reach into her purse and grab the nearest scrap of paper — an old VISA receipt or a deposit slip from her checkbook, and with a thick pencil, which she always carried, would stand in the aisle and sketch.

Between projects she felt scattered and tense, her hands fluttering nervously at her sides, itching for the feel of color and the smell of her paints.

She had been between projects for such a long time that the initial anxiousness she always experienced had drifted into a sort of malaise, a dead space, where she got up, wandered through the day, and then went to bed again.

It was midmorning, and she sat at her kitchen table and wondered why she couldn't keep her hands still. She rose, walked through to the living room, and sat down again. It was a stupid idea; she didn't even know what Anna Coffin looked like. She had no *relationship* with Anna Coffin. But then the other side of her mind would argue, why not? Artists had taken on stranger projects, and didn't everyone down at Wellingtons tell her there was already a portrait? Anna had lived here alone, like she did. They shared that much of a connection, didn't they? She dialed Roland's number.

He said to her, "I think it's marvelous that you want to do a portrait of Anna. The one we know about was the one that Gilbert commissioned."

"Where can I see it?"

"I have a very unsatisfactory photocopy of it. The original is in the Bosuns Harbor Historical Society Museum, which would be a marvelous place for you to begin your research. I can loan you my Anna Coffin file. Later on today I'm heading over to Augusta, but I'm here for a while. I wouldn't mind a visitor if you want to come for them now. I could even be persuaded to put the teakettle on."

"I'll be there."

The inside of Roland Irons's house looked like a page out

of the Southwest edition of *House Beautiful.* Colorful Navajo rugs were scattered on the polished hardwood floors. Blankets and throws were draped artfully on chairs and couches. Hardwood railings were polished to a high gloss. The prints on the walls were expensive ones, she could see. She followed him through a wide hallway and out onto a windowed sunporch along the south wall. This room was hot in the summer, he told her, but marvelous in the fall and winter, just marvelous. This was his office. On a large wooden desk were a computer, modem, phone, and fax. Behind the desk were floor to ceiling bookshelves, filled with what looked like leather-bound volumes.

"You have some nice things," Margaret said.

"Genevieve's influence. She was the decorator. She collected art and first editions."

He opened up an oak filing cabinet, fingered through it, and finally handed her a thin manila folder. "Here it is, my Anna Coffin file."

Margaret was disappointed by the size of it; she had hoped for a thick file bulging with pictures and memoirs and original pages from original diaries. She couldn't help herself. "It's small," she said.

"I'm afraid there's not much here. There's not been much anyone has found about her life. I just stumbled onto her story when I was researching the account of the Bar Harbor fishermen. But I found her story so intriguing, I decided to do the chapter on her."

"Maybe that's why my parents didn't know of her."

"I would suggest checking with the historical society. It's located just off the town square, in a white building."

"All the buildings around here are white."

He laughed and said, "Now about that tea?"

Margaret followed him into the kitchen. She'd force herself to drink tea if it meant more information from Dr. Irons.

Like the rest of his house, the kitchen was spotless with gleaming pots hanging on an island near the center. The room was a study in blues. Deep blue ceramic floor tiles and pale blue countertops.

"Nice kitchen," Margaret said.

"Genevieve. Again."

"You must miss her very much."

He plugged in the kettle and procured some loose tea from a canister.

"I do. I'm thinking, actually, of selling this place. Too many memories. We would go for walks every morning."

When the tea was ready, Margaret took a sip. It was surprisingly good.

"Thanks for your help," she said.

"It's nothing really. I enjoy this."

Roland opened up the manila folder. "Photocopies," he said. "Of letters and information about her story. She wrote quite a few letters that were preserved. There's nothing about where the body was buried or where the shawl and flute ended up, but here, you're welcome to what I have."

"You said you had a photocopied picture?"

"Yes," said Roland, shuffling through the file. "Here at the back, very poor quality, I must say. You really should see the original."

He lifted out the photocopy and handed it to Margaret. She held it up and looked into the face of Anna Coffin. In the portrait, the young woman was standing, her left hand close to her chest clutching the ends of a white shawl. She was wearing a long, light dress and black button-up boots. Her hair looked dark in the photocopy, although it could have been any color. It was done up in a series of combs and ringlets that framed her face. She wasn't especially beautiful, perhaps a bit chunky in body, but there was something haunting about her, a vulnerability, an innocence, a sadness. The face did not smile, but held a look of surprise, almost as if she had been caught unaware by a camera.

"So, this is Anna Coffin," she said.

"That is Anna Coffin. The one who lived in your house."

"Amazing. Yes, I will paint her, although a lot will have to come from my imagination."

"The best place."

TWENTY-TWO

Clark was sitting at the kitchen table halfway through his second cup of coffee when Pat walked in and demanded to know why he wasn't at work yet.

"Do you see the time? That brother of yours is going to fire you and with good reason."

"I'm about to give him a taste of his own medicine," he said with a smirk.

Pat was wearing a faded pink terrycloth bathrobe belted loosely enough around her ample frame to reveal a pale blue nightgown of some flimsy material. Lately she was spending more and more of her days in this housecoat.

"So you're not going in at all?" she asked.

"I'll go in later. Donna's there today. They'll be enough people there today."

Pat poured herself a cup of coffee and leaned against the counter. Her blond hair hadn't been combed yet and stuck out in brassy tufts around her head.

"Leo's coming today," she said.

"Leo!" He stared at her. "How come nobody told me?"

"I don't know. Maybe you should listen more."

"How do you know Leo's coming?"

"Sylvia told me. Some big meeting with Monty. If you ask me it's got something to do with Margaret." She reached into the deep pocket of her bathrobe and withdrew half a pack of cigarettes.

"Pat, you know how I hate cigarette smoke."

"So leave, then. It's my house, too."

"You'd like me to."

When she exhaled, Clark waved his hands in front of his face. He asked, "What does Margaret have to do with anything?"

"I dunno. Just a feeling, and if you paid a little more attention to things you wouldn't be sitting here asking me about it."

The phone rang and Pat answered it. He watched her lift one tan leathery arm to the receiver. Pat still lay in the sun every summer day for at least four hours on her chaise lounge, basting herself with a spray bottle of water every so often. Apparently no one had told her about the dangers of too much sun.

"It's for you." She handed the receiver to him.

"Who is it?"

"How should I know? What am I, your social secretary now?"

He grabbed the receiver from her. It was the PI, Chris Rikken, the guy he'd gone to see the night before.

"I've decided to take the case," was all he said.

"Good."

"But I'll need to meet with you, get more particulars, anything at all. I'll begin by doing a search of Leo and Monty, driver's licenses, bank records, all that."

"You can do that?"

"It's my job. It's what I get paid to do."

"Good." Pat was watching him curiously, head cocked to one side.

"Can you talk?" asked Chris.

"Not really."

"I figured so. How about we meet at the Bulldog Cafe tonight at eight. Can you make it?"

"Sure."

104

"Who was that?" asked Pat when he hung up.

"A guy from work."

"What guy from work?"

"A guy who wants some lumber."

"Yeah, right."

TWENTY-THREE

The warm day had a lazy feel to it, and instead of heading directly back to Coffins Reach, Margaret drove down to the waterfront and found a parking spot behind a tan jeep. She placed the Anna Coffin file in her backpack and walked along the harbor front. There were a number of yachts moored in the bay as well as fishing boats that had pulled up to the wharf. Such a scenic place, she thought, the stuff postcards are made of.

She bought a coffee to go at a corner convenience store, the kind that sells little bags of chips, candy bars, and cans of pop. The coffee smelled old, as if it had been sitting in that discolored glass pot since early morning. She bought it anyway. The pink-skinned, white-haired man behind the counter looked as sleepy as the store itself. The place resembled an old drugstore, apothecary they called them then, the kind of place where druggists mixed up concoctions from bottles rather than dispensing manufactured pills like they do today. When she asked for a lid for her coffee he looked at her blankly. She repeated her question. Finally he pointed to a counter that contained lids, little round plastic containers of cream, and paper squares of sugar and artificial sweetener. The wooden floorboards creaked under her feet as she walked through the door, and on her way out she noted a calendar on the wall dated 1947. I really am in the twilight zone, she thought.

She walked up toward the town square and sat on an empty bench. She'd read through the file and then go and have a look at Anna's portrait.

Dr. Irons's file contained a number of photocopies of pages from other books, plus copies of the actual letters that Anna and Gilbert had written to Geoffrey and Sarah. Most of the photocopies came from a book called *Life and Legends: People on the Coast of Maine*, which was published, she noted, in 1944. The letters all came from the historical society archives. She read through them paragraph by paragraph and realized that there was much that Dr. Irons hadn't included in his chapter. There was far more to this woman than a white shawl and a missing gravesite. She put the letters in chronological order and started at the beginning. At first the letters told of her daily routine, the helping to clean the house with a housemaid (and friend) named Emily. (Dr. Irons's story had given the impression that Anna lived there alone.) Her letters described in great detail the shorefront, calling the two-humped island Dragon Back Island. A perfect name for it, thought Margaret.

She read on. These early letters portrayed Anna as playful and energetic. In one she described the two of them, Emily and Anna, rowing out to Dragon Back Island. "It took us an hour to get there, but once we did, we ran the length and breadth of it. So deserted it was, not a human presence did we see, not even the dragon!" And then, "Emily and I raced along the shore. I, being faster, won! I am glad Gilbert or Sarah was not here to see me grab up my skirts and behave like a child."

And in another, "We did not feel like cleaning today so we went walking along the beach. Emily found a jellyfish and said it reminded her of Gilbert's face. I admonished her for that. But later I laughed when I thought of it."

Gradually her letters took a different tone. "Gilbert has admonished me for my playful countenance. I will try to act my age when he is about. Perhaps that is why God is punishing me."

Punishing me? thought Margaret.

"Gilbert says God never laughs except in derision. Is that true? If that is true, then I am the worst of infidels. Gilbert said that is why God is cursing me with barrenness. I will try to be more faithful to my serious call when Gilbert is away."

Margaret read the next letter. "I am still barren. Gilbert said that God is punishing me because I would rather worship God by the seaside than in a church. Is God only in the church? I asked Gilbert this question and he slapped me across the face. Sometimes I am so stupid. Gilbert tells me that."

The letters became more desperate, more lonely as time passed. Toward the end every one seemed to be stuck on only one theme — her inability to bear children. "Emily has left. She had to go back to England to care for her mother. So I am alone. I know Gilbert will come back to me if only I can give him a son."

A small breeze lifted the papers in Margaret's lap, and she caught them before they fluttered away from her. How many times had she thought those same thoughts: God is punishing me. If I were a better Christian, then maybe God would give me a child. If I do all the right things in the right order; go to church every Sunday, read the Bible and pray every day, then God will look down in favor and grant my wish.

At the very back of the folder she saw a half piece of paper, less dog-eared than the rest of the material. In it, Anna wrote to her sister that Gilbert had brought her a flute.

"I am surprised at this, for Gilbert doesn't care for music as I do. But I will play this flute until God gives me a child, or until I die."

Margaret read all of the offerings with a sad interest, but when she looked down at the picture of Anna again, she wondered. How had she missed that look of despair?

She got up, her legs feeling strangely heavy; perhaps if she saw the original painting. She made her way across the grass to the white building behind her. "Bosuns Harbor Historical Society" was lettered on a wooden sign above the door. She walked up the wide steps. The door was unlocked and opened into a generous foyer. She stood for several seconds waiting, but no one came. The walls were lined with photos of tall sailing ships, of Bosuns Harbor circa 1867, 1899, 1902, and 1946. Unsmiling faces looked out in grim relief. She also saw a picture of *her* house in Coffins Reach. The wide porch, the widow's walk.

"Can I help you?" The voice startled her. She turned. The gray-haired woman standing behind her was someone she recognized. She groped for a name. Vivian. At Wellingtons the night before. The woman spoke first.

"Margaret, I thought that was you. How nice that you came."

"Hello, Vivian. Stu's wife, right?"

"You have a good memory. It's nice to see you again. Would you like a tour? We even have a bit here about your Coffin Mansion."

This was the first time she had heard it called that. Usually it was referred to as "the Old Ochs house." She liked "mansion," even though that term might be a small exaggeration.

"If it would be no trouble," Margaret said. "And I'd love to see that portrait of Anna Coffin."

Vivian talked as she led Margaret on a tour of the downstairs rooms. "That portrait used to be in an attic storeroom; no one even knew it was there. No one even knew who she was. Now, with Roland's book, we've had to take it out and display it, so many people ask about it."

Vivian, who was smartly dressed in a plaid woolen skirt and shawl, looked far different than the woman in the rubber boots and khaki jacket who had sat and looked at her over her half-glasses the evening before. "It's upstairs, but we'll tour the main floor first. It will give you a flavor for the area."

Margaret was shown models of sailing ships and told that Bosuns Harbor was once a major ship-building port. "This was the place to be back then," Vivian said. In another room she viewed artwork and crafts by local artists and artisans that depicted the area's history. Margaret noticed Dr. Irons's book on display there. She walked through replicas of storefronts and was led into a full-sized replica of a local apothecary. "The building is still in existence," said Vivian, and Margaret recognized the corner store that had sold her the bad coffee. She wandered through rooms and rooms of old farm implements, foot-pedal sewing machines, cream separators, cookstoves, antique glassware, and cutlery.

The portrait of Anna was in the last room they entered. The painting was larger than Margaret had imagined, at least five feet high and four feet wide. There she was, Anna Coffin, clutching her white shawl in her left hand. In her right she held a small bunch of flowers, their flower faces down, almost as if she didn't know she was holding them. Margaret hadn't noticed that in the photocopy. There was a look of surprise in her dark eyes, but the fear was unmistakable.

Margaret finally spoke. "She looks so sad."

"She had a sad life."

She shook her head. "It's more than that. Frightened, maybe. I can't explain."

"Everyone has that reaction when seeing her portrait for the first time, and doesn't it look like her eyes are following you everywhere you move?" She paused. "Did Roland tell you about the curse?"

"The what?"

"After that first book came out he learned about the flute

and about the curse. I think he's planning on a new chapter in which all will be included."

"What curse?"

"Apparently Anna Coffin put a curse on the house before she died — that no one who lived there would ever know any kind of happiness. It would always be surrounded by death and barrenness."

Margaret's eyes widened. "My house?"

Vivian smiled and nodded. "Roland would just laugh it away, however. He is a skeptic, our Roland is. Curses and ghosts. He loves to make fun of them."

Margaret looked into the face of Anna Coffin again. Was there really fear there, or was there something else? A sneer? A taunt? A look of "I dare you"?

TWENTY-FOUR

Twilight, that part of the day caught between daylight and darkness, had descended along the coast as Margaret drove home.

She decided that to put any credence in the curse was ridiculous. She thought of Robin's mother. She could picture her talking about the power of God being stronger than any evil. She thought briefly of calling her, but she put that idea out of her mind almost as quickly as it entered. She used to be close to her mother-in-law. But not anymore. Not since Margaret had walked into her kitchen and stated that she was abandoning God because God had abandoned her. What kind of a God gave something just to take it back eight years later? She must not have gotten it right. She told her that she was tired of pleasing a God who would not be pleased.

Anna, Anna, I understand, she thought. I understand a rage so strong, a hatred so cruel that one leaves a curse for all generations to follow.

She had walked out of Robin's mother's kitchen that afternoon leaving the stunned woman sitting at her table. Margaret had not been back. A few weeks later Robin had left.

The night deepened as Margaret turned off the main road and headed down toward her house, a crooked murky structure growing out of the ground, all odd angles and jutting black fingers against the bruised sky.

Ruth Godwish was standing on her small cement back porch, her hands raised above her head, her face lifted toward the bleak sky. An odd gesture, almost a gesture of worship. She ignored Margaret.

As Margaret walked toward her own back porch, something felt wrong. Hadn't she left the light on? She always left the porch light on. Perhaps the bulb had burned out. Maybe that was all it was. She fumbled for her keys in the blackness, dropping them once. Ruth Godwish was still there. Was the woman staring at her? She was finally able to unlock the door and step inside. She reached for the light switch.

"Donna!" she cried out.

Her cousin was sitting cross-legged on a rocking chair beside the woodstove. She looked up and smirked.

"You gave me such a start!" Margaret said.

"That was the whole idea."

"You scared me out of my wits! Why are you in my house? How did you get in?"

Donna placed her hands behind her head and stretched her catlike body.

"How did you get in here? How? I demand to know!"

"The door was unlocked."

"The door was *not* unlocked. I *always* lock the door. How did you get in?"

"Well, cuz, it was unlocked this time."

"It *had* to be locked! I always lock it. I'm very careful about that."

"Will you quit with the broken record already? I'm telling you the door was unlocked. Instead of going on and on about the door being locked, why don't you ask me what I'm doing here?"

Margaret sighed. "What are you doing here?"

"I came for a visit." Donna uncoiled her legs from around each other and rose. "Figured you wouldn't mind."

"Well, I do mind." Margaret's voice rose shrilly at the end.

"Oh, touchy."

"Why didn't you at least have the light on?"

"I like scaring people." Donna walked toward Margaret, raised her hands and said, "Boo!"

"Donna! This is not funny."

"It was a practical joke! Don't get your undies in a knot." Donna was wearing all black again, from her black hair down to a pair of high-heeled patent leather boots.

"It wasn't funny." Margaret willed herself to stop shaking.

"I like your scream. You have a good scream. You should try out for Stephen King movies."

"I didn't scream."

"Well, loud sigh then, moan, maybe. *Donna!*" She mimicked Margaret's cry. "*Donna! Donna!*"

"Why are you here, Donna?"

"I came to see you. Ruth Godwish, the old witch, told me you were out. She told me that you usually go for a walk every morning, but that this morning you had breakfast with Roly Irons, *Doctor* Roly Irons as he likes to be called, the pompous fool, then you went out. And that you hadn't been back."

"How does Ruth Godwish know so much about what I do?"

"Ruth Godwish knows everything."

Margaret walked to the south window and pulled down the blinds. If Ruth Godwish had been watching from her house, she couldn't help but notice this deliberate snub.

Donna was continuing, "Ruth Godwish has 'second sight.' "

"What?"

"Second sight. She can see things other people can't. Some people would call her a witch. I call her a witch in another aspect."

Margaret hung her backpack on the back of a kitchen chair. "This whole town is crazy. A bunch of lunatics live here!"

114

Donna only smiled. Margaret turned on her. "Why did you come and what do you want? And how did you get in?"

"I've told you a dozen times that the door was unlocked. It was unlocked. Read my lips: the door was unlocked." She paused and smiled. "Actually, I came to see if you'd like to go to Bangor with me on Friday." An innocent look on her face. A searching look. A child's face.

"You want me to go to Bangor with you?"

"Don't look so surprised. I'm trying to be nice here. Neighborly and all. I go once a week. I could show you all the good watering holes. All the best shopping." That look of innocence was gone now, replaced by a hardness.

Margaret shook her head. "I don't know."

"Sometimes Bradley comes with me."

"Bradley Godwish goes with you to Bangor?"

"Yeah. Why so surprised?"

"Why does he go with you?"

"We go way back, him and me." Donna rose, took Margaret's coffeepot, and proceeded to rinse it out and fill it with water.

"What are you doing?" Margaret asked.

"I'm making coffee. You want some?"

"That's my coffeepot."

"Oh, duh. So sorry I didn't bring my own."

Margaret sat down at her kitchen table.

"Where's your coffee, cuz?"

"In the freezer."

"The freezer? You keep coffee in the freezer?"

"It keeps it fresher."

"That's not true, you know. It dries out the oils."

This was ridiculous, Margaret thought, having to defend her own culinary habits to this interloper. She rose. "Here, let me."

115

"Thought you'd never ask. I'm terrible at these domestic niceties. I'm sure you're so much better, having been a wife and mother and all."

The words stung, but Margaret ignored them as she placed a clean filter in the coffeepot and scooped in dark coffee. A few minutes later the two of them sat at the kitchen table drinking coffee while Donna talked. She talked of exploit after exploit in Bangor — of men she'd met, of movies she'd seen, of restaurants she'd visited, of the time she even worked for one whole day in a bar. "I wore this little skimpy number. But I had to quit at the end of the day. Had to get home."

Margaret had met people like Donna before, always wanting to tell you how much they know about absolutely everything, from coffee to men in bars, when deep down they are hurting children. She had an idea that somewhere in there, Donna was a confused child, a struggling soul. Sometimes her eyes gave her away, and every so often her long fingers shook as she wrapped them around the mug, blue fingernails intertwining. Margaret wanted to ask her, "Why didn't you ever leave Maine?" But somehow the question never formed on her lips.

An hour later, Donna stood and stretched. "I better be getting home."

"How did you get here?" Margaret asked.

"I drove. How do you think I got here?"

"I didn't see your car when I came in."

"It's over at Godwishes'."

Margaret watched from her back door as Donna walked next door, got into her car, and drove out fast. Margaret could see the face of Ruth Godwish framed in the window of the kitchen, watching her leave.

Back inside, Margaret bolted and locked the doors, including the doors to the cellar and the attic. She sat down at her table and poured the remaining black liquid into a mug. Then she dialed Dr. Irons's number.

"Why didn't you tell me about the curse?" she asked him.

"The curse?"

"The curse that's supposed to be on my house."

"The curse is another slip-up on my part, I'm afraid, which is why I want to give the entire Anna Coffin story a fuller treatment, perhaps in another book. Not much is known about the curse, and nothing was known before I wrote the chapter, but apparently — and Vivian loves this part of the tale — Anna Coffin put a curse on her house that no one who lived within its walls would ever have happiness, only barrenness. So you see," Roland went on, "the curse has little or no effect. There have been plenty of fruitful families within those walls." He smiled.

Margaret frowned. "Have you ever heard of something called second sight?"

Roland chuckled. "Ah, you have been in conversation with the locals, I can see."

"What is it?"

"Sometimes it's called second sight, sometimes, the sight. It's the belief that certain individuals are endowed with psychic abilities to see things. It's more than fortune-telling; it's the ability to sense what people are thinking and feeling."

"Sort of like intuition?"

"Exactly! That's exactly what it is. Some people are more intuitively aware of their environment. That's all it is. That's exactly what it is. Some seem to want to link this with magic arts."

"Witchcraft then?"

"Witchcraft, magic, religion are all man's attempts to reach that entity known as God."

"So you don't believe in God then?"

"You say 'believe in God,' as if God were some outside entity or force and even personality. I believe God is in human nature. God *is* human nature. Even the Bible, that most sacred religious book, says that the kingdom of God is *within* you. Within you. Within me. We are all there is. Therefore curses and hexes and what have you really have no power unless we give them power."

"What do you mean?"

"If someone truly believes he has been cursed he will act accordingly. Conversely, if someone believes God has 'blessed' him, he will *act* blessed. Studies have shown that a student will excel when a teacher tells him he has special gifts and talents, even when none exist. And conversely, a 'gifted' student can be relegated to the ranks of the mediocre if what he does is constantly criticized or belittled. A curse is just the nth degree of criticism."

"But my sister was killed in that house."

"Coincidence, Margaret. Do you have any idea how many children are killed every year in random accidents? Drownings, car accidents, sports accidents, and on and on the list goes. And what about all the people who summered in your house year after year? Have they experienced the ramifications of this curse? No. And the reason? They didn't think about the curse. They probably didn't know about it, which would give it no effect over them."

That night Margaret again dreamed about Anna Coffin. This time Margaret was inside her house and Anna was standing on the outside looking at her through the front bay window. The house was locked and Margaret was desperate to get outside. Something horrible was going to happen to her if she didn't. She could sense it. She raced from room to room on the ground floor, but everything was locked up tight. Even the windows were boarded up, locked, nailed shut with heavy beams she could not pry off.

"Help me!" she called through the glass to the still figure. But outside, Anna stood silently clutching her shawl with her left hand, letting the flowers drop from her right, her eyes following Margaret. Desperately she called, but Anna did not move.

Something compelled her to go upstairs. On the landing, the door to the third floor was opened wide. Quickly she ascended the steep steps. She stood there. One door in the entire house stood open: the door to the widow's walk. Slowly, one foot in front of the other, she walked toward it.

TWENTY-FIVE

Donna drummed her fingers on the cash register, for once glad that she was working today. She wouldn't have to be at home when Leo and Dolly pulled up in their fancy car, cow-faced Dolly smelling of perfume and mink coats, getting out like she owned the place — not just the hardware store, but the whole town.

Then there would be the hugs, the kisses in the air beside cheeks, with the herd of white poodles they always brought, chirping around their feet like a flock of pigeons.

It wouldn't be too long before Dolly would start complaining. First it would be about the weather in Maine, and then it would move on to how terribly *provincial* the whole place was, stringing out the word provincial with her nose in the air as if the word itself smelled bad. Yeah, as if Portsmouth is any great shakes, thought Donna.

Maybe she should go to Bangor by herself tomorrow instead of waiting until Friday. But that thought made her head hurt. Not unless it was Friday. She couldn't go unless it was Friday. Her world was ordered now, and she feared changing that order, even for a day, even for a minute. Last night she had thought that she might be able to go on a different day if she could persuade someone to go with her. At first she thought of Bradley. She had even gone so far as to go to his house. Huge mistake.

"Bradley isn't well," his mother had said.

"Liar," she wanted to say. Instead she said, "Can you tell him I'm here?"

"He's not well, Donna."

"I just want to see him."

Donna had stood there, staring into the little witch face of Ruth Godwish, the setting sun slashing across her face like knife marks.

"Just let me talk to him."

"No, he needs taking care of."

"I could take care of him. You know I could."

But Ruth Godwish had slammed the door. So Donna had no choice but to go over to Margaret's. Finding the place dark and the door unlocked was a bonus. So what if Margaret seemed a little spaced-out. She had always been a bit of a wimp anyway, younger than all the rest of them, tagging along even when she wasn't wanted, all the time, always there.

Across the length of the store Clark was arranging screwdrivers in bins, jabbing the sides of the bins, jabbing, jabbing. He was scowling, as usual.

She'd wait until Friday. She'd go on Friday. Get out of this place on Friday. But the fact that it was Friday might not be enough. Not this time. Not with Leo and Dolly here. She might need someone to go with her, even if it *was* Friday.

TWENTY-SIX

Margaret took her sketch pad down to the beach. She planned to do some preliminary sketches of the point and the shoreline before she attempted to paint Anna. She drew everything — the abandoned MacGregor cabin (she must go and explore that place sometime), the fishing boats, Dragon Back Island. Her fingers felt good and comfortable around the thick pencil. Andre was wrong. She would not lose her talent.

Her back was to the Godwish home, and she didn't have to look behind her to know that the curtains were drawn and a wood fire was burning. But it was such a fine day even the presence of Ruth and Bradley Godwish couldn't dampen her spirits. She remembered with a small tinge of guilt her promise to go over and watch videos with Bradley. Maybe later today. But with the morning light this good, she would be a fool not to take advantage of it.

For several hours Margaret sat on a rock and sketched, the sun warming her back. Even a fraction of peace in her troubled soul was a treasure.

She filled half a book with sketches before her rumbling stomach told her it was lunchtime. When she walked to her front door, Ruth Godwish was outside, sitting on her own small front step, a basket between her legs. She looked up at Margaret but didn't respond to her wave. Undeterred, Margaret walked toward her.

"Good morning, Mrs. Godwish," she said cheerfully.

"And you," replied the woman. She still did not look up.

"Fine day it is today."

"Indeed." Various mounds of dried green vegetation lay on her porch. Some looked like seaweed, some were common herbs that Margaret recognized such as basil and parsley, and there were some that looked exotic and foreign.

"What do you do with those things?" asked Margaret, bending down to take a closer look.

"These are herbs."

"I can see that, but what are they for?"

"My, we are asking a lot of questions, aren't we?"

"I'm just curious."

"And you know what curiosity did to the cat."

"I promised Bradley that I'd come over to watch videos with him. Is he inside?"

"He's not here today."

"Where is he?"

"He's at the workshop, that hateful place of bad spirits."

"Does he like it there?"

"I never ask him."

Margaret reached down and fingered a piece of dried green fluff between her fingers.

"Don't touch!" Ruth screamed. "You are too nosy for your own good. I said that to myself the moment you came back. Nothing good's going to come of it. Just be stirring up more trouble. Trouble that's best left stilled after all these years. I said that the minute I saw you come back, Hannah. That's what I said."

"Mrs. Godwish, I'm not Hannah."

"Norma Ann is dead, that's what I keep telling Bradley, but when he saw you again it was like it just happened. The murder. 'Norma Ann's mama's come back,' that's what he told me."

"Mrs. Godwish, Norma Ann was not murdered. She fell. It was an accident. It was in all the reports. And my mother is dead, too. I can't help it if I look like her."

"The reports!" She spat out the word. "That's what they told everyone." As she spoke, Ruth Godwish gathered up her herbs and went inside, leaving Margaret on the porch.

After a quick lunch, Margaret looked up an address in the phone book, got in her car, and headed out toward Bosuns Harbor. She passed a hand-lettered sign which read "Bosuns Harbor Ceramic Factory Up Ahead, Visitors Welcome."

A mile later she turned right into a gravel parking lot. The ceramic factory was located in a small square cottage surrounded by a white picket fence that looked newly painted. A handicapped passenger bus was parked next to the side door, along with a few cars. Hers was the only car in "Visitor Parking Welcome."

The cottage was fronted with window baskets full of flowers, still fresh, still blooming. She got out and walked the flagstone path to the door.

A sign on the door read "Walk Right In." Margaret did so and a jangle of overhead bells announced her presence. She stood alone for several seconds in a room filled with shelves of dishes, coffee mugs, lampstands, and painted ceramic frogs, the kind that hold plastic dish scrubbers. In the back she could hear chatter and music.

A short, round, bespectacled man approached her from the back and introduced himself as Arnie, director of the handicapped workshop. "I'd shake your hand, but I'm not sure you'd want to." He held up his clay-covered palms. "Have a look around if you'd like."

"This is quite a place here."

"We're quite proud of it. We're working on being completely self-sufficient."

"I'm just new to this area. My next-door neighbor works here. I think he's here today. Is there any way I can see him?"

"We're happy to have you drop by, and you most certainly may see your neighbor." He was smiling broadly. "And if you're new to Coffins Reach, we're always looking for volunteers."

"This is very nice," she said, looking around, "but I'll have to think about volunteering. I'm not sure how long I'll be here."

"Oh, don't mind me. I try to buttonhole everyone who comes in here," he said with a laugh. "Are you a summer person?"

"No," she said with hesitation. "I'm more of a *fall* person."

She followed him down the hall from the display room. "Who is your neighbor?" Arnie asked.

"Bradley Godwish."

He shook his head. "Bradley, Bradley, Bradley."

"He and his mother live next door to me."

"You know him well?"

"We grew up together."

"That poor fellow would do a whole lot better if he didn't have five mothers hovering over him."

"Five mothers?"

He began counting on the fingers of one hand. "First there's his real mother, God bless her pea-sized heart, then there's Sylvia Ochs, then Dolly Ochs, who isn't here much, thank the good Lord, not to mention Donna Ochs and Pat Ochs."

"Donna Ochs?"

"She's one of our volunteers. She seems to have a special interest in our Bradley."

"We all grew up together. Bradley, myself, my sister Norma Ann, and Donna, my cousin."

"Donna's your cousin?" He squinted at her through his

glasses. "I've never seen you before."

"I've been away. Living in Canada."

"The Ochses seem to have claimed Bradley as their pet project. Now, don't tell me you came here to check up on him, too." Arnie's voice was still friendly, but held an edge of something else.

"No, I've only spoken to him once since I've come back. But I'm curious, his mother seems to have no use for this place. So I wonder why she would enroll him here?"

"Community pressure," said Arnie, pushing his glasses up on his nose and leaving a smear across the front of them. "I mean, she has to appear to be doing something for her son. At least the Ochs family are good for one thing. They've taken him under their wings. Perhaps it has something to do with the fact that, as you say, you all grew up together."

"Maybe they feel a kind of obligation to him."

"Maybe. Still, I'd like to see him in something else, something that would challenge him more. I could get that fellow into a group home, an independent living situation with four or five other fellows and a caretaker." He raised a chubby finger. "So he doesn't like the beach, so what? We get him into a home away from the beach. Then we work on that problem. I've got an opening. It would do him a world of good to get away from that mother of his. If you have any influence with her, will you do *him* a favor and talk to her?"

"I'm afraid I don't have much influence there at all."

They were standing in the doorway of the room which ran across the back. Inside was a large Ping-Pong-sized table. People were sitting around, forming bowls, painting, chatting. They didn't seem to notice her. She was also introduced to a number of workers and volunteers. The idea of Donna being here, with her black hair and skinny tights, wearing a clay-stained apron and leaning over the shoulders of clients, did not fit.

A doorway led into a kitchen, and through it she could see the large shoulders of Bradley Godwish bent over a double sink. She walked toward him. "Bradley," she said.

He turned suddenly, dropping the dishcloth into the sink.

"You startled me. You shouldn't have startled me." He turned to Arnie. "She startled me."

"She's okay," said Arnie, placing a hand on Bradley's shoulder. "This is your neighbor. She came to visit you."

He peered into her eyes, and when he recognized her, a look of terror crossed his face. He shoved his dishwater fists into his eyes. "Can't go. No! Can't go to the beach. Can't go, Norma Ann!"

"Hey," said Arnie. "Hey buddy, it's okay."

Arnie led the whimpering Bradley to a kitchen chair. By this time other clients were peering their faces around the side of the door. Margaret stood there, helpless. "I'm sorry," she said to both Bradley and Arnie. "I'm sorry." Margaret backed out of the room and raced down the hall.

The last thing Margaret heard as she opened the door was Bradley whimpering loudly, "I didn't stop them. I didn't stop the bad people!"

TWENTY-SEVEN

Chris sat down in the cabin of his boat, notes and papers spread over his chart table, his laptop computer with modem plugged in and whirring quietly. He already had several pages of notes, all in his tiny meticulous hand, that he was transferring from the little spiral-bound notebook to his computer. As he two-finger typed, he thought about the fictional detectives — Sam Spade, Travis McGee, Spenser — who never seemed to spend much time at home typing notes into a computer. From page one, they found themselves right in the action, following leads, traipsing all over the city, and ending up in a gun battle or car chase. In real life, detective work was a lot of time on the telephone, searching through data banks at local papers or libraries, and more recently, searching the Internet. Chris had a gun, but he never used it. As a PI he'd never been in a gun battle in his life. His work seemed to fit into two categories: getting the dirt on one half of a divorcing couple, which he hated, and finding missing people, which he loved.

Clark had brought him up to speed on Monty and Leo. Chris learned that collectively they were worth more than ten million dollars, tied up in three hardware stores plus a number of real estate holdings along the Massachusetts coast.

Clark Ochs, on the other hand, was the poor relation. He was employed by Monty and Leo in the hardware store for $12.50 an hour. He had twelve thousand dollars in a savings account at the bank, plus a checking account with just enough money to cover the expenses each month. His wife had her own savings account with about two thousand dollars. Clark had been involved in a number of business deals that soured. He'd scrimped and saved and bought a condo in Connecticut. Six months later it burned to the ground. Clark was underinsured and lost his shirt. He once bought a tour boat that sunk; another house he purchased (a "sure thing" in the Fairfield area of Bridgeport, Connecticut) was condemned. He bought a small motel for an inflated price and a year later turned around and sold it for far below its market value. "Clark, Clark, that's not the way that's supposed to work," said Chris shaking his head.

By scanning the bank records provided to him by a police contact, Chris learned that Mitch Ochs, now deceased, had received a check in the amount of $500,000. Chris double-checked the date — a week after his daughter died. Paid off? Paid to leave? Why?

Chris made a list of people he needed to talk to face-to-face: Monty Ochs, Sylvia Ochs, Leo, Dolly, Donna Ochs, Margaret Ochs, maybe even some of the cousins who had left Maine. He'd have to come up with some pretext or other. He took out another juice box, this time a blend of five tropical fruits, and sucked on the straw while he worked.

TWENTY-EIGHT

For the next two days, Margaret spent her mornings working on sketches of Anna, her afternoons scrubbing and cleaning her house, and her evenings listening to music and reading. She was trying to forget about the curse, Bradley's reaction to her, Donna sitting in her unlocked house.

On the morning following the disastrous trip to the ceramic factory, she called and apologized to Arnie.

"I seem to have such a bad effect on him, and I don't know why."

"Bradley is a complex person," Arnie said. "Unfortunately, I'm not a psychologist. I do a bit of counseling, comes with the territory. I've spoken at length with him. But there seems to be a block there. I'd like him to get some help. Unfortunately, that's the last thing his mother would agree to."

"I don't know if there's anything I can do. I wish there was."

"Perhaps time is all he needs."

Time, thought Margaret as she hung up the phone. He had had lots of time. I've moved to Bangor, finished high school, gone to university, married, moved to another country, had a daughter, and begun a career as an artist, all the while Bradley has sat in front of videos.

On the second day her friend Joyce from Fredericton called and they talked for half an hour. Margaret, forcing herself to sound upbeat, gave a carefully worded account of her new Anna project. She avoided any reference to the ghost and that her house was the ill-fated recipient of a hundred-year-old curse.

"Don't be a Christmas letter, Margaret," Joyce said.

"A what?"

"A Christmas letter. You know, those things people force themselves to write and mail to everybody they haven't seen or spoken to in twenty years, saying things like, 'We're all of us so thankful that Bill is able to spend more time with the family.' Translated: 'Bill was fired from his job again.' And then there's, 'Joey's new boss is quite happy with his performance.' Translated: 'His parole officer is quite pleased that he hasn't lit any fires recently.' "

"Joyce, you never fail to make me laugh."

"My intention is to make you think. You don't have to be all Christmas cheer for me. I'm your friend, remember?"

"I'm fine. Really I am. Really."

"Really?"

"Yes, really."

"Too many reallys. Methinks the lady doth say the word really too much. Speaking of Christmas, what are you doing for Christmas?"

"Were we?"

"Were we what?"

"Speaking of Christmas," Margaret said.

"We were. Remember Bill and Joey? The Christmas-letter people? So, what are you doing for Christmas?"

Margaret ran her fingers through her hair. "It's a while yet."

"Warning, dates on your calendar are closer than they appear."

"I don't know."

"Robin's back."

"You've seen him?"

"I've done more than see him, I've talked with him. He

came over to see me. He wants me to persuade you to come home. He says he wants to talk to you."

"He's had all summer to talk to me."

"I'm not going to tell you what to do. But I want you to know you're invited here for Christmas. I could smuggle you in and out, and no one, not even Robin, would ever have to know you were back here if that's what you wanted."

"I'll think about it."

After the conversation with Joyce, Margaret went into her kitchen and brewed herself a pot of coffee. While she waited for it to finish, she laid her cheek on the cool wood of the table. She missed her friend, and a pang of acute loneliness overcame her. What did she have here? Just an old cursed building. No warmth. No sitting with friends around the fireplace, sharing a glass of wine. No children running through its halls. Just this building, neighbors who wanted nothing to do with her, a strange cousin, and odd dreams and even odder visions. Some of her first sketches of Anna were scattered on the table. She regarded them coolly. How could she have thought that the two of them shared a bond? When Anna had cursed her house she had cursed Margaret. Death and barrenness had been her companions as well. Well, Anna dear, you have won. Your curse has come down through the ages and settled itself upon me.

The late afternoon was turning cool and cloudy, and Margaret decided to put her mind to work once more. If she did sell the house, it would have to be clean. She ascended to the third floor again, and got to the scrubbing of the topmost story, mopping out corners encrusted with decades-old leavings of bugs. When she had left her Bangor home, it was without a backward glance. She had never even brought Robin or Aislin down to meet her father, afraid that if they came they would find him sitting in his chair, newspapers and magazines stacked beside him. When she was still living with him, she was the one who had made the meals, carried the laundry to the laundromat, mopped, and vacuumed. There was nothing wrong with him. The doctor had told her that. Nothing physically wrong, that is, the doctor had said, a concerned look on his face as he tapped his pencil on the desk. I would recommend admitting him for a while. He'll be fine.

The day after her father was admitted to the psychiatric ward of the hospital, Margaret left for university. She had never been back.

Out of guilt, she had written a few letters and Christmas cards filled with photos and cheery messages such as "Why not come up to Fredericton this summer? All of us would love to see you." But she knew her father would never come, and for that she was relieved.

She continued her mopping. A good cleaning. That was all that was needed here. A good cleaning.

TWENTY-NINE

"Hello." The woman who opened the door to him looked to be in her mid-thirties, intelligent eyes, face smudged with dirt, an air of weariness about her. Her dark hair was a mass of unruly curls which descended like corkscrews around her forehead. She was wearing jeans, smudged at the knees, and a navy sweatshirt, the sleeves rolled up above the elbows. She made an attempt to wipe the smears of grime from her face with the back of her hand, which only worsened them. She'd obviously been into some heavy-duty cleaning, he thought.

"Hi, my name is Chris Rikken, private investigator." He stuck out his hand. "I'm looking for Margaret Ochs."

The woman cleared her throat. "No one by that name lives here." Her voice was soft.

He pulled out a binder and pretended to look through it. "I'm sorry. My records show that a Margaret Ochs lives here. The daughter of Mitchell and Hannah Ochs."

"Well, your records are wrong." She started to shut the door. He grasped the edge of it with his right hand.

"I'm sorry." He tried another smile. "I'm just wondering, do you happen to know where she lives?"

"There is no such person as Margaret Ochs." She spoke quietly.

He leaned forward. "I'm sorry?"

"I said, there is no such person as Margaret Ochs."

"Okay, uh, fine. It's just that I needed to talk with a Margaret Ochs about a matter that concerns her father and her deceased sister."

She looked up suddenly. That look did not escape him. He peered at her more closely. Margaret would have been around ten at the time of her sister's death. He remembered a little girl, long dark braids, who hugged a teddy bear, eyes wide and wondering while the investigator Jon Smith talked with her aunt and uncle. That was his only glimpse into the person called Margaret Ochs.

Faded pictures began to play in the far reaches of his memory. A young woman, the mother of the girl who'd fallen to her death, sitting small and hunched on the couch, knees together, Kleenex balled up in her lap, while her husband paced behind her, clenching and unclenching his fists. There was something about the woman who stood before him that made him remember that woman in the far-off picture.

"You are Margaret," he said softly.

Her eyes widened. She attempted to shut the door.

"No, please," he said. "I'm not here to hurt you. I'm here to help."

"Who are you?"

He stared at her for a moment then said, "My name is Chris Rikken. I'm a private investigator."

"You said that. What do you want?"

"I'm sorry. It's just that you reminded me of someone I met years ago. Hannah Ochs was her name."

"If another person tells me that I'm going to sign up for plastic surgery!"

"You are her daughter Margaret then?"

"I'm her daughter, Margaret. But you look too young to have known her."

"You flatter me, but I was a rookie deputy at the time. I was one of the officers who investigated your sister's accidental death."

"Why are you here now? Are they reopening the case?"

"No, not officially. I've been hired to look into monies paid out after her death."

"What money? Like insurance?"

"That's fairly confidential at this point."

"What did you want to talk to me about?"

"I'd like to talk to you about your father and your uncles. Can I come in?"

She looked at him warily. "I don't know. Can I see some identification?"

He pulled out his wallet and showed her his PI's license.

She looked at it doubtfully. "I don't know."

"Well, if it would make you feel any better we could talk here."

"Are you with an insurance company?"

"An insurance company?"

"You're here about some money."

"Yes, but not insurance money. I'd like to ask you a question."

"Go ahead."

"Why did your family move to Bangor after your sister died?"

"Isn't that obvious?"

"No, not to me."

"Living here was too painful. My parents needed a fresh start."

"Did they get one?"

She wiped her hair away from her face. "I don't know what you mean."

"A fresh start. From what I understand your mother died two years later, and your father had to be hospitalized for depression. That doesn't sound like a fresh start to me."

"How do you know so much?"

"I'm paid to know these things." He tried his most winsome smile on her.

"Why do you need to know this?"

"Among other things I've been hired to find out why your father was paid $500,000 to leave Coffins Reach and never come back."

She stared at him. "That's not true. Why would someone pay him to leave?" She said it very quietly.

"That's what I'm trying to find out. Let me ask you something, was your father employed in Bangor?"

"Yes, my father was employed."

"Did he work a lot?"

"What are you getting at?"

"Or was he off sick a lot?"

"I don't know. I don't remember."

"And yet you were well off there?"

"I don't know. I didn't pay much attention."

"But you had all of your university education paid for, and you were left a handsome sum upon his death."

"I resent those questions. That's personal information. Why are you asking me these questions?"

"I believe your father was blackmailing someone."

"What!"

"Do you have any personal papers of your father's, bank statements and the like? I'd love to be proved wrong on this."

"No, I don't have anything of my father's."

"Not even when you came down for the funeral?"

She leveled her eyes at him. "I didn't come down for my father's funeral."

Silence. He cleared his throat. "Well, okay then. I'm sorry if I upset you." He spoke gently, as gently as he could. "I'd love to be proved wrong on this."

"I'll prove you wrong," she said. "I'll prove you are dead

wrong. Because none of this is true, you know. My father wasn't paid money to leave and never return. And if I had those papers I could prove that to you."

"Well, let's hope you're right."

Before he left he handed her his business card. She crumpled it in her fist and went back inside.

"Call me," he said. "If you want to talk about anything."

THIRTY

After he left, Margaret threw the bolt across the door and leaned against it. She felt unsettled and jittery. Blackmail? It was not possible. Grumbling, she rinsed out the coffeepot. Loudly, she clanged pots and cups together as she tidied up her kitchen. How dare that stranger come barging in here with such accusations! Who was he and what did he have to do with her father, anyway? Well, she'd prove him wrong.

As she rinsed out the sink, wiping it with a wet sponge, she began to wonder not only about her father's papers but about all of the other things. She had been cleaning and scrubbing in the third floor for two days now, never noticing, never questioning, never even casually wondering where all the boxes and trunks had gotten to. Where were the clothes, her dolls, her mother's dolls, even her old report cards and school projects? Where were the faded lace curtains, the musty suits hung on padded hangers, her grandmother's dresses, the costume jewelry, the music boxes? Had they been moved to Bangor? She had never seen them there.

Maybe the papers were still in this house somewhere. Perhaps things were hidden away somewhere. She decided to look. She would begin in that most dreaded of rooms, the cellar. She grabbed a flashlight, pulled back the bolt on the door, and started downward. The light switch was at the bottom of the steps. Poor placement, she thought. The moldy, dank smell of it rose to meet her. She padded across the cement floor and onto the dirt. There was a bit of a crawl space along the front of the house, and bending down, she illuminated the darkness with her wide beam of light. Nothing. Just more dirt, and a few graying boards with nails so rusted they turned to dust when she touched them. She backed away, and feeling chilled, she hugged her arms around herself.

As a child she had always hated this place with its low ceiling and the one lone bulb that dangled like a detached eyeball. When her mother would ask her to go down for a canning jar of this or that, she would open the door, hold her breath and run down the stairs as fast as she could, grab the jar, and head back up before taking a new breath. It became a game with her — to see how fast she could go down and be up again. Usually she had to gasp a breath halfway up the stairs, but sometimes she made it all the way. Today she was breathing in the stale air. Just a few more places to check, although she was sure no boxes were down here. She would have seen them when she was down here with Roland, she was sure of that.

Nevertheless she walked around the perimeter of the room, examining the foundation stones for cracks. (Secret rooms? Anything was possible.) She found nothing, just boards caked with centuries of dust and rodent droppings. The canning cupboard yielded nothing, and when she tried to close the door, it creaked ominously. The new gray furnace that hummed in the corner was almost anachronistic. She felt around its edges. Nothing. Behind the furnace were more foundation stones, piled edge to edge, mortar added to their joining pieces. She tried to picture Anna and Gilbert arm in arm, looking on as masons placed stone on stone, the marble arriving by sailing ship from New York and then drawn by horse to this construction site.

There were various shelves to the left of the furnace, thick boards, graying and layered with dust. This part of the cellar was dark, so she shone the light on the shelves. There on the bottommost shelf was a stack of old newspapers, yellowed and brittle with age. Gingerly she pulled them out, plunked them down on the floor, and shone her light on them. There were about four of them in the stack, tied together with string. They were all the same edition of the September 14, 1973 issue of the *Bosuns Harbor News*. On the front was the eighth-grade picture of her sister. Her hair was long and straight and combed off her heart-shaped face in the style of the day. In the photo she was smiling, grinning really, her face tilted slightly sideways as she gazed at the camera.

She read the article:

Norma Ann Ochs, daughter of Mitchell and Hannah Ochs of #2 Coffins Reach Road, fell to her death from a third-story porch in a tragic accident at her home yesterday. Detective Jonathan Smith stated, "It is a tragedy. The porches of these old houses should only be ventured upon with great caution." Her mother said the small porch facing the beach on the third story was a favorite spot of Norma Ann's even though she was warned of its dangers.

Norma Ann is survived by her parents, Mitch and Hannah Ochs; one sister, Margaret Ochs, age 10; aunts Sylvia, Dolly and Pat Ochs; uncles Monty, Leo and Clark Ochs; aunt and uncle Dr. Peter and Margaret Mahone; grandparents, Florence and William Whyte. She is predeceased by grandparents Esther and Earnest Ochs. Norma Ann had an outgoing personality and was described as a model student. "She will be missed," said teacher Evelyn Parker. "This is such a terrible, terrible thing."

When the furnace started up, Margaret gasped and jumped. She rose from her crouched position, and holding the dirty papers away from her, carried them upstairs. She locked the door to the basement, and then placed the newspapers on the kitchen table.

The phone rang.

"Margaret, this is Sylvia. Just wondering how you're keeping over there, and to tell you that your Uncle Leo and Aunt Dolly are up from New Hampshire for a visit. We'd love for you to stop by and see the clan. When I told them you were in town, neither one of them could believe it. Can you make it for supper tomorrow night?"

"Fine, supper would be fine."

"And I hope you're keeping okay over there by yourself."

"I'm cleaning and sketching. That's about it. Found something interesting in the cellar just a minute ago."

"Oh, what's that?" Did Sylvia's voice take on a note of something else, or was Margaret only imagining it?

"A stack of old newspapers, the ones with the account of Norma Ann's death. There are about four or five of them here, yellow and old. Would you like to see them?"

"I'm sure that would be the last thing I would care to see at this point."

"I was wondering about something else, Sylvia. I was wondering where all the trunks and boxes are. Do you happen to know?"

"What trunks and boxes are you talking about?" Her voice had taken on a definite iciness.

"The ones that were in the attic all those years, the dresses and dolls and even my old pictures and paintings."

"I have no idea where those things are. I can't imagine why you'd even be interested. I just *assumed* they found their way to Bangor."

"I don't remember seeing them there."

"You were young then. Maybe you just don't remember."

"Maybe."

"Margaret, when your father died, did you come back and see to his things?"

Margaret hesitated. "No."

"Well, there you go." Sylvia's voice was suddenly light. "They were probably sold or auctioned off, or just plain junked. Maybe Brown & Brown would know. Or the lawyers."

Margaret was too embarrassed to say she didn't even know the name of her father's lawyer. When her father had died, she received a call from a lawyer telling her. At the time she hadn't even bothered to jot down his name.

On that day the lawyer had said, "There will be funeral arrangements to be made. Will you be down to see to them?"

"It's impossible for me to get away right now. Can someone down there make them?"

She remembered the lawyer's long sigh. "We will see to it then. He has left explicit directions and enough funds to cover the costs."

"Fine."

When Robin came home from work that day, Margaret did not tell him her father had died. They ate supper in silence. Later, Robin went out to a meeting. She didn't tell him the next day either. Nor the next. They weren't talking much anyway, plus the timing was never right to tell him. Then it became too late. *Oh, by the way, my father died last month, just thought I'd let you know.* She told no one her father had died.

Now she stared at a spot on the kitchen wall, a water spot. "Sylvia?" she said.

"Yes."

"I had an interesting visit today from a private investigator. He made the claim that my father was paid a large sum of money to leave Bosuns Harbor when Norma Ann died."

"How outlandish! How horribly outlandish! What a horrible thing to say to you after all these years. What's that detective's name? I'll tell Monty about him. That's not right, troubling you after all these years."

"It did strike me as strange."

After she hung up she decided to call Brown & Brown. She gave her name and asked for Maizie.

"You mean Mavis?"

"Yes."

"Margaret, dear," Mavis said when she picked up the receiver. "How can I help you? Have you decided at last to get rid of that white elephant?"

"No." Margaret hesitated. "I'm just calling for some information."

"Go right ahead then, anything we can do to help we surely will."

"It's about my father's estate. I was just wondering if you knew where his other personal effects ended up?"

"Personal effects? You mean like clothes and things, that sort of thing?"

"Right."

"Well, Margaret dear, we only handle real estate in this firm. We can't be expected to be responsible for *clothing* and things, my goodness, we're not the Salvation Army!"

"No, I don't mean that. I just wanted to know if you knew what happened to his things?"

"Have you checked with the lawyers?"

"No. I was wondering if you might know the name of his lawyer."

"You don't know the name of the law firm that handled your father's estate?"

"Well, I did know it. I had it in Fredericton, but I didn't bring that information down here, and I've forgotten it."

Mavis sighed. "Let me go look. I've got a client coming in

144

momentarily. If he comes in I'll just have to hang up, you understand that, don't you?"

"Of course. Clients come first."

"They do indeed."

She was put on hold and treated to elevator music.

A few minutes later Mavis was back. "Margaret dear, I have the name here. Do you have a pen?"

"Yes."

"Okay, here it is. His name is George Hamish."

As Mavis read the name and address, Margaret jotted them down on a piece of blank paper. Maybe a trip to Bangor was in order, after all. Maybe she'd take up her cousin's offer.

"Now, Margaret dear, you call, you hear, when you want to sell your house. I've a number of clients who are interested. A *number*. Why, the people coming in to see me momentarily are interested in beachfront property in Coffins Reach. They mentioned it by name, they said Coffins Reach, just like that. As soon as you're interested in selling you just give me a shout."

"Good-bye," Margaret said.

THIRTY-ONE

When the telephone rang at quarter to nine the following morning, Margaret had been up for about an hour. In her robe and
slippers she had been touching up her Anna sketch and thinking
about going for a walk.

"Are you game to go to the city today? It's Friday." It was
Donna, and her voice was full of morning cheer.

Margaret hesitated. "Well, I don't know. I'm not dressed
yet, and I'm supposed to be back at your house tonight to
have supper with Leo and Dolly."

"Oh them. We'll be back by then."

"What would we do in Bangor?"

"Go shopping, have lunch. Later, I have to go to the airport."

"The airport?" Margaret said.

"We could shop in the morning, I could show you around,
then we could have lunch, I know a good place, and then I
could drive you wherever you'd like, drop you off someplace,
go to the airport, and then come back to get you."

Maybe she could use the afternoon to visit her father's
lawyer, Margaret thought, find out about his effects — not
that she planned to call that detective back again — and then
there was always the possibility that Donna might know
something about the attic boxes. "Sure, why not?" she said.
"When do you want to leave?"

"When can you be ready?"

"Half an hour."

Forty-five minutes later the two women were driving out

of Coffins Reach toward the city of Bangor. Donna wore a slim brown leather jacket and matching high boots. Her hair was yellow blond today, cut square along her shoulders with long bangs brushing evenly across her eyebrows. Margaret had stared at her open-mouthed when she first got into the car.

"What's the matter, cuz?"

Margaret smiled a greeting, tried not to stare.

"It's my wig, isn't it? Do you like it?"

"It's . . . unusual."

"Everyone should wear wigs. I don't know why everyone doesn't. I can be different people, anybody I want." She swung her head from side to side and the synthetic banana hair swished on her leather collar.

"It's very nice," said Margaret, feeling that such a reply was required.

"I like it," Donna said.

Donna drove her little sports car extraordinarily fast. She rounded a corner out of Coffins Reach, and Margaret placed her palms on the dashboard.

"Am I going too fast for you?"

"Where did you learn to drive, the Indy 500?" Margaret tried to keep her voice light.

Donna grinned.

Later on Margaret said, "Do you remember much about Norma Ann?"

Donna turned her head abruptly, causing the car to swerve into the neighboring lane.

Margaret, her hands on the dashboard, continued, "I guess it's because I'm here now and living in that house that all of this is coming back to me. The other day I was upstairs — I'm scrubbing out that old place, you know — and I got to thinking about the times we played up there when we were children. Do you remember? I got to thinking about all those old boxes and stuff, and all of a sudden it hit me, where is all that stuff?"

Donna said nothing but her driving slowed. "Are you asking me?"

"No, no, I guess I was just thinking out loud."

The car was quiet, the only sound the tires against asphalt, the wind whistling through the seams of the vehicle.

"Have you seen Bradley lately?" Margaret asked.

"What do you want to know that for?"

"Just curious." She said it lightly, lightly. "I hear you volunteer at the ceramic factory."

"Who told you that?"

"I was visiting there. Someone named Arnie told me."

"That weasel." She frowned and gripped the leather of the steering wheel even tighter. "What else did he tell you?"

"Nothing. Just that you work there sometimes."

"Why did you go there?" Her question sounded like an accusation.

"I wanted to see the place and I wanted to visit Bradley."

"Why?"

"Just curious."

Donna turned to her. "I could be curious too, cuz. I could ask you all about Robin and Aislin."

Margaret blinked at her. "How do you know about Robin?"

"I know everything. Me and Ruth Godwish. We know everything."

Margaret studied her. It was possible, she guessed, that her father had kept them all informed of her whereabouts.

"Okay, here's the deal. I don't bring up Robin and Aislin, and you don't talk about Bradley and Norma Ann."

"But Norma Ann was my sister," protested Margaret.

"You never knew her."

"She was my sister."

"I repeat, you didn't know her. Subject closed."

Donna was glowering, her crayon-red lips set in a rigid line, long fingers flexing around the steering wheel like a cat pawing in. Her features were fine-boned — angular nose, thin lips, a bit pinched perhaps. Her face seemed to have a permanently hurt look. She had nothing of the full-lipped, high-cheeked, round-eyed look the fashion world measured beauty by these days, but her cousin was certainly not unattractive.

Donna tuned the radio to a rock station and turned up the volume, making all further conversation impossible.

Thirty silent minutes later they reached the outskirts of the city. Donna turned to her. "Where do you want off?"

"Excuse me?"

"I said, where do you want off?"

Flustered, Margaret groped in her purse for the small slip of paper with the lawyer's name on it. She stammered the address to Donna.

"That's by the river. You should have told me it was by the river before I got this far," she said angrily. She made a sudden right turn and an oncoming vehicle screamed by, horn honking. "Jerk," Donna said.

When they reached the address of the George Hamish Law Associates, Donna said, "I'll pick you up here at four."

Margaret gaped at her. "Lunch?" she ventured.

But Donna had reached across, pulled the door shut, and was screeching away. Margaret stood there watching until Donna's car was out of sight. Great, ten-thirty in the morning in the middle of a strange city with no car. She turned and walked slowly up the wide sidewalk to the law offices. The building was a gleaming white, many-storied structure, an enlarged, much-shined-up version of her own place. The entire street was lined with these old majestic houses, and many, she saw, housed doctor's offices, law offices, insurance, and real estate agencies.

Inside the large front door, a pear-shaped woman wearing a pink cardigan buttoned at the neck was sitting at a desk near the door punching a computer keyboard. Oval glasses hung from a silver chain around her neck. She looked up when Margaret entered.

"Yes?" she said.

"I'm looking for Mr. George Hamish. I wonder if it would be possible to see him for a few minutes?"

"It's Dr. George Hamish, and he's with a client right now. Was there something you needed to see him about?"

"Yes, there was."

"And what might the nature of your business be?" The woman sounded as if she was from Boston.

"The nature of my business might concern a former client of his."

"And what might your name be?"

"My name might be Margaret Collinwood."

"Is that your name?"

"Yes."

The receptionist consulted a large brown leather appointment book. "It looks like he won't be free for at least another twenty minutes, maybe half an hour. Can you wait?"

"I can wait."

"There's a lovely little coffee place just on the corner if you'd like to wait there."

"Can I wait here?"

"By all means."

Margaret sat down in an overstuffed chair in a nook by the front window and leafed through old *New Yorker*s and *Finan-*

*cial Post*s. It could be worse, she thought. Dr. Hamish could be out of town and it could be raining.

Fifteen minutes later the door behind the receptionist opened and out walked a rumpled man in a brown suit, carrying a folder. He was frowning. He left through the front door without looking at Margaret.

It was a full five minutes before the receptionist rose and said, "The doctor will see you now."

For a moment Margaret thought she had stumbled into the wrong professional office. Dr. Hamish's office was deep, dark, cavelike, and spoke of academia. There was a faint aroma of pipe smoke. A large man with a thick handlebar mustache and a shock of white hair was seated behind a desk. He wore a gray wool sweater and looked more like a university professor than a lawyer.

"You wanted to see me about something?" he said. She recognized the deep, metered voice that had called her in Fredericton when her father died.

"Yes. It's about my father, who was a client of yours. He passed away about a year ago. Mitchell Ochs."

A change in demeanor. A narrowing of the eyes for a split second. Steepling his hands on the desk, he scrutinized her. Finally he said, "Mitchell Ochs. I thought there was something familiar about the name Margaret Collinwood."

She smiled hesitantly, unsure. "Yes," she faltered. "You called me, I think."

"Yes, and if I recall correctly, you were too busy to come down."

"There were circumstances."

"I'm sure there were, but as I told your gentleman friend just yesterday, I will not release information unauthorized to him and I won't to you."

"What?"

"I don't know what your business is, why this sudden interest in Mitchell Ochs's personal papers, but like I told your friend, I cannot release his papers."

"You'll have to excuse me, I really don't know what you're talking about."

"Your friend, coming in here, wanting to see his papers or personal effects. If this is just his ploy, having you come in here, well, you can tell him it just won't work."

Margaret ran her fingers through her hair. "What friend? Who came to see you?"

"He came in here with some cock-and-bull story about money paid out after Mitchell Ochs's death."

Margaret opened her eyes wide and stared at the lawyer. "He's no friend of mine," she said. "I have nothing whatsoever to do with that person who came to see you yesterday. I am Mitchell Ochs's next of kin. I've been back in Maine for a few weeks now and I'd like to finally clean up his estate."

He leaned back. "Well, I would say that it's about time, wouldn't you? That is, if you are really who you say you are." His smile was not friendly.

"I'm Margaret Collinwood. I can show you identification. Mitchell Ochs was my father, and what I came for was just to see if you had any of his personal effects, belongings, or if you know where they are."

"You're not part of this insurance scam?"

"Definitely not!"

He regarded her, then he said, "His personal effects were cleared away as per his instructions."

"What do you mean, cleared away?"

"Auctioned off, thrown out."

"Why?"

He glared at her. "Because none of his heirs came to claim them."

She wanted to scream at this man *I didn't come to his funeral, I didn't, I didn't, because he didn't come to Aislin's! He never called. He never even sent a card! I sent him so many things down through the years, but when he never called, never wrote, I thought why bother? I never visited him because he showed no interest in me!*

But she looked down into her lap and said, "Were you friends with my father?"

"About as close as anybody was, if that's of any interest of yours."

"I'd like to see his papers now, if I may."

"Looking at you I have no doubt that you are his daughter. You are the exact image of his late wife. If it wasn't for that, you'd be out of this office like that fellow yesterday."

"Then can I have my father's personal papers?"

"No, you may not."

"I may not?"

He rose. "You may look at them here, or I will get Louise to photocopy the contents of your father's file. Only then will you be able to take them with you."

"I'll wait for you to photocopy them."

He muttered, "For the love of heaven, don't ask me why I'm doing this." He motioned to her. "Wait out front."

Margaret sat in the chair she had recently vacated and watched while the receptionist took a thick file and disappeared around the back.

A quarter of an hour later, Louise grudgingly handed her a thick sheaf of white photocopied papers. They barely fit inside Margaret's backpack, and edges of paper sprouted out of the top like an unruly spider plant.

Maybe a cup of coffee would go well with this stack of reading material. The corner coffee shop was an espresso bar with long windows facing two streets. She bought an extra-

153

large regular coffee and a low-fat cranberry muffin from a somnolent looking man in a green apron. She was the only customer in the place, but she suspected that the room filled to capacity during lunch hour as well as during coffee breaks.

She took a seat at a booth by the window, unwrapped her muffin, and dumped the contents of her backpack onto the table. The wills were the first papers she saw, both her mother's and her father's. She skimmed through her mother's first. It was pretty straightforward: All of her assets were willed to her husband. Peradventure the two of them should die together, their assets would be divided equally between their two children, Norma Ann and Margaret. Odd, thought Margaret, that this will was not changed when Norma Ann died. Her father's will was next. His was current. All of his assets were willed to his surviving daughter, Margaret Ochs Collinwood, Fredericton, Canada.

Next was a threefold glossy full-color brochure advertising a cemetery, a place called Forest Greens in Bangor. It looked more like an advertisement for a hotel or health spa. Her parents were both buried there, she read, her father having purchased his plot prior to his death. It was next to his wife's.

Norma Ann was buried in the small graveyard behind the Congregational church in Bosuns Harbor. Margaret had been there only once in her life, when as a ten-year-old girl she stood beside her mother while Norma Ann's casket was lowered into the ground. The cousins were all there, and the relatives, a sea of Ochs faces. Everyone threw in handfuls of dirt on top of the box as they walked by. Margaret didn't.

She had been to her mother's grave twice. Once when she was buried, and then on the first anniversary of her death, when she and her father placed a flat of fresh pansies on it, her mother's favorite.

She had been to Aislin's many times. She had come to

154

know well the granite stone that marked the place in the earth like a bookmark. At first she would kneel and pray. Gradually her prayers of sorrow turned to cries of rage as she thought of the body of her little daughter rotting in a box underneath all this cold, worm-infested ground. It enraged her that God would do that.

Underneath the wills were pages and pages of photocopied bank statements. This sort of thing might interest the detective. She'd look them over carefully.

Underneath were copies of news clippings. The first one, the account of Norma Ann's death, she recognized from the papers she had found in her basement. There were many other copies of clippings; articles about the business successes of Mitch and Monty. Every time there was a new acquisition, it seemed, there was a write-up about it. She scanned them all, accounts in the business section of the purchase of the hardware store chain, a marriage of a cousin now living in California. Why would her father cut out and save every single article ever written about his brothers?

Something underneath made her stop. Aislin! A wallet photo of her daughter was photocopied onto the center of the white paper. She was smiling in that picture, chubby hands folded in front of her dress. Despite herself, Margaret thought about that day, and about Aislin's blue dress and about how ten minutes before they were scheduled to see the photographer, Aislin had dropped a chocolate bar onto her lap. She had stood there wailing while Margaret frantically tried to remove the stain, making it worse in the process, and then there was Robin telling the both of them that if they didn't all leave right now, this very moment, they'd miss the appointment, and what was wrong with another dress, for Pete's sake.

The photographer was a young woman with a lot of

Raggedy Anns in her studio. She was able to successfully move the folds in the skirt so that no chocolate stains showed.

Margaret picked up the white paper and stared at the picture. The edges of the snapshot looked creased, as if the original had been scrunched into a wallet. She thought about that, her father carrying around his granddaughter's picture in his wallet.

Underneath the snapshot was a copy of the long chatty letter that Margaret had written to her father when she had sent the picture. She skimmed through the hastily written note.

Dear Dad . . . Things are going well here. Robin is as busy as ever in school and in his music productions. I swear, that man never quits. Aislin is growing like a weed and I'm sending along a picture of her for you. As you can see, she's cute as a button and really keeps us on our toes. She's enjoying piano lessons, and doing quite well. Dad. . . . I'm sure you would love her if you could come up and see her.

Like all of the other ones, her father hadn't answered this one, but he had *saved* it!

Underneath was a poem written in Norma Ann's flowery hand, a few lines on a page. Margaret finished her coffee, ordered another, and read through it carefully.

Anna and I
Anna and I wander the lone beach together.
We both wear white, but she is like me
And I know her.
And she knows me.
We share a name

Margaret read it again. Did Norma Ann know about Anna Coffin? Why would her father keep this poem, this one poem about Anna? There was so much that confused her.

The last item was a copy of the police report, dated September 14, 1973. She read it through in its entirety.

She finished the last of her coffee and stacked all of the papers together and placed them in her backpack. It was noon now.

Outside a light mist was swirling in the fall air. She hugged her arms around her and decided to take a cab to the nearest mall. She spent the next two hours wandering through brightly lit, noisy stores. She read Norma Ann's poem. She had pizza in the food court for lunch. She looked down at Aislin's picture. She drank more coffee. She looked at her sister's picture. At three she remembered Donna saying she was going to the airport. Maybe she could find her there.

"Which airline?" said the cab driver as they drove up the road to the Bangor International Airport.

"Any door is fine. I'm meeting someone in the lobby."

He dropped her off and she walked through the automatic doors. She scanned all the airline terminals. Perhaps Donna was buying a ticket; maybe she was going somewhere. The top of the escalator opened into a large carpeted area lined with shops. She did not see Donna. She wandered through the stores, looking at the T-shirts from Maine and the ball caps with lobster claws growing out of them. Robin collected ball caps . . . well, he didn't really collect them, he just seemed to have a lot; they seemed to keep appearing. Ball caps and coffee mugs, he would say, you put two of them together on a shelf and the next day you'll have three.

She should buy him this one with the lobster claws for his Christmas stocking. He would get a kick out of it. She picked up glass beer steins and coffee mugs with lobster caricatures and stuffed toys. Something for his mother, maybe this vase, or better yet, this book of downeast Maine traditional recipes; something for her sister-in-law Stephanie, maybe this anthology of short stories by Maine local authors. She put every-thing back except the book of short stories. She bought that for herself and left the store.

That's when she saw Donna, or rather the back of Donna's yellow head. That was Donna, all right, that hair, brown leather jacket. Her cousin was sitting very still on an airport chair facing the window, knees together, hands motionless in her lap. Margaret started to go over and sit beside her, tell her there were no hard feelings, that her day had been fine, really. And how about they stop and get coffee somewhere before they headed back?

But something stopped her. Donna's face — eyes closed, pale cheeks wet, lips moving ever so slightly as if meditating, weeping yet not weeping, for the face bore no expression. Her head remained upright, not bowed.

Margaret felt she had invaded someplace very private, very spiritual, very intimate. She backed away slowly and left her cousin sitting in the chair.

In front of the airport she caught another cab back to the law offices of Dr. George Hamish. At the corner she ate a muffin and read her new book until forty-five minutes later, when Donna came, smiling, regaling her with tales of what she had done all day.

"Did you ever get to the airport?" Margaret asked.

"Not today, too busy. Much too busy. Maybe next Friday."

THIRTY-TWO

Donna had learned that sometimes the best way to get rid of the demons was to sit very still. The airport was a good place for sitting. Nobody came and asked if they could help you. No one much noticed you if you sat in an airport. She had been fine, really fine, until Margaret had started talking about Bradley and Norma Ann. She closed her eyes.

As soon as she had dropped Margaret off she had come here. She spent most of every Friday in the airport. She would sit and watch the planes take off and land, watch the people rush forward to greet travelers, listen to the screeches of delight, the laughing reunions, watch the hugs and kisses, the lingering good-byes between couples who waited until the flight was called for the final time. She had been coming here so often that certain faces became familiar to her, the same businessmen in suits carrying overcoats on their arms, arriving in Bangor every Friday at the same time. Never anyone to meet these people, nor the women in their suits and heels and coifed hair. But they were so self-assured they didn't need anyone. Just walked out, got their cars out of long-term parking, and drove home.

When she tired of watching the people, she would watch the airplanes, huge machines people trusted with their lives. She watched the men in their heavy orange jackets, bright orange earmuffs, wave long lights as they guided the planes in. Like a dance it was, so choreographed, first one arm and then the next. She watched the men drive the long carts that snaked out onto the tarmac with all the luggage.

Then she watched the tanker trucks drive out to fuel up the planes.

Donna Ochs watched them all.

THIRTY-THREE

Donna chatted the entire way home. Margaret said little, just nodded every now and then while Donna went on and on about fashion boots, hair color, all the places she'd visited that day. Margaret found herself looking at her cousin. What had she been doing in the airport? The thought exhausted her. It was a relief when Donna finally pulled down her driveway and she could escape.

An hour later, showered and wearing a long brown knit dress, she drove through the twilight mist to Bosuns Harbor.

The first person she saw when her knock was answered was her Uncle Leo. Another carbon copy of Monty, although bigger and broader, and where Monty's hair was gray, Leo's was black as coal. Leo had the characteristic thick Ochs eyebrows, which fringed both eyes and gave him a faintly sinister look. The two brothers, Leo and Monty, completely dwarfed the younger Clark, who was leaning against the sideboard in the dining room, a can of beer in his hand. It was hard to believe she was related to all these big-faced strangers.

Leo took her hand, pumped and pumped it. "Look at you, Margry! Hey Monty, you didn't tell me what a knockout our little niece turned into. You know what, I bet everyone tells you this, but you look just like Hannah. Doesn't she look just like Hannah? Everyone, doesn't she remind you of Hannah?"

Even though he smiled effusively, there was a harshness about Leo that Margaret found disconcerting.

Dolly, Leo's wife, was the next to greet her, with her bouffant silver hair and heavy earrings. There was a largeness about Dolly that was more than just body weight. She said, "Margaret, Margaret, what a surprise! When Sylvia told me you were back, why, I just couldn't believe it! Not one word of it, I said to Leo, I'll have to see her for myself before I believe it, and look, you're here."

Margaret smiled and remained pleasant. She didn't see Donna until it was time to sit down for dinner. When Donna walked down the stairs she was wearing ratty jeans and a tattered sweatshirt. Her own brown hair lay flat and thinning against her scalp. Her mother said, "Donna, can't you come down here looking a little better than that?"

Donna gave her a look and sat down.

During supper they all wanted to know in great detail what Margaret had been up to since she had run off and married a foreigner.

"Canadian," she said.

"Same difference," Leo said.

She gave them her practiced version, the version that didn't mention Aislin, the version that had her husband studying music in Ontario.

"Oh, you poor, poor dear," Dolly said. "It must be so difficult to be apart for so long. He sounds like such a nice young man."

"Yes."

"But you'll see each other at Christmas?"

"We hope to."

They asked about her work, her artwork, and she told them in great detail about Andre and the shows she had been in.

"Do you teach art?" asked Sylvia.

"A bit, sometimes, yes."

"That must be quite rewarding."

"Monty tells us you have quite a studio in that old house

out there," Leo said. "Are you working on anything?"

"Actually, that's an interesting question. I've met with Dr. Irons a few times and gotten a lot of information from him. He's quite an interesting man. I'm working on a series of paintings of Anna Coffin. She's the ghost that is said to inhabit my house."

Sylvia clapped her hands together and said, "Oh my, that must be quite an exciting project."

"It is, yes."

During the meal Margaret noticed that Monty talked very little. Clark said nothing at all. Leo was the effusive one, the gregarious one. There was a definite pecking order among the three brothers. And Clark Ochs was at the very bottom.

Partway through the meal Margaret said, "Today I was able to get a piece of poetry that Norma Ann wrote. Do you know if she knew about the Anna Coffin story? How could she, I keep asking myself, and yet her poem talks about it."

It was as if her question had sucked the air out of the room. In the vacuum, Sylvia said, "What poem?"

"I found it with my father's things. I was at his lawyer's today."

"What lawyers?" Leo asked.

"My father's lawyer. I thought I'd clean up everything to do with his estate before I sell."

"I didn't know Mitch still had papers at the lawyers," Leo said.

Margaret nodded pleasantly. A look passed between Monty and Leo.

"Were there other papers?" Sylvia said tentatively. "Things of that nature about your sister?"

"No, just that one poem."

Leo took a bite of his salmon and regarded her evenly. "I'm glad you're selling that place. That's no place for a sin-

163

gle woman; the winters can be vicious right by the water there."

"I agree," Pat said. "That's no house for one person to live in. It needs so much upkeep."

"And the heating," said Dolly, placing her hand upon her ample bosom. "The cost of it doesn't bear thinking about. I'd get out before winter comes."

Other Ochs heads were bobbing, nodding, agreeing that she should sell and leave, the sooner the better.

Sylvia rose. "Would anyone care for coffee?"

Before Margaret left for home, Sylvia took her aside and said, "Now, don't you let anyone talk you into selling that old place. You make up your own mind about it."

Margaret smiled, glad that she had at least one ally in this household.

There were two messages on her answering machine when she got in the door. She listened to them while she shed her dress and pulled on her comfy robe and slippers. The first was from Roland Irons, who was wondering how she was doing on the Anna project and how about getting together again. The second was from Chris Rikken, who said he had to see her on an urgent matter, and could she call him when she got in, no matter what time it was. She jotted down the number.

She called Roland. They chatted comfortably for a few minutes and then agreed to meet for coffee the following afternoon at Wellingtons.

She called Chris Rikken. "I've got something I want to show you," he said. "Can I come over?"

"Now?"

"Yes, it's urgent."

"It's late, I've had a tiring day, and I'm heading for bed in about three minutes. I also have something for you. I have some bank statements of my father's. They prove he wasn't being paid off."

"Great. How about I come over tomorrow morning first thing?"

"How first thing is first thing?"

"Seven-thirty?"

"Too first thing. Make it nine."

"Fine."

THIRTY-FOUR

At nine the following morning a grinning Chris Rikken was standing at Margaret's back door, a bag of muffins in his hand.

"I've got blueberry, whole-wheat blueberry, low-fat cranberry bran, high-fiber whole-wheat raspberry, carrot and pineapple, and my personal all-time favorite, chocolate chip."

Margaret stood at the door; she was not smiling.

"I knew you'd have coffee," he continued, "that's why I didn't bother bringing any. You strike me as a coffee drinker. Every time I come here the smell of coffee wafts up."

"Every time you come here? All one time?"

"My point exactly — you should invite me over more."

"What was so urgent? Surely not muffins from Dunkin' Donuts or the smell of coffee."

"I'm here to make peace. I know I came on kind of strong the other day." He pushed his wire-rim glasses up on his nose. "That plus I found a bunch of your family possessions."

"What family possessions?"

"A trunk and some boxes."

"Where?"

"It's a long story. If you let me in, I'll tell you all about it." He could smell coffee from within. "I'm telling you the truth, it really is a long story."

Unsmiling, she opened the door a crack, just enough for him to brush past her, walk into her kitchen, place the muffins on the kitchen table, and sit down. She remained standing.

He began, "Okay, you wanted to know — it was while I was in Bangor yesterday."

"You were in Bangor yesterday? I was in Bangor yesterday!"

He looked up. "No kidding? We could have had lunch. I was there the day before, too."

"Yeah, I know."

He looked at her, eyebrows raised.

She said, "All right, if you did find something, boxes and trunks as you say you did, why have you come here? I'm not your mysterious client. I don't even like you."

He winked at her. "You would if you got to know me. I'm one of the good guys. Anyway, after I looked through the things —"

"You looked through my things?"

"Oh, all of a sudden they're *your* things?"

"You said so yourself — family possessions. I can't believe you actually went through private property."

"Well, to put your mind at ease, I didn't find anything useful so I brought them to you. They're yours. They mostly contain curtains and things."

"How nice of you."

He grinned. "Can I be so bold as to ask for a cup of coffee?"

"No, you may not be so bold. I'm not pouring you a cup of coffee until you tell me what you found and where."

He shrugged his shoulders and ripped open the bag of muffins, carefully laying them side by side on the opened paper bag. "That coffee sure smells good."

"Your story first."

"Okay, you want my story, I'll tell you the story."

He had gone to Bangor the day before yesterday and after getting nowhere with the geriatric lawyer of her father's,

167

drove to the house she and her parents had lived in.

"How did you find out where I lived?"

"I'm a detective. Don't try this at home."

She smiled at him.

"That's the first time I've seen you smile," he said. "You're pretty when you smile."

"Shut up and go on."

The new renters were a young couple with twin toddlers, who had never heard of Mitch Ochs nor where any of his things were. The young woman had told him, "Some people were packing up stuff when we looked at the place. I assumed it was family, or maybe the neighbors."

A quick check of the neighbors revealed nothing. Most didn't even know Mitch Ochs, who many said kept to himself. One long-time resident, an elderly lady named Sophie Farmer, remembered Margaret. Sophie had said that when Margaret left, Mitch had become more and more antisocial. "Never said boo to a soul." Sophie was sure she'd seen an auction company come in and take care of the household effects.

"I remember her," said Margaret, picking up the whole-wheat blueberry. "She was old then; she must be ancient now. She used to let me come over and plant marigolds in her garden."

"That would be her," Chris said. He said that he began calling auction companies. The sixth one he contacted had handled the Ochs estate. The receptionist on the other end of the phone bought his insurance story hook, line, and sinker. She told him there was nothing unusual about the Ochs auction. He could hear her flipping through papers.

"So everything was sold; relatives didn't claim any of it?"

"Except for the stuff to be trashed," the receptionist said.

"What stuff?"

"Stuff that was worth nothing, stuff we couldn't sell."

"And you personally threw out all of this stuff?"

"Not personally, no. If I remember correctly, it came in late and was taken by the landlord. Yes, I think that was it. At least that was the impression we got." She paused. "Who are you?" Her voice took on that cautious edge that indicated maybe she'd said too much already.

He obtained the address from the current residents and decided to visit the landlord in person.

It turned out that the landlord was a bit of a packrat. A jolly, talkative fellow, he wore a grimy button-down white shirt rolled to the elbows underneath a pair of oversized jeans held up by wide suspenders. They were incredibly baggy even for his portly frame. He guided Chris through his house, which was a maze of add-on rooms and additions with the patterned linoleum flooring not quite matching from room to room. The entire small house looked as if it had been decorated with rug samples, curtain swatches, and linoleum remnants scavenged from the dumpsters at Floors R Us.

"People tell me I'm crazy," he said. "They say, why don't you move into that other house you own? It's a whole lot nicer than this place. I say why? Why should I move? Besides, what would I do with all my junk?"

On their way down the basement steps he told Chris, "Let me tell you the truth. I actually bought that place over there to move into, get out of this place into something half decent, but call me lazy, call me whatever, I've never been able to get up the energy to pack up and move. So I've rented out that place all these years and lived in this one. As you can see, I never throw anything out."

The basement was wall-to-wall boxes, trunks, pieces of old beds, furniture legs, haphazard piles of mattresses, toilet seats, an old wringer washing machine, and chaotic stacks of rusting tools. He climbed over his junk and located a trunk and five dusty boxes sealed with packing tape. "Here we go," he said. "I'm feeling generous today. If you can cart these things out of here, they're yours."

Chris took the last bite of his chocolate chip muffin and looked at Margaret. "So I rented a little U-Haul trailer and loaded them up. Okay, now I get coffee?"

"Where are they now?"

"In a safe place."

"What safe place? Don't get all 'detective' with me. These things belong to me. I should have them."

He looked steadily at her. "Look, Ms. I-Want-My-Rights, how long ago did your father die? How long have you had the chance to get these things that you are now demanding?"

She placed her palms around her coffee mug. He waited. "You know nothing about my life." She said it very quietly.

"I'm sorry."

She rose. "You're looking for money stuff, bankbooks and things, to prove my father wasn't paid off, right?"

"More or less."

"I might be able to help you. I picked up my father's personal papers at the lawyer's yesterday. I'll let you have a look at the bank statements. They'll prove that my father wasn't being paid off. There's no mention of any $500,000 deposit."

"All right," he said.

"But first you have to get the boxes."

Chris left, telling her he'd be right back with everything. It wasn't until he was out on the highway that he realized he never did get his coffee.

THIRTY-FIVE

When Chris returned a few hours later, Margaret was upstairs in her studio and didn't hear his car or his knock. She was standing back and studying her sketch of Anna Coffin and frowning. The watercolor had a misty aura — the sea, the salt, and Anna sitting on a rock, pale skirt clinging to her wet knees, silver flute at her lips. But it was her eyes that made Margaret frown. Something about them was wrong. Something she couldn't quite define. She peered at the tiny photocopy of Anna's portrait that she kept propped against her easel. It wasn't her intention to paint a portrait of the real Anna Coffin. That had already been done. Her desire was to paint the mythical Anna, Anna of the flute, Anna of the white shawl and the sea, Anna of the rowboat to Dragon Back Island, Anna of the wind, Anna who had walked out into the sea and never returned.

The Anna she had seen her first night in Coffins Reach.

"That's very good."

Margaret spun around to the voice. Standing at the head of the stairs was Chris, glasses slightly askew on his face, wide smile, carrying two cups of Dunkin' Donuts coffee in a cardboard tray.

"Don't you knock?"

"I did for about an hour. Then I called. Then I tromped up the stairs loud enough to wake the dead, calling all the time."

"I'm sorry, sometimes when I get engrossed in a project . . ."

"I brought coffee. Seeing's I didn't get any the last time I

171

was here." He placed the tray on an empty table in her studio. "You have a great view up here."

"I like it."

She hugged her arms and looked at him. Why did he unnerve her so? Maybe it was that confident manner, his loose-jointed body, brown hair mussed with a hint of gray around the edges, the kind of hair mothers love to run their hands through.

"I got the boxes in the U-Haul outside. You want me to get them?"

"Let me help. How many are there?"

"Four or five and a steamer trunk."

Outside, when he opened up the back of the U-Haul, she recognized the trunk. "That was in the attic," she said. "It will have drapes and bedspreads. Maybe some tablecloths."

"I know," he said hefting a box. "I rented a U-Haul to cart around old kitchen curtains."

They placed the boxes on the dining-room floor, and from the sideboard drawer she produced the sheaf of papers.

"These are just a loan; you can copy them," she said.

The copy of the police report lay on the top of the file. He picked it up and said, "My first foray into the jaded world of police detection. How not to write a police report." He waved it in front of him. "That's what this is an example of."

"What do you mean?"

"Maybe it was because I was just out of the police academy, not even twenty, and with everything still fresh in my mind, but it seemed to me that the detective on the case sat down with the families and came up with their version of what happened, instead of conducting a thorough investigation."

"What do you mean?"

"Well, I've no doubt that your sister probably did fall to

172

her death, and it was probably completely accidental, but you'd never know it by the way the investigation was handled. We do forensics a whole lot different now, a whole lot more thorough. The search we did on this place could be in a police training video on how not to secure a crime scene."

Margaret had stopped on one word. "What do you mean, probably, as in 'it was probably an accident'?"

"Okay, I'm putting weird ideas into your head and I don't mean to. Essentially, I came up here with the detective, right into this house, right up these stairs. The detective spent a total of about five minutes wandering around, and then about five hours with the Ochs brothers, who explained in great detail what should go into the report and what should stay out. The whole thing had this stink about it — I'm sorry, I'm talking about your family here. This house was never cordoned off; it was never an official crime scene. When I mentioned this to the officers in charge, they laughed at me."

"What are you saying? That my sister didn't die accidentally?"

"Not at all, I'm not commenting about your sister's death, that's not the issue here. All I'm talking about is the way this investigation was conducted."

But Margaret's head was spinning.

"Well." He downed the rest of his coffee, threw the cup into a garbage can, put the papers under his arm, and winked at her. "I better be off. I bought you a coffee," he said, pointing.

"You can't leave," she told him. "You can't just all of a sudden come out with 'it was probably an accident,' and then leave."

"It was probably an accident."

She watched him leave, her mind still reeling with questions. She wanted to call him back, demand that he tell her everything he knew about her sister, about her uncles, about why the investigation wasn't correctly handled. Instead she watched him drive away, and then she turned and walked back into her kitchen, exasperated.

In the dining room she began with the trunk. She was right. It did contain stacks of curtains and tablecloths, creased by their years in the trunk. She lifted out the pieces, one by one, unfolding them carefully and laying them out on the dining-room table. She held a lace curtain up to the light. It was delicate, intricate, and she wondered how the lace would stand up to a gentle hand washing. There were also a couple of bedspreads and a few lace tablecloths, badly in need of repair. She recognized the pale blue bedspread that had been on her parents' double bed. She lifted it out. Not in bad shape. She decided to wash it; maybe she would even use it.

Carefully, using a sharp knife, she slit open one of the boxes. Clothes. Her mother's dresses. Her grandmother's dresses, boots and belts, creases in their dark leather like wrinkles on an old face.

Her grandfather's suits were at the bottom. There were three of them, and she pulled them out and laid them side by side on the table. In the pocket of one of the suit jackets she found a pocket watch. The shiny brass timepiece was heavy in her hands. She turned it over. The inscription on the back read: Earnest J. Ochs. She had only seen pictures of the grandfather she had never met, the progenitor of the Ochs clan.

The rest of the pockets were empty.

She exhumed dusty felt hats with feathers and pins. She pulled out one of the long pins and wondered if it was even possible to buy these anywhere anymore. She found dresses, vintage clothing, costume jewelry, chair-arm doilies and dozens of cotton handkerchiefs.

One cardboard box contained a number of smaller boxes — Whitman's sampler candy boxes and hinged cigar boxes. In a cloth-covered jewelry box she found a small object wrapped in tissue paper. She unwrapped it. It was a small wooden bagpiper, probably six inches tall. She held it up and examined it in the light. What was familiar about it? Why did it make her feel uneasy? The little carved figure was clad in a blue-green kilt, red waistcoat, and gray hat, the colors still bright even after all these years. She turned it over. The artist's name was not noted on the piece. Where did this come from? She set it on her kitchen windowsill. Perhaps seeing it here regularly would jog something in her memory.

She also found her mother's porcelain dolls with their crack-lined faces, soft bodies, and eyes that closed when you laid them down. At the bottom of the box were file folder after file folder stuffed with crumpled papers — dozens of her and Norma Ann's report cards, pictures, and class photos. She found a small book with "autographs" scripted across it in gold. The first page contained the message: *Property of Norma Ann Ochs.* She flipped through the book and read at random:

To Norma Ann,
Remember A
Remember B
But most of all
Remember me
From your friend, Clara Morton

and

To my friend Norma Ann:
I wish you much

I wish you plenty
I wish you a husband
Before you're twenty
From Kathy Swanson

Margaret closed the book and placed it on the table. She picked up a small box that clinked with shells. She remembered these shells. She had collected them on a family vacation to the New Jersey shore.

Underneath was a folder of her own artwork and a tin box of watercolor paints, round disks of faded colors hardened over time into tiny rock spheres. She looked at these paintings — houses with chimneys and smoke, trees and ponds and ducks.

At the bottom was a diary, the kind with a lock. The lock was easily broken with a nail file, and Margaret began through the entries, reading here and there:

September 7: Went to school today, nothing interesting happened.
Sept. 11: I'm bored, bored, bored. I may go to Bosuns Harbor to the movies.
Sept. 20: Valerie says that J. likes me. Ugh!!
Sept. 22: Margry's bugging me again. She's always bugging me, follows me everywhere. Mom says I have to be nice, but sometimes I wish she would just go away. She's too little.

Margaret smiled, but felt a pang. If Norma Ann had grown to adulthood, what kind of sisters would they be to each other? Would they share coffee and lunches in restaurants? Would they laugh at the same jokes, cry at the same movies, read the same books?

Halfway through, an entry caught her eye:

Nov. 9: Donna said it's stupid to believe in God. We had a big fight about this. She said that the Ochses don't go to church, that the Ochses don't have to believe in God. She said it's part of our heritage to be self-sufficient. I don't know what that means.

Nov. 10: I had to write this right away. Donna and I have made up. I'm glad about that. I asked Mom about God but she wouldn't tell me anything. She said she went to Sunday school when she was little. But now she doesn't go anymore. I asked her why but she didn't say anything. Do you know why I'm wondering about God, Diary? It's because I was reading a book and it talked about God, and it got me thinking why our family doesn't go to church. Other people go to church, but I don't know why we don't. I started praying on my own. And you know what? I think there is a God. I can't tell anyone this, though. I asked Mom if we could go to church in Bosuns Harbor sometime. She said, when dad's away we might, she said might. But when he's home he wouldn't allow it.

The entire middle section of the diary was empty, page after blank page, almost a year of blank pages. Near the end she read:

April 5: I can't tell anyone about the miserableness of my life. Bradley knows. That's all. Not even Donna. And of course I can't tell Margaret. She's too little.

Tell me what?
On the very last page of the book she read:

April 7: I feel like killing myself. I prayed for the pain to go away. No one understands. Why doesn't God take the pain away?

Margaret ran her fingers over the pages, over the handwriting of her sister, tears squeezing out of the corners of her eyes.

What had changed the normal, happy preteen girl who was "bored, bored, bored" into this one who was praying that God would remove her pain? Who would know? Donna? Somehow she knew that her cousin wouldn't talk. Just bring up the subject of Norma Ann and she'd be stranded in Bangor again. Sylvia? Maybe Sylvia.

A new and fierce thought began demanding Margaret's attention. Could her sister have been responsible for her own death? Could her sister have flung herself down from the porch? *I feel like killing myself.*

She sat cross-legged on the floor, sat that way for a long time, the only sounds the wind against her house, the flipping of pages in Norma's book as she read back through them page by page, until she realized that she was supposed to meet Roland at Wellingtons at two. It was now a quarter till.

Before she left, she took the wooden piper, wrapped it back in tissue paper, and placed it in her jacket pocket.

THIRTY-SIX

Donna didn't go to the ceramic factory that morning. She was scheduled to, but didn't. She knew this would eventually mean another "talking to" by Arnie, who would call her into his office and pace while he went on and on about how you can't run an organization with only halfhearted commitment from volunteers. She would sit there, head bowed as if she were in the principal's office, while Arnie strutted back and forth in front of her. It had happened before.

She never meant to miss work. She had left that morning, the same as she did every Tuesday, but instead of turning in at the ceramic factory she drove past it, out onto the highway towards Coffins Reach. She took the gravel road down past the Godwishes, past Margaret's place, and kept on going. She parked between the hedge of beach grass and the stone embankment. She'd been here before, and she knew no one could see her car from the road. She climbed over weeds and rocks to the abandoned cabin. This was where she came when she couldn't hold the edges of herself together anymore.

This was the place where they found her that time so long ago, that time when they came and took her to the hospital. That time when they stood above her whispering. She knew they were talking about her. Most everyone did. She wanted to scream at them, to make them talk louder so she could hear what they were saying, but she was mute. All she could do was to swing her head from side to side, fiercely, but it was held tight between warm palms.

Carefully, very carefully this time, she unlocked the back

179

door with the key she kept under the rock by the back porch. No one would see her here. No one would know she was here. Not this time. That time, Old Man MacGregor was living in the cabin when she had slumped on his doorstep, clothes torn, body scratched and bleeding from her jagged fingernails. It was quite by chance that this was where she ended up on that night. Old Man MacGregor called the doctor, and they came and took her away.

But he had died a long time ago.

Inside, the cabin was dead cold, as she knew it would be. She hugged her arms around her and grabbed a gray woolen blanket from the bed. She huddled into it and sat in a rocking chair and looked out toward the ocean through the cracked window. When they were children, all of them, they would visit the strange old man who lived in this house and he would give them candy canes, even in summer.

Something was peculiar about the sea today. It looked seething and unsteady, like water in a kettle just before it comes to a boil. Maybe it had to do with the unsteadiness of earth. She was sure, had been for a while now, that time had begun to speed up. Something had come undone in the center of the planet and it was beginning to spin out of kilter around the sun. It wasn't a sudden thing, this speeding up, but gradual, so gradual that only she noticed. Nights were coming around more quickly. It was night and then suddenly it was night again, the next night.

Donna rocked back and forth in the chair, back and forth, back and forth so fast that the floorboards squeaked, the chair rungs groaned. She couldn't stop. She was as powerless as the planet upon which she lived. Faster. Maybe this had started twenty-five years ago. Because how could twenty-five years have passed so quickly with nothing changed? Faster. She rocked and hummed tunelessly while she watched the sea, ready to boil over its banks.

THIRTY-SEVEN

By late afternoon the sun had sliced through the gray and was casting long cathedral shadows through the windows of the Bosuns Harbor Public Library. Margaret sat at the microfiche reader going through old news clippings. She had already seen most of these in her father's files: snapshots of her uncles glad-handing the mayor; a smiling Leo Ochs holding his Citizen of the Year award; check presentations with Leo and Monty and Mitch, arms around each other (where was Clark in all of this?), donating to the United Way, the YMCA, the hospital, the handicapped society. But these were only mildly interesting to her. What she was looking for were accounts of her sister's death. After Chris had left with the pronouncement that the investigation into her sister's death wasn't all it should have been, she decided to find out herself.

Earlier that afternoon, she'd had coffee at Wellingtons with Roland. The usual eclectic crowd was there — graybearded men, and women with chin-length silver hair and hiking boots — the philosopher kings of the Maine seacoast. They had moved their chairs into a semicircle and were debating the pros and cons of the government's new antipoverty bill when she entered. Roland was already involved in the conversation, citing his opinions on each of his ten fingers. Margaret poured herself a black coffee and helped herself to something that looked like quiche. When she pulled out her wallet, the little piper fell to the floor.

Lorne reached down and picked it up. "Interesting icon," he said.

"It was with some things that belonged in my house," Margaret said.

He fingered it. "It looks like it's from the Black Watch regiment."

"Have you ever seen anything like this before?" Margaret asked.

"Are those the Black Watch colors?" Stu asked. "Are you sure, Lorne?"

Lorne turned it over. "I would say definitely yes. And to answer your question, Margaret, these regimental bands lead the troops into war."

"I was hoping actually to figure out where it came from. Why does this little bagpiper make me feel as if it has something to do with the curse on my house?"

Roland chuckled and clapped his hands. "The old cursed house again."

Margaret looked at him. "I had a sister who fell to her death from the widow's walk there. My parents both died as a direct result of her death. A hundred years previous, Anna Coffin drowned. There is a lot of death associated with that house."

"And you think this little wooden bagpiper is involved?" This was asked by a woman she hadn't met.

"I don't know. All I'm saying is that this piper gives me a creepy feeling when I look at him. I think it's associated somehow with my house."

Vivian said, "Well, he does look rather sinister, wouldn't you say so, Helen? But there's nothing in the literature about a bagpiper, isn't that so, Roland?"

"Not that I know of. We know there was a flute, but a member of the Black Watch regimental band? I don't know. I'm heading down to Freeport to do some more research on our Anna. I'll let you know if a bagpiper fits into the mix."

"Now, take Vivian, for example," Stu said. "She really believes that house is haunted, she's totally convinced."

"Don't go on about that, Stu," said the woman named Helen. "You'll frighten her."

"I'm not afraid," Margaret said. "Just curious. So many deaths."

That had been an hour ago. The little marching bagpiper now stood at attention on the library table beside her, its dot eyes looking beyond her to some private war. She sped the microfiche through the years and saw more of the Ochses and their "generous donations." She was surprised to discover that in 1972 her Uncle Leo was a town selectman.

Then she saw the article she had found in multiple copies in her basement. She reread the account of her sister's death. She sped through several weeks of issues after this, months of issues, but her sister was not mentioned again. She flipped back. No byline. She closed her eyes, massaged her temples. It had to have been a suicide. She knew that a lot of papers don't report suicides, especially small-town papers. That could be why nothing else was mentioned. A suicide would explain her mother's eventual demise and her father's depression.

The *Bangor Daily News* was next. There was an article about the death of her sister similar to the one in the Bosuns Harbor paper, except for one small detail. The final sentence of the story stated, "The police are not ruling out foul play." She stared at that line for a long time, a new, more fearful thought entering her consciousness. She thought of Ruth Godwish's wild suggestion. She jotted down the byline of the reporter, a Simon Schultz.

She found no more articles. No more stories. No more "generous donations." Nothing. It was as if the day after her sister's death, the generosity of the Ochs brothers suddenly dried up.

On her way home, Margaret decided to stop in at Sylvia's. Her aunt seemed delighted to see her and explained that Monty was still at the store and that Donna was at the ceramic factory, and how nice that they could get together, just the two of them. She offered to make tea and settled Margaret into a cozy sitting room, while she went to the kitchen. Margaret fished the photocopy of the Bangor story from her backpack and flattened it out on the coffee table. When Sylvia arrived, silver tray in hand, she stopped and looked down.

"What have we here?" she asked.

"An article I found at the library. *Bangor Daily News*, September 14, 1973."

Sylvia sat down, lifted her glasses from the chain around her neck, and picked up the photocopy. Several minutes later she handed the article back to Margaret. "Did you have a question about this?"

"The last line," Margaret said.

"The last line?"

"The last sentence."

Sylvia peered at the paper again, taking her time. She handed it back to Margaret and said lightly, "I fail to see why that has you concerned."

"Foul play. Doesn't that mean murder?"

Sylvia laughed then, a throaty nervous laugh. "You're beginning to sound like Ruth Godwish. You know how reporters like to make things more sensational than they really are. It was to sell papers, that's all."

"Why would they write that?"

Her aunt tapped her finger on the paper. "Simon Schultz. Yes, I remember him. We had trouble with him. I think he went on to work for one of those supermarket tabloids, a totally unscrupulous young reporter if memory serves."

Margaret looked at the older woman steadily. "Then if she

184

wasn't murdered, did my sister kill herself?"

"Oh dear, no. What a preposterous idea, the idea of suicide. Oh, my goodness. The police said it was an accident."

Not all of them. "I have a copy of the police report," Margaret said.

Sylvia looked at her.

"I have a copy of the police report," Margaret repeated.

"Why on earth would you even want a copy of the police report?"

"It was in my father's personal files, the ones I told you about."

The elderly woman stopped and put a hand to her cheek. "Was there anything else in there?"

"Lots of things."

It was several minutes before Sylvia spoke. "You are so full of strange ideas today, Margaret. Well, I guess it's to be expected. We had to deal with your sister's death plus your father's estrangement a long time ago. And now that you've come back, well, I guess you have to find all these things for yourself and come to some peace with it all."

"I read lots of articles about all those generous donations that Monty, Mitch, and Leo made."

Sylvia visibly relaxed. "You will know that the Ochs family is historically one of the most generous families along the Maine coast."

"Historically. But not anymore."

Sylvia's hand fluttered nervously to the pearls at her throat. "Business profiles change, Margaret. We experienced gains during the 1950s and '60s. But that changed."

"When my sister died. The *day* my sister died. That's what it looks like. It may surprise you that a detective is investigating this whole thing. He says the police investigation was not conducted the way it should have been."

Sylvia took a sip of her tea. "Oh, my goodness, I forgot the sugar. I can't forget the sugar. You take sugar, don't you?" She left.

When Sylvia returned, silver sugar bowl in hand, she said, voice like the sugar she carried, "That may seem to be the way it was, but I can tell you, it is purely coincidental. And as for the investigation, it was thorough, most thorough. We were questioned time and time again."

Sylvia took a long sip of her tea and then topped off Margaret's cup even though she hadn't taken a sip. Margaret watched as Sylvia's hands adjusted the napkins, the cookies, arranging them just so on the silver plate.

"Why won't anyone talk about my sister?" Margaret asked. "I bring up her name and Donna leaves me stranded in Bangor. I talk to you and you run off and get sugar. I'm not sure how Bradley fits into all of this, but he can't even stand to look at my face, while his mother watches every move I make from behind her curtains. And then there's this whole Anna Coffin thing, and the so-called curse on the place. Is that why my father left? Because of the curse? Or was he paid off?"

Sylvia gasped. "These cookies are not sweet enough. I told Donna to add more sugar, but that girl never listens."

Margaret looked steadily at her aunt. "Why did my father leave?"

"There are some things you need to know, I guess. We begged them to stay. Your mother would have stayed, I think, but your father wanted to get away, the sooner the better. When they left we tried to keep in contact with them, but they would have none of it. We finally had to content ourselves with the thought that grief does strange things to people. We had to let him go. Hannah and I were very close. Her leaving was a great loss to me."

186

"How did my sister die?"

"She fell. It was an accident."

"I don't think that's what happened. I think she committed suicide. And while I'm here, I plan to find out why."

Margaret left without touching her tea.

THIRTY-EIGHT

By the time she left, the sun had disappeared and the winds had come up rather suddenly; the leaden clouds swooped down like a swarm of ravens. She could feel her little car pitch and reel on the highway.

As she pulled into her driveway, the crinkled face of Ruth Godwish looked out at her from the window. Inside her own house, she shut all of her blinds and pulled the phone toward her. She soon discovered that Simon Schultz had not worked for the Bangor paper for more than twenty years. No one knew where he had gone or where he was living. Next she pulled out her old address book and looked up the last phone number she had for Margaret Mahone, her mother's sister. The person who answered was not her aunt and had never heard of her. Some detective I'm turning out to be, she thought.

She filled a glass with tap water, picked up Norma Ann's diary from the drawer where she'd left it, and went into the living room. She would sit in the bay window, watch the storm, and go through the entries again, especially the ones she had missed.

Jan. 4: There's a teacher in my school, Miss Parker, and she's been explaining the Bible to me.
Jan. 15: Miss Parker said I could go to church with her some-time, but Mom won't let me. I said why not and she said Dad won't allow it. I told Miss Parker that, and she said that was okay, that she'd tell me things from the Bible. She is helping

me with my writing.

April 5: Miss Parker told me the story of Anna Coffin. I don't know why. Maybe to try to get me to think about something else. She said maybe I could write some poetry about it. I told Mom about the story. She didn't know it. But it was in the library and Miss Parker knew. She showed me the book. Anna Coffin killed herself. She just walked into the water and didn't come out. Sometimes I feel like doing that.

The phone rang. Margaret decided to let it ring. Her answering machine kicked in after four rings and she heard Chris's voice. She picked up the living room extension.

"Hi, I'm here," she said.

"You were monitoring your calls," he accused, laughing.

"Isn't that why people buy answering machines?"

"Well, I'm glad you thought me worthy to talk to."

"I need to talk to someone sane."

"And I'm the only sane person in the state of Maine."

"I keep thinking to myself, am I *related* to all these weirdos?"

"My thoughts exactly every Christmas."

He asked her if her Uncle Leo had ever sent her any money.

"My Uncle Leo? I barely knew my Uncle Leo."

"Margaret, did you look through these statements very carefully?"

"Yes, I never found anything about $500,000."

"That's all you looked for?"

"Well . . . yes."

"Well, for starters, these are not your father's bank statements."

"They're not?"

"These are for a savings account in the name of Leo Ochs."

189

"Leo Ochs? Why would my father have Leo Ochs's bank statements?"

"Remind me never to hire you to work for me," he said with a laugh.

"Remind me never to give you my résumé. Why would my father have a copy of Leo Ochs's bank statement?"

"Six copies, to be precise. Here's the deal. I have six bank statements, all for the months of September. I've got September 1973 right up to September 1978. On September 13 there is a withdrawal of $20,000. Leo paid someone or something $20,000 every September. And since the statements were in your father's files, I would assume that this sum was paid to your father."

Margaret ran a hand through her short curls. September 13, the day her sister died.

"You still there?" he asked.

"I'm here."

"Do you have any thoughts on this?"

"Maybe he was giving it to charity. My uncles were always giving money to charity."

"The great generous Ochs brothers. Let me ask you something, Margaret. When you were growing up in Bangor, did you have much money?"

"We had enough. Not a lot that I remember. My father could have sold this house. I don't know why he didn't. That would have brought in something. After my mother died, I remember my father couldn't work anymore, well, not a lot. As a teenager I didn't pay much attention, just when my father would give me a fifty-dollar bill and tell me to go buy groceries."

"So your father had money, you never starved, and he, according to what you just said, didn't work much."

"Haven't you ever heard of pensions? Or dividends from the company?"

"Your father's share of the Ochs Brothers' holdings was bought out. He was paid one lump sum before you left. He was no longer a partner when he moved you to Bangor."

"How'd you find that out?"

"It's a matter of public record. And your father left you quite a bit, didn't he?"

"That's none of your business."

"And your entire university education was paid for, wasn't it?"

"That doesn't prove anything. We had money from before."

Later, she sat in the bay window and thought about Chris's words. If what he said was true, why did Leo continue to send her father money? Because Mitch was his brother and he felt some sort of a family obligation? She watched the sea, which was inklike and restless. Ahead of her the trees on Dragon Back Island were bowed in the wind.

Toward the point she saw her again. The woman in white, standing as she had the night Margaret arrived, facing the sea, waves lapping her bare feet. Margaret raced to the kitchen, pulled on her boots and a rain jacket with hood. She forged her way through the wind and rain, but by the time she got to the point, the woman had gone. Margaret ran around the point to the lee side, holding her jacket around her with wet hands, frantically searching for the ghost woman.

But she had disappeared.

THIRTY-NINE

"Evelyn Parker?" said the woman behind the desk at the Bosuns Harbor Junior High School. The woman, whose nameplate said she was Carmen, looked to be in her mid-twenties, very tall, rake thin, with an overabundance of pale yellow hair. When she stood up she reminded Margaret of a sunflower.

"She would have taught here in the late sixties, early seventies," said Margaret.

"Hold on. Let me check."

She turned and walked into an inner office while Margaret waited. Mid-September and the junior high had been in session for only a few weeks. The floors, the desks, the tables, even the teachers and students wore that shiny freshness of a new school year. Groups of jean-clad students with backpacks slung over their shoulders brought in notes from parents, late slips, permission slips, delinquent school fees. Teachers carrying stacks of photocopying scurried into and out of the office. And loudspeaker announcements of this meeting or that meeting being canceled or changed, shattered what little silence there was.

Five minutes later the receptionist returned.

"I've got an Evelyn Parker here. She retired in 1979."

"That's probably the one."

"Was she a teacher of yours?"

"She helped a special friend of mine through a bad time once and I want to personally thank her."

"I do have an address, but I can't guarantee she's still there. It's a local address, but I'm sure she's moved. I haven't heard of this name and I've been here for eight years. But I'll give you the address if you'd like; perhaps whoever's living there knows where she is now."

Margaret thanked the sunflower woman and made her way through the tangled knots of students in the hallway. The address was on Shore Line Drive. She wondered if Evelyn Parker lived near Roland. Small world if she did.

Leaving the school grounds she hung a left and drove down to the waterfront. A mile or so past Roland's house, she parked her car beside a small white cottage trimmed in dark shiny green. A silver Volvo was parked in the driveway. This gave Margaret hope. An old Volvo would be just the kind of car a retired single lady teacher would drive. Her knock was answered by a broad-bellied man in his forties. He was wearing a faded Boston Red Sox sweatshirt with the sleeves rolled up. He was frowning. The TV was on and loud, a game show. Perhaps Margaret had called him away from a marathon TV-watching session and now he'd have to start all over again.

When she asked if an Evelyn Parker lived there he said no, he had never heard of an Evelyn Parker. He'd been in this house for fifteen years. Did he know where Evelyn Parker had moved to? Not a clue, he said, shaking his head, not a clue. Could she know the name of his landlord? "House is mine," he said. "Been here fifteen years."

"Who did you buy it from?"

"Who are you, the IRS? I don't have to answer your questions."

"You're right, and I'm sorry. It's just that I'm desperate to locate a former resident of this house."

"Yeah, well, I don't know any former residents of this place. I bought it from an agent."

"And you don't remember the former owner's name?"

"Don't know, don't particularly care."

Margaret turned to go. "Sorry to bother you."

"Yeah," he said, slamming the door.

At a phone booth in town, she pulled Chris Rikken's business card from her wallet and dialed his number. It was worth a try, wasn't it? And he seemed helpful enough.

"Hello." His voice was strong, authoritative. All business.

"This is Margaret Collinwood."

"Margaret, hi there."

"You're a detective, right?"

"Right."

"I was wondering if you could locate a person for me."

"A missing person?"

"Well, actually three people. The first one's a retired school teacher. I mean, she could be dead for all I know, but the last address I have for her is in Bosuns Harbor and she doesn't live there anymore. The second one is a former reporter with the Bangor Daily News, and the third is a lady named Margaret Mahone. You can find people, right?"

"I do it all the time."

"Good."

"Renewing old acquaintances while you're back in town?"

"Sort of."

"Okay, if your old friends aren't trying to hide, they should be fairly easy to locate, provided they're still alive."

"What do you charge?" She knew her question sounded hopelessly unsophisticated, but she had never hired a detective before.

He laughed. "Let me put it this way, if my quick search comes up with your names, how 'bout you buy lunch one day?"

"Deal," she said.

FORTY

Within ten minutes of starting an Internet search, Chris had come up with four Evelyn Parkers in New England and one Margaret Mahone near Albany, New York. He hadn't been able to locate any Simon Schultzes in Maine, but found 137 in New York City, and a total of 73 in the New England states. He pressed *print* and tapped his fingers on the edge of his computer while he waited. Used to be only the police and a select few individuals and businesses had access to crisscross directories, which matched names and addresses with the chronological listings of phone numbers. Now, virtually anyone with a computer had that same information. Even the bad guys.

He remembered a demonstration at a convention he attended a few years back in Boston where down in front a smiling, three-piece-suited computer guru plugged the latest CD-ROM phone book into his machine, and then up there on the screen was the complete phone book of everyone in the good ole U.S. of A. He also had one for Canada. "Get both of them at this one low convention price!" He chose a "volunteer" from the audience, keyed in his phone number, and then proceeded to tell him the names, addresses, and phone numbers of his next door neighbors. That was a few years ago. With the Internet, things were even simpler.

Now, there was no guarantee that these Evelyn Parkers and this Margaret Mahone were ones that Margaret wanted. They could have moved to sunny Arizona for all anyone knew and taken Simon Schultz with them.

He leaned back against the bulkhead and looked outside

through rectangular portholes. He never minded rain. He pulled on a raggy gray wool sweater and went outside. Plenty of time to call Evelyn Parker and Margaret Mahone, plenty of time to find out why Leo and Monty had paid off Mitch. He sat in the cockpit under his blue canvas bimini and listened to the rain splat against the canvas overhead. He knew this was the kind of morning that most people liked to spend sitting in front of a fireplace with a good book. But Chris had done enough sailing in the rain that he'd grown accustomed to it, even liked it.

He looked out into the murky bay. By this time of year the marina was practically deserted. A lot of the fair-weather sailors had already pulled their boats out for the season, and they sat on cradles in the boatyard covered with tarps or shrink-wrapped in white plastic. He was the only one in the Belfast marina who lived on his boat year-round.

He hadn't always lived on a boat. Like everyone else, he'd lived in a house once. He had a wife, a dog, and two kids, and they lived in a bi-level in Bosuns Harbor with a nice view of the bay. He had known his wife, Ginny, since high school. A whirlwind courtship ended in whirlwind marriage which ended in a whirlwind divorce. That's the word he liked to use when describing Ginny — whirlwind. She left him the first time during their second year of marriage. They were reunited two months later when she came to him weeping that she loved him, would never leave him again, and that she was pregnant. Their first child Suzanne was born six months later. There were more breakups and more makeups, the two of them always making up with as much passion as they fought. In all of this, Chris never thought she'd really leave for good. When she did, when the weeks passed and the months passed and she did not return, he began drinking and missing work. As a result he lost any custody of his two daughters that he could have hoped for. In the end he lost the house, the good car, the kids, and the dog. Eventually Ginny and the girls moved to Deerfield, Illinois, where she married an accountant.

The one thing she didn't take was the boat. Probably, if someone had realized at the time that this old boat was some sort of asset, it would have been seized as well. He moved his few possessions aboard and quit the police force before anyone could fire him. For months he moved through his days in a kind of drink-induced stupor. Morning, afternoon, dusk, dark, it was all the same to him.

And then one afternoon his seven-year-old daughter Suzanne phoned. All by herself from her home in Illinois. He asked about school and she told him about her new friends, about their dog Floppy Tail, about their new house, about her new bedroom. She told him she missed him, and when was he going to come and visit?

That phone call woke up something inside of him. No matter what happened he was still their father, and always would be. If he was ever going to see his girls again, he had better get his life together. He had been handed a raw deal and he had two choices. He could either go on feeling sorry for himself, drink himself to an early grave, or he could get up and make the best of it. He decided on the latter.

The next day he found the closest AA meeting and started attending, two or three times a day at first, and then every other day. He also began sailing again, not just sleeping and drinking aboard his boat. He cleaned it up. He tightened and repaired the rigging. He replaced the frayed sheets and repaired the sails. He took it out into the bay, got to know himself, his boat, and every inch of coastline from Belfast to Florida, and across the Gulf Stream to the Bahamas.

When his daughters came for summer visits, he took them

sailing, teaching them port from starboard, how to pull the sheets in on a tack, and how to bend on the jib. At night they would anchor in some secluded bay, sit down in the cabin and play games of SORRY!, tell jokes, and eat licorice whips and peanut butter sandwiches.

His sweater wasn't keeping out the damp, but he was reluctant to go back inside. When finally he did, he shut the hatch and turned back to his computer. He did have work to do, after all. He decided to begin with the list of Evelyn Parkers. The first one he phoned was a potter in Bar Harbor who'd never been a school teacher. The second one was a computer technician in Barrington, Rhode Island, who'd also never been a school teacher.

The third Evelyn Parker answered his query with, "Oh, you must be looking for my aunt, Evelyn Parker. She was a teacher in Bosuns Harbor for a long time. She lives down near Portland in one of those self-contained apartments for seniors."

He jotted down the address and phone number from this pleasant-voiced stranger, appalled at how quick people are to divulge vital information. How did Evelyn Parker, the niece, know that he wasn't an ax murderer? He thanked her and hung up.

The real Evelyn Parker's phone rang, and on the fourth ring a pleasant, elderly voice announced that Evelyn Parker wasn't in right now, but if you would kindly leave your name and number she'd get back to you just as soon as she could. He hung up without leaving a message.

He decided to go and see Margaret. He changed into a clean sweater, put the printouts of addresses into an envelope, and left.

When Margaret saw him at the door, she took the envelope and said, "Thank you." But she seemed distracted and looked past him, toward the house to the south.

"Are you all right?" he asked.

"Okay, I guess."

She started to close the door.

Like before, he put his hand along its edge. He said, "I don't mean to pry, but you don't seem fine. You were fine this morning, and now you're either tired or afraid."

Quietly, almost to herself, she said, "Maybe I should just leave, make that Mavis person a happy camper and go back to Fredericton."

"Why would you want to leave?"

"I don't know."

"You must know."

"I don't know why I should tell you, you're probably in cahoots with all of them."

"All of who?"

"The people around here."

"Can you be a little more specific?"

"Why should I?"

"Because I'm the only sane person in Maine."

"Well, you and Roland, except he talks too much."

"I don't talk too much. I'm told I'm a good listener."

Sighing, still not smiling, she opened the door. "Come in, then."

She told him that coffee was made and if he wanted a cup they were in the cupboard next to the sink. She said all of this in a monotone, as if she offered everyone who walked in here coffee by rote. Her own coffee she drank out of a gigantic white mug that looked more like a soup bowl.

"Do you think you drink too much coffee?" he asked her.

"They're going to have coffee in heaven." She wasn't smiling when she said this.

"Do you want to talk about it?"

She got up. "This place is making me crazy. I really

opened a can of worms coming back here." She paced around her kitchen, adjusting things, opening and closing the fridge until she looked at him and said, "Someone's been here, that's why I'm feeling weird. Someone's been here."

"Someone burglarized this place?"

"Sort of."

"Did you call the police?"

"Nothing was taken. But I could tell someone was here. Little things," she said, spinning around. "Little things, little things, things not exactly put back where they belong. I could tell, you can always tell. I think it was Ruth Godwish. That lady watches me all the time."

"How would she get in here?"

"She walks through walls, I don't know. She's some sort of witch or something."

"Ruth Godwish?"

"That's what my cousin told me."

"Your cousin says Ruth Godwish is a witch?"

Margaret nodded. She was sitting down across from him now, hugging her arms.

"You're afraid," he said.

"I just don't know who to trust anymore."

"Maybe talking to that old teacher will help. Was she a special friend?"

"I don't know her. She was my sister's teacher. I think she knew about my sister's depression. I think she had schizophrenia. From all that I've read, it often comes on in early teens, and back then, no one would have recognized it, maybe no one but this teacher. It's the only explanation that makes any sense."

"Why don't you start at the beginning," he said gently. "I don't mind listening."

She did. She told him about the diary, about her sister's

depression, about reading the articles in the paper, about Simon Schultz and how he had written "foul play" in his story.

"Where's the diary now?" he asked.

"In my backpack. I had it with me. I was hoping to show it to Evelyn Parker."

She told him she was sure that her sister had taken her own life because of mental illness.

"Maybe whoever broke in here wanted that diary," Chris said.

"But why?"

"It talks about her depression? I don't know, maybe whoever it was wants to cover up Norma Ann's mental condition at the time of her death."

"Why?"

"I don't know. Keep talking, maybe something will make sense."

She told him about Bradley's strange behavior, and about Donna leaving her stranded in Bangor, and her aunt's odd behavior as well. "She had always struck me as being the levelheaded one in the Ochs family. My Aunt Pat was always a bit spacey, and Aunt Dolly was totally loony tunes, but Aunt Sylvia was okay. But yesterday she acted so strange, I just couldn't understand it. I told her I was going to find out why my sister committed suicide. Now I think I know. I think she was suffering from a mental illness that no one understood or treated. That's why I want to talk to her teacher. Maybe she'll have some clue."

"How about you and I go there? It's down near Portland. It's about a three-hour drive. I could make the arrangements."

"You'd do that?"

"I would."

"I can trust you?"

"With your life," he answered her.

201

FORTY-ONE

The following morning at about eleven o'clock, Chris and Margaret pulled in front of apartment 4B in the Ocean View Estates near Portland, Maine. The apartment complex was one of those high-priced retirement homes with a lot of pale wood, decks, and meticulously maintained grounds. A small, dark-haired man in coveralls was raking nonexistent leaves from the yard beside 4B. He didn't look up when they approached.

The door was answered by a tall, slender elderly woman in navy creased slacks and a white cashmere sweater. Her straight white hair was expertly cut to her chin. She smiled pleasantly when she saw them.

"You must be the ones here about Norma Ann?"

Chris extended his hand. "I'm Chris Rikken and this is my friend Margaret Collinwood, Norma's sister."

Evelyn Parker nodded. "What a tragedy that was."

"So you remember her?" Margaret said.

"Like it was yesterday. You were her sister? I never had you, did I?"

Margaret shook her head. "We moved to Bangor shortly after she passed away."

"Come in." She held the door wide. "I've iced tea ready. And some white cake."

"Great," said Chris.

They admired the apartment, the view, Evelyn Parker's taste in decor, and accepted tall iced drinks and pieces of cake on white china plates. Then Margaret said, "I've recently come to own my parents' old house, and I've been gathering

202

some of my sister's things together. I've found her diary and one of her poems."

"Were you close to your sister?"

"As close as we could be, I guess. She was older than me. I was a little kid to her, I think."

"She was a thinker, that one. And a poet."

"I've started reading her diary. Did you know that my sister was depressed before she died?"

Evelyn nodded. "She was depressed. That I remember. In those days she became so . . . how shall I put it, so unreachable. We used to talk, she and I. Maybe it was her poet's heart, but she had a keen spiritual side. And then suddenly she changed. Overnight she changed."

"That's what I've discovered in her diary." Margaret pulled out the little book from her backpack. "I have a theory. I think she was suffering from some mental condition, maybe something as serious as schizophrenia. She never got help for it and eventually, she died. I think she may have committed suicide. That's what I think."

For the next half-hour the three of them pored over Norma Ann's diary.

"It was so strange," said Evelyn at one point. "In the fall of seventh grade she was a cheerful, happy, good student, full of life, running for student council, and by the spring she was a different person."

Evelyn Parker rose and brought back a stack of old yearbooks and photo albums. It had been a long time since Margaret had looked upon the junior high face of her sister, but there she was, smiling sweetly in little square snapshots that marked the years.

"Did my sister share anything with you that would account for her strange behavior?"

Evelyn shook her head. "No, she did not."

"What do you think about my theory of mental illness, then?"

Evelyn surprised Margaret by shaking her head. "I'm not sure of that. She didn't seem as if she were losing touch with reality; that's not the impression I received. I got the feeling that there was something going on in her life, something she couldn't share, something that was causing her great pain. I remember the day she died, she had come to my class before school and said that she had something she needed to talk to me about. We made a date for after school. She never showed up. I looked for her, even called her at home, but no one answered. That was the last I saw her. She died that afternoon. I wish to God I had pursued her more, made her talk to me, made her confide in me."

"What about suicide?"

Evelyn looked past the two of them out the large picture window toward the white sand and the ocean beyond. She said, "The one thing I am sure of is that it was not an accident."

FORTY-TWO

Halfway home, Chris pulled in at a tiny clapboard-looking shack for, according to him, "the best chowder in the state of Maine." He smiled and winked at Margaret, who protested, "It's been such a day. I just want to go home."

"You need some cheering up, and Paul's chowder will cheer you."

"It's that good, eh?"

"It's that good."

Paul's Fish House had an order-through window, boarded up for winter now with a piece of graffiti-covered plywood. A few broken-down picnic tables, painted with gull droppings, were stacked to the right of the door. During the summer, presumably, you could get your fish meal and sit outside. The place offered no view, however, unless looking at highway traffic was your thing.

Despite its lack of decor the small room inside was warm and full of boisterous chatter. Margaret and Chris found a square rickety table near the back. A white plastic tablecloth covered it and was stapled to its underside. She ordered coffee with her chowder and he ordered a large orange juice with extra ice. For a while they chatted amiably. He told her he lived on a sailboat, and she said she had been on a sailboat once.

It was a long time ago when friends of Robin's had invited the three of them, her and Robin and Aislin, out on their Tanzer 26 on Grand Lake. It was a sunny and windy Saturday morning when they left, baloney sandwiches, bathing suits, towels, and a case of pop in hand. Aislin, wearing a bright orange life jacket, had scrambled around the deck the entire time, loving it.

She didn't tell Chris that. She had never told Chris about Robin or Aislin. She had never even told him she was married. Should she? But wouldn't that be odd, working that into the conversation now? *By the way, in case you're interested, I'm married.* If she told him that now, if she brought it up in the midst of all this comfortable chatter about boats and sailing and the best chowder on the coast of Maine, it would seem as if she were trying to draw attention to it.

She folded both of her hands on the table so that her wedding ring showed.

"So you liked it?" he asked.

"Liked what?"

"Sailing."

"Sailing? Yes, we . . . I loved it."

"You'll have to come out with me sometime."

"Yes, that would be fun." She said it quietly, looking down into her chowder.

This past spring, right after school ended, Robin had told her, "I'm going away for a week."

"Going away? Where?"

"I have to go away by myself. I have to think things through."

She said nothing. The silence lengthened.

"We'll destroy each other if we stay here together," he had said. "We never talk. I'll be gone just for a week. When I come back we'll figure out if we have a future."

She had watched as he folded T-shirts, underwear, socks in rows in the bottom of his suitcase. Next came the jeans, which he folded in half and laid on top. It was odd for her not to pack for him. When he'd go away to teachers' conferences and band trips, she always packed for him, carefully laying his pants on the bottom and the shirts on top. She always made sure his clothes, and especially his band director's tuxedo, were clean and pressed. It was odd and wrong for her to be watching him pack, and not reminding him to remember his toothbrush, his deodorant, his razor.

He was saying, "I can't think. We should have been more aware of her flu. She was crying at ten o'clock. Why didn't we go in and check on her?"

"I did. I went to her door, asked how she was."

"But you didn't check her, see if she was feverish. If you had done that one little thing . . ."

Careful, they had been so careful not to blame each other, guardedly walking around the edges of their conversations for months, and he had said it. Finally.

If you had done that one little thing.

He left that day, for a week that turned into two and then three, then the rest of the summer. He never called her. At the Regent Mall one afternoon she ran into his principal, who asked how Robin was doing. When she said fine, he said, "Maybe this year's leave of absence will do him good. You two have been through a lot."

She looked at him, uncomprehending. When school started and Robin didn't come back, she understood. At the beginning of September, Mavis had called and Margaret had left for Coffins Reach.

"Where are you?"

Margaret looked up and into the face of Chris Rikken. So different he was than Robin. Robin was witty and smart, with soft-sweatered shoulders and a ready smile. Chris was rugged and long and lean, with rumpled hair and crooked glasses.

"I'm here. Just thinking."

He looked at her and said, "Why did you come to Maine?"

"It's a long story."

"I've got time."

"Not for this one."

"All right."

On the way home, she fell asleep, her head against the flat coolness of the window pane. At her house he followed her in. She turned. "I'm okay."

"I want to make sure. You said you thought someone was here before. I want to make sure no one's here now."

In the kitchen she glanced at her answering machine. Three messages. She'd get to them later.

"I want to check the place out before I go," he said.

"It's really not necessary. I think I was just imagining things anyway."

Chris wandered around checking closets and turning on every light. "How about upstairs?" he said.

"No! Really. Everything is okay. Please, I just need to rest."

"Well, okay then, if you're absolutely sure."

"I'm sure."

When he drove away she pressed the playback key on her answering machine. The first one was from Mavis in her TV shopping-channel voice urging her to call back as soon as she possibly could, she had an offer that she didn't think Margaret could possibly refuse. The second was from Sylvia. "I should apologize for my behavior yesterday. You must think I'm rude, but I'd had an odd day, and then you came with that and it just unnerved me. Please do call me when you get in tonight."

The third was from Robin. "Margaret. It's me. Can you phone? I'm home now. In our home. Can you call me, please? We need to talk. I'm sorry. I'm so sorry I left. I was wrong about that. I was wrong about a lot of things. I need to talk to you."

If you had done that one little thing.

She clicked *erase,* poured herself a glass of red wine, and walked upstairs.

At the top of the steps she stopped; a hand flew to her mouth; the glass she held shattered at her feet, wine spattering the walls like fresh blood.

There in the center of her portrait of Anna Coffin, right through the white dress, right through the heavy watercolor paper, was a knife, its heavy wooden handle jutting out. An obscenity in that tranquil ocean scene. For several minutes she stood there, shaking, shivering, entirely cold.

The phone rang. She gasped and jumped. She answered the one by her easel, keeping her eye on the knife. It was one of the kitchen knives, one that was here when she moved in, one she seldom used. What does one need with such a heavy-bladed knife as this in an ordinary kitchen?

"Hello." Her voice was barely above a whisper.

"Margaret, this is Sylvia. I'm so glad you got home. First of all, I want to apologize for how I acted. I haven't been myself lately, but that's really no excuse I guess. But the second reason I'm calling is that Mavis called. I know she can be a bit of a pest, but I guess she really does have someone who wants that old house of your father's, someone who's willing to pay you a huge sum of money. She wanted to know where she could reach you. You really should call her. She said the offer wouldn't wait."

"Okay." Margaret couldn't get her voice to function normally. She was finding it hard to breathe.

"Margaret? Margaret, are you there?"

"I'm here." She stared at the knife.

"Margaret, are you okay? Has something happened?"

"Yes. Something has happened." Her words were slow and measured.

"What happened?"

"I can't . . . can't."

"Margaret, are you sick?"

"I don't know."

"Margaret, now you hold on. You stay put. I'm going to get Monty and maybe Leo and Dolly, Clark and Pat too. We're all here. We're going to come right over. Don't you move. Do you want me to call 9-1-1?"

"I can."

FORTY-THREE

Donna was in the living room watching TV when she heard the commotion. Sylvia and Monty rushing, calling — something about Margaret being sick. Sick? Maybe an accident. Sylvia was shouting to Dolly and Pat that she didn't know for sure, but from the sound of things it was *something*. They all better get going. Right now. All of this while the poodles yelped underfoot.

From the window Donna watched them leave in her father's car. She had stood at this window (this very one?) when the call had come about Norma Ann. The same rushing, the same grabbing of jackets. Donna put her hand to her mouth. Could Margaret be . . . ? No, it couldn't be. Not twice. Not two times from that porch. But if it happened to Norma Ann and then Margaret, would she be next? Donna grabbed her keys and ran out, leaving the TV on.

Her father's car was there, Donna saw, as she drove down the gravel lane towards Margaret's. Donna turned right and pulled up along the south side of the Godwish home. Her family wouldn't see her car here, see her running along the path to Margaret's. Ruth Godwish saw her, however, her face pressed against the window. Donna laughed out loud and waved to her. The face moved away and a curtain fell across the glass.

All the lights were on in the house. Donna tried the back door. Unlocked. Quietly, like a cat, she entered. No one was there. But of course not. They would be upstairs, on the third floor, the place where Norma Ann had fallen.

She stopped. There on the kitchen table stood a little bagpiper. What was it doing here? An omen? It had been here when Norma Ann fell. Now Margaret? She grabbed it, clenching it tightly in her palm, and headed up the stairs.

On the landing she saw the seven of them before they noticed her — her mother and father, Pat and Clark, Leo and Dolly, and Margaret, who was sitting on a chair, shoulders slumped, chest heaving. Sylvia was rubbing those shoulders and making cooing noises. So it wasn't like the last time. Margaret hadn't fallen. Not like Norma Ann had done. Margaret was okay. And for the time being Donna was safe.

And then she saw it, the thick wooden handle of a butcher knife protruding out of a half-finished portrait. The painting was of a girl sitting on a rock, a flute to her lips. Donna cried out when she looked at the face of the girl in the portrait. She covered her mouth with her hand, but it wasn't soon enough.

"Donna!" said Sylvia dropping her hands and looking over at her. "What are you doing here?"

But Donna was staring at the picture wide-eyed. Out of the corner of her eye she saw Uncle Leo wiping his wide moist brow with a large handkerchief. When he saw her, he walked over to the painting and grabbed the handle of the knife with both hands.

"That's enough of that," he said, pulling it out.

But Donna stared at the picture, couldn't stop staring, small animal sounds coming from someplace within her as she clutched the little bagpiper. Finally she said to Margaret, "Why did you paint *her?* What would ever possess you to paint *her?*"

Margaret looked up at her. "Anna Coffin?" she asked.

"No. Norma Ann. Why would you paint Norma Ann?"

FORTY-FOUR

The two police officers who came shook their heads and kept asking Leo over and over why he had removed the knife.

The older of the officers, a man in his mid-forties with a graying mustache, kept saying, "You had no idea that you may have been tampering with evidence? Destroying any chance we had of finding the person who did this?"

Leo just shrugged and said the whole thing was so upsetting to his niece, and he couldn't have that. He just couldn't have that. None of them could.

The police officer said, "You could have moved everyone away from the painting and gone downstairs, for example. Made tea." He sighed, looked at the younger officer, a lanky fellow with large hands, and said, "I don't know. We'll dust for fingerprints. We'll be able to do that much."

They were sitting downstairs in the living room now, the eight of them, including Donna, who sat sullenly and quietly in the window seat fingering the bagpiper. No one noticed that she held it.

The officers walked among them, talking. In answer to their questions, Margaret told them that nothing was missing. She told them about the other day when she had come home and had the distinct impression that someone had been there.

"You didn't call us?"

"I thought maybe my imagination was running wild. I've had such strange dreams here."

"Nothing was taken?" asked the older officer.

"Then or now?"

"Then and now."

She shook her head. "Nothing as far as I can see."

"Any significance about the picture? Who's it of?" asked the younger officer, leaning toward her.

"Anna Coffin," Margaret said.

"Who's Anna Coffin?"

"A person who lived in this house a hundred years ago."

"Any reason why someone would want to put a knife through her heart?" the young cop said.

The older officer gave him a look and said, "I'm thinking vandalism. Pure and simple. Could've been any number of local kids."

But Margaret disagreed. Her house had been locked up tighter than a drum, she told them, with new locks even on the windows. The officers took a tour of the house then, with Monty expounding the virtues of the new locks he had installed.

"They look strong enough," said the older officer. But when they came to the basement door he said, "Aha."

"What aha?" asked Monty.

"This lock is loose. Look at this thing; it's practically off its hinges. Let's get some fingerprints on this one, Jeff."

"I don't remember it being that loose," Margaret said.

"I didn't put a new lock on this door, figuring it was an inside one," Monty said sheepishly.

"Well, at least we know now how the culprits got in. I'm willing to bet someone came in through a basement window. These old houses, the basement windows, half of them can be kicked in with a good boot. That's all it takes for some of these places. Someone gets in through a basement window, gets upstairs, jimmies this lock and bingo, they're in."

"You're sure about that?" Leo asked.

"It's the only explanation that makes sense. I'm going to be talking to neighbors, too."

"I only have one," Margaret said. "Ruth Godwish lives with her son right next door to the south. The next house is out on the north point, quite a distance from here, and it's abandoned."

For the next half-hour, Margaret and her three aunts sat at her kitchen table while the two officers dusted for fingerprints, spreading a white powder over every surface of her door, the basement windows, and her studio upstairs, while Monty and Leo looked on. Donna sat in the kitchen with her back against the wall, the bagpiper still in her hand. Clark stood in the kitchen uncertainly. Sylvia made a full pot of coffee, which they all shared. Dolly was going on and on about how Coffins Reach used to be such a safe place to live, and how terrible things were now. Everywhere, said Dolly, crime is everywhere. There's no getting away from it.

During a lull in their talk, Margaret turned to Donna, whose eyes were closed, and said, "Why did you say that painting was of Norma Ann?"

Donna didn't answer, just shrugged her shoulders.

Her aunts looked at Margaret, unspeaking, for a moment or two. Finally Dolly said, "But Margaret, it *is* a picture of your sister. All of us assumed you were doing a picture of Norma Ann. That's what all of us thought, didn't we, Sylvia?"

Sylvia nodded. "Margaret, it's a beautiful picture of your sister. The resemblance is uncanny. You've captured the very essence of Norma Ann."

Margaret blinked at them, blinked again. Norma Ann? Did her unconscious mind paint the face of her dead sister on the body of Anna Coffin? She was ten when her sister died, and the only pictures she had seen since then were the snap-shots in Evelyn Parker's book and the yellowed one in the basement newspapers.

"You think it looks like Norma Ann?"

"It's Norma Ann precisely, to a tee," Dolly said. "That expression in her eyes. You noticed it too, didn't you, Pat?"

"I did, yes."

Margaret stared at them while Dolly went on about what a nice memorial this was. Behind Dolly, she could see the officers approach the Godwish home. She could see from the window the little figure of Ruth, hands on hips, shaking her head. Funny thing, the mind. Remembering things long forgotten. Almost she could see Ruth Godwish standing there the way she used to look, pixielike and tiny, pretty, her long dark hair in two braids down her back.

Sylvia laid her hand on Margaret's shoulder.

"Margaret, maybe it's time to think about selling this old place. Mavis really wants you to call. Some people came by, history buffs, I think. They know your house and want to buy it. They want to turn this place into a bed-and-breakfast, if you please. Maybe it's time you sold it, got away from this place. Look at the crime. Tell me, how many times were you broken into like this in Fredericton?"

Margaret just shrugged. Sell the place? There was still so much to think about.

Donna rose then and plunked the little bagpiper down in the center of the table. The voices stopped immediately.

FORTY-FIVE

At the hardware store the following morning, Clark was quietly bobbing a tea bag up and down in a mug of hot water. Leo was sitting in the staff room, grunting over the morning paper. When Monty walked in, he went over to Leo.

"Just thought you should know. There's a detective been asking a whole bunch of questions."

Clark looked up suddenly.

"Who? What detective?" Leo said. "You mean that cop from last night?"

"No, someone different. A detective."

"What kind of questions?"

"Stuff about the death of Norma Ann, stuff along the lines of the police investigation into her death not being thorough enough, that sort of thing."

"How do you know this?"

"Syl told me."

"The police have reopened that case?" Clark said innocently, stirring a sugar lump into his tea.

"No," Monty said. "Just some private investigator. Not a police detective."

"Why?" Clark asked.

"How should I know?"

"I wouldn't put it past Margaret," Leo said. "She's been awfully curious about a whole lot of things since she came back here."

"Now Leo, let's give her the benefit of the doubt," Monty said.

But Leo shook his head, his brow furrowed.

"What I'd like to know," said Clark, "is how my little bagpiper, you know, the one that disappeared, happened to end up on Margaret's table last night. That was the one I gave you, remember Leo?" Clark was feeling quite confident this morning.

Leo growled, "I have no idea what you're talking about."

"I remember, Leo," Clark said.

"You remember what?"

"I remember where that little piper came from. I remember what happened to it."

"Enlighten me, dear little brother, because I don't have a clue as to what you're blabbering on about."

"I gave it to you for the Blueberry Harvest Art Show."

Leo was shaking his head. "You're hopelessly mistaken, little brother, hopelessly mistaken."

When Leo and Monty left, Clark smiled to himself. He did remember. That was the one thing he was sure of in all of this.

He had been working on figures from the Black Watch bagpipe regiment before Norma Ann died. He was quite proud of them. Leo was in charge of the art show, having donated most of the prize money. It was Leo who would hire and pay the jury, who would decide which pieces were shown and which were not.

"You want your soldiers in the art show, I take it?" Leo had said, looking down at the box Clark had brought with him that day so long ago.

Clark nodded. It was a real case of bad luck that put Leo Ochs in charge of the art show this year, Leo who didn't know art from a hole in the ground. It killed Clark to have to stand here and grovel in front of him.

"Just show these to the jury, that's all I ask."

"You think that just because you're my brother I can give

you all kinds of special treatment?"

"That's not what I'm asking for. Don't even tell them where they came from. Just show them."

Leo said, "You'd be better off, little brother, if you worked at a real job, the hardware store, for example, instead of carving little soldiers from wood."

"If you're so against local artists, why donate the money?" Clark asked.

"It's called politics, baby brother. Politics."

"Just show these to them, and if they're not accepted, I promise I will quit this dream and come work at the store."

Leo reached into the box and picked up one of the tissue-wrapped figurines. "I'll just take one."

Two days later Norma Ann was dead and the piper was missing. When Clark went to ask Leo for it, Leo had said, "Sorry, pal, you never gave me a bagpiper. I may not be sure of a lot of things but of that I am sure."

"You're lying," said Clark, storming out of Leo's front door. "I stood right here and handed it to you day before yesterday!"

After the funeral, after Mitch and Hannah and Margaret moved away, Clark never carved soldiers again. The art show came and went without Clark. He lined up his wooden soldiers in shoe boxes and buried them beneath tools and spare car parts in the shed.

On this gray morning Clark looked into his tea and wondered how his life had turned out so wrong. Coward, that's what Pat called him. Maybe she was right.

FORTY-SIX

"I hear there was some excitement at your place last night," Chris said to Margaret the following morning.

"News travels fast," Margaret said into the phone.

"You want me to come over?"

"Why would you want to come over?"

"Because I'm the only sane person in the state of Maine?"

"That's good enough reason. I'll put the coffeepot on."

"I'll bring the muffins."

When she hung up, Margaret raced a comb through her hair, cursing the rainy weather that was making it spiral all over her head. The previous evening, after the police officers had left, and after her uncles had repaired the lock and boarded over the basement window, and after Sylvia had insisted for the tenth time that Margaret come home with them for the night, and after Margaret had said, "No, I'd rather stay here," Margaret took her book of short stories and headed upstairs again.

She stood on her landing and surveyed her studio. The room looked curiously naked without Anna there, looking out at her every time she walked by. The police had taken both the portrait and the knife with them. Evidence, they told her as they dropped them clumsily into plastic bags. She had spent a lot of time on that work, feeling that she was finally beginning to capture the essence of the woman on the beach. It had taken her a lot of hours to get it perfect. The thought of starting over gave her a stomachache.

She was afraid she wouldn't sleep, but after barely one

short story, she fell into a dreamless sleep that was only inter-
rupted by the sound of the rain pelting on her eaves. It was
morning.

Half an hour after she woke, Chris had called. She barely
had time to shower and put the coffeepot on before he arrived, a Dunkin' Donuts bag held out sheepishly in front of
him with both hands.

"You have shares in that company?" she said.

Margaret offered to make her special scrambled eggs, and
he readily accepted. While she whipped up eggs and cheese
and green peppers, she asked him, "You're the detective; why
would someone want to destroy one of my paintings?"

"They didn't take anything else?"

"Not that I can find, and my CD player was right there.
They didn't take that. It was like they purposely walked upstairs and stuck a knife through the center of that particular
painting."

"Maybe that's just what they did."

"But why would someone do that?"

He shrugged his shoulders. "How did they get in?"

"The basement."

"The basement?"

"Yes, they knocked out a basement window and then
came up the stairs and jiggled the lock somehow. That's what
the cops said."

He put down his coffee and walked over to the basement
door. He spent a lot of time examining it.

"That's a bunch of hogwash," he said.

"What do you mean?"

"What the police told you is a bunch of hogwash. This
lock's tight as a drum. They didn't come in this way."

"No, it's been fixed since then. Monty and Leo put new
screws in it and fixed it all up before they left."

He looked at her. "Was it secure, do you remember, yesterday, say the night before last when you went to bed? You said you always check it."

"Always, and it was as tight and secure as it is now."

"If it was tight then it would have been virtually impossible for someone to break in from the other side. Believe me, I know. I've tried. And there's no damage to the door, none that I can see here, and there would have been if a person tried to jimmy the door open from the other side." He pushed his glasses up on his face. "No, your thief didn't get in this way."

"But the police . . ."

"Let's go downstairs and have a look at that broken window."

"It's been boarded up."

"Where's the light switch for downstairs?" he said, heading down.

"Down at the bottom. I hate it down there." She put the egg mixture aside and followed.

"Come with me. I'll protect you from the creepy crawlies."

He put his arm on her shoulder as they descended. Downstairs, he looked at the boarded-up window and bent down to examine the shards of glass swept into a neat pile on the floor.

"This is all the glass there was?" he asked.

"There's more glass outside. I haven't cleaned that up yet."

"Those cops are idiots. Anyone can see that your painting stabber didn't come in this way. If the window had been kicked in from the outside there would have been more glass in here than out there. I'm willing to bet there's a bigger pile outside. My guess is someone came in through the door, loosened up the basement lock, then came down here and

222

smashed out the window. That would give the impression that the burglar came in this way. That's my take on what happened."

"But why?"

He straightened to full height and looked down at her.

"Maybe someone wanted you to think they were a common burglar."

Back upstairs at the kitchen table again, he took a small notebook from his jacket pocket and began taking notes. She watched the pages fill up with arrows and diagrams as he talked. "Okay, let's try to figure out why someone would want to stab that particular painting. Let's go with that angle for a minute here. What was the painting of?"

"It was a painting of Anna Coffin."

"That ghost lady you talked about?"

"Anna's the woman this house was built for way back in the 1800s. The point is named after her, but the weird thing is that the picture reminded my aunts and my cousin of my sister Norma Ann. I must have subconsciously been thinking of my sister when I was working on the face."

He raised his eyebrows. "Okay, let's look at the sister angle then." He was writing rapidly on the paper. She looked at it quizzically. "My own shorthand," he explained. "Why would someone want to stab a painting of your sister, a sister who's been dead for twenty-five years?"

The thought made Margaret shiver. She wished it would stop raining.

He went on, "Maybe it wasn't the subject of the painting at all. Maybe it was a warning."

"A warning?"

"I'm brainstorming here, thinking out loud, coming at this thing from all angles. Okay, let's go with the break-in itself. I want to ask you something. Remember the other day when I walked all the way up the stairs and you didn't even hear me? Does that happen very often?"

"I'm an artist. I get into these muses and I can't even hear what else is going on around me."

He looked at her over the top of his glasses. "This happen a lot to artists?"

"I don't know. Some."

"Do you keep your door locked when you're inside here going into these muses?"

"Seldom."

"So anyone could come in, walk all around downstairs, sing a song, do a dance, pick up your key, take it out, make a copy, bring it back . . ."

"You're making fun of me."

He grinned. "It's just that I never met a real artist before."

She looked at him wide-eyed. "Do you think that's what happened? Someone just came in and got my key?"

"Could be." He paused. "You said someone was in your house the other day, that you *felt* someone had been in your house. Maybe they came in to get the key."

The phone rang. It was Mavis going over that incredible offer, that offer that just wouldn't wait, not one more day.

"I've decided not to sell," Margaret said into the receiver.

"That's it?" Mavis said.

"That's it."

When she hung up, she told Chris about the offer, the too-good-to-be-true offer. He surprised her by frowning.

"Someone's pulling your leg," he said.

"What do you mean?"

"This house isn't worth that. Not in a million years."

"You don't think my house is worth that? It's waterfront property!"

He shook his head. "I know waterfront property. It's my

224

life. Those huge mansions down the beach aren't even going for the price she's offering. Something's screwy."

"Mavis seemed to be on the up-and-up."

"Then *her* leg is being pulled." He paused and looked at her for a long time before continuing. He seemed to be considering. Then he looked back at his notebook and said, "Let's work on this a bit more. Let's say someone broke into your house from the outside, using the back door. I say we go next door and talk to the neighbor."

"Ruth Godwish?"

"Yeah."

"The police questioned her yesterday. She didn't see anything."

"Now that I can't believe. Every time I drive down here she's looking out of that window."

"Her son Bradley is even stranger. He lives right on the water but never goes near the beach, never even looks out the front windows. The curtains are always drawn."

"I remember I had to spend time with him when your sister died," Chris said. "He was so out of control. He kept going on about the bad people."

Margaret stared at him. "That's what he said to me."

"He made no sense, and we couldn't get anything out of him. Then it was ruled an accidental death and that was the end of it." He rose. "Let's go next door."

Margaret was shaking her head. "I'm telling you it won't do any good. We'll just be standing out there in the pouring rain and she won't say a thing. She won't let us see Bradley."

It was just as Margaret had predicted. The two of them stood on Ruth's back steps, water dripping off their umbrella as she vehemently shook her head. She had seen no one, heard no one.

"You're lying, lady," Chris said. "You got your head

poked out of that window every time I come down here. You seem to know every time Margaret even goes to town. You can probably tell us what we had for breakfast. I don't believe that you didn't see a soul here yesterday."

"No one was here. I would have seen if they were."

"Someone came down here, broke the basement window of Margaret's house, destroyed a valuable piece of artwork, and you didn't see a soul?"

"That's right."

Chris stared at her. "I would like to talk to your son."

"I'm afraid that is impossible."

"Why?"

"He's leaving shortly for his workshop."

"Fine, we'll wait, we'll talk to him when he comes out. We've got all the time in the world, haven't we, Margaret?"

"You may not talk to him. I have to be insistent on that."

But Chris had put his hand on the doorjamb and was pushing the door open. She was no match for his strength.

"Chris, it's okay," Margaret whispered.

"It's not okay. And I'm not leaving until I get a chance to speak to Bradley."

The commotion had drawn the man from somewhere in the house, and he walked toward them. Chris pushed forward into the warm, damp kitchen and Margaret followed.

"Bradley Godwish," he called. Bradley was backing away. "I'm not going to hurt you. We just want to ask you a very important question. Did you see anybody come to Margaret's house yesterday?"

He shook his head slowly from side to side.

Ruth said, "Bradley will have seen nothing. You notice that our curtains are drawn. Bradley never looks past the curtains. He never looks outside."

"Because of the bad people?" Chris asked. "Is that because of the bad people, Bradley? What happened when Norma Ann died? Who did you see then, Bradley? Who?"

But Bradley was whimpering loudly, fists pressed into his eyes.

"I will not have my son harassed in this way!" Ruth said.

Chris glared at her. "You saw something yesterday. I know you did. I can see it on your face. You both saw someone drive in and go into Margaret's house yesterday. You know who it was, lady. I don't know why you aren't talking, I don't know what your game is, but one thing I do know is that you saw someone come by here yesterday and you know exactly who it is!"

She glared up at him. "Get out! Get out of my house and don't come back!"

Chris slapped his business card down on the counter. "Give me a call if you change your mind."

She threw the card after him as he and Margaret headed back to Margaret's in the rain.

FORTY-SEVEN

"She knows something; did you see her eyes?" Chris was talking loudly as the two of them shed their wet raincoats at Margaret's back door. "I hate liars, and that woman is lying. And then those bozo cops who come in here. Random vandalism? Give me a break. It's this very kind of incompetence that made me quit the force and go out on my own. This very thing!"

They were back in the kitchen now and Margaret was resuming her whipping of the scrambled egg mixture.

He frowned and looked around him. "This whole house thing has me wondering, too. This isn't California. No way should someone be offering you such a huge amount of cash for this old place."

"Well, it does have a nice view, plus its own ghost," she offered.

He was sitting at her table now, his head in his hand, his face furrowed. He hadn't shared with her his deepest fears, that Margaret was in danger, someone wanted her to leave, and was willing to pay almost a million dollars to make her do so. If she took the money she wouldn't be the first Ochs to be paid off and told to leave. He watched her ladle the eggs into a sizzling frying pan. And wasn't it a little too coincidental that Sylvia happened to phone Margaret yesterday as soon as she got in? And that Leo just happened to remove the knife from the painting. He didn't share his suspicions with Margaret. He couldn't make sense of what had happened. It would take some thinking. She dished out the eggs in silence. They ate them with the muffins Chris had brought.

"I came down here for some peace and quiet," she said. "I just wanted everyone to leave me alone. Why can't it at least stop raining?"

"Margaret, tell me more about this Anna Coffin."

"There's not that much to tell, really. I read about her story in Roland Irons's book on Maine ghost stories and was fascinated to discover that my house was the one she lived in. Her husband was a sea captain and built this house for her. I saw her picture at the historical society and decided to paint her. She was an abused wife. I don't know, I sort of identified with her."

He looked at her, said gently, "Were you an abused wife?"

"Oh, no, not at all, don't ever get that idea. No, I identified with her in other ways." Her face was turned away from him when she said these things, and when she turned back she was wiping the corners of her eyes with a Dunkin' Donuts napkin.

"Are you okay?"

She nodded. "Just tired. There's so much here that is making me so tired."

"It's pouring rain outside. I can't sail, I can't go for a run. I've got plenty of time to listen to that long story if you want."

She looked at him, then down at her hands. Quietly she began. She told him about Fredericton, about Robin and about Aislin. While she talked, the rain pelted like fine stones against the windows, a backdrop of continuous sound. She told him about the night Aislin died, about Robin leaving, about feeling alone, about the ghosts that followed her here, about the ghost of Anna.

"I used to believe in God. I don't anymore," she said.

"Why not?"

"God took my daughter away from me. He's the only one I can blame. I think sometimes it'd be easier for me if she'd been killed by a drunk driver or something. I'd have someone then to blame, someone to catch my anger. But no, God killed her. He's the only one I can blame."

Chris looked steadily at her. "God kills people, does he?"

"He could've prevented it."

"I always thought God gave life, not destroyed it."

She looked at him. "What do you know about God?"

He told her about Ginny and his daughters. He told her about quitting the police force, about drinking. "I joined AA a bunch of years ago. I still go occasionally. When I was there I got to thinking all about the higher power thing. It made a lot of sense to me then, still does."

"And you never turned away from God when your wife left?"

"I think the whole thing may have brought me closer to a god, or closer to searching for a god." He smiled slightly at her. "I've never told this to anyone before, this searching for something out there. Big macho PIs are never supposed to have these feelings."

"You go to church?"

"Not very often. Sometimes. I'm still in search mode."

"I hope you find what you're searching for, Chris."

"Yeah."

She took a sip of her coffee. It was cold. She put it down again. He said to her, "You had some happy memories, right? Some good times with that daughter of yours and that musical husband — he in a band or something?"

She laughed. "Well, he directs a band, at the high school. He also sings. He's really quite wonderful."

He looked at her for a long time. "He's a lucky guy."

"I don't know if I will ever get over losing my daughter. And you know the thing that scares me the most? That I'll forget what she looks like. I keep going over her face in my memory. I lie awake at night thinking about her, trying to keep her face in front of me. Chris, what if I forget what she looks like?"

"You won't." Chris was talking gently now. He reached across the table and took both her hands in his. "Would you like to go out tonight? I know this great little restaurant in Bangor. We could spend an evening away from all these mixed-up things."

"Yes." She smiled at him. "I think I'd like that very much."

"Great." He rose. "Now, I'm not being paranoid. Trust me in this. I'm going to take a quick run into Bosuns Harbor to buy some new locks for this place. I'll be back in about half an hour to install them."

"Fine," she said.

FORTY-EIGHT

Donna hadn't slept well the previous night. She kept seeing the little bagpiper, one knee in front of the other, leading the troops into battle. The little face had filled her dreams from the time she had put her head on the pillow until the time she got up. All night long she heard the drone of the pipes in her dreams.

Early in the morning Donna sat up in bed, looked out into the dawn, and thought about the day Norma Ann had died. It had been a day like this day, misty, foggy, the sky promising rain. On that day Donna had caught the bus to school as usual, expecting that Norma Ann, who got on first in Coffins Reach, would save her a place like she always did. But when Donna boarded, she saw with dismay that there was already someone sitting next to Norma Ann. It was pimply faced Jackie Smokeman, who was enamored with Norma Ann and didn't care who knew.

"Get lost," said Donna when she saw him. "This is my seat."

Jackie just sat there with his ears poking straight out and brown patches of hair sticking out all over his head. "Your name on it?" he said.

"Norma Ann," Donna said, "how come you let snotnose sit next to you?"

But Norma Ann didn't look up. She didn't look at Donna. She didn't look at Jackie. She just sat there fiddling with a little wooden figurine; around and around she turned it in her hands. Donna sighed and took the seat directly behind her cousin, and then horror of all horrors, greasy Bella Comstock from the trailer park sat down next to her. Bella was just about as obnoxious as Jackie. She spent an inordinate amount of time combing her hair, standing in front of the girls' room mirror arranging it just so, putting on layer after layer of makeup. Bella was known to smoke in the girls' room, as well, and had gotten kicked out of school for it once already.

To keep her body from touching Bella's, Donna leaned forward in her seat and onto the shoulder of her cousin. Norma Ann didn't move, just sat there, not speaking, not even turning around when Donna tapped her on the shoulder and said, "Are you all right? You sick or something?"

Donna looked down at the figurine. It was a little wooden statue of a bagpiper in a kilt.

"What's that?" asked Donna.

Silence.

"Norma Ann, are you deaf or something?"

"Can't you see she doesn't want to talk to you." This came from Bella.

"Yeah, and that's none of your beeswax!" Donna said. She hunched against the window and stayed that way for the rest of the trip.

School had been in session for just a few weeks, and they were both in their second year of junior high school. Their first year had been full of fun and promise, but during the summer between seventh and eighth grade, Norma Ann began to change. She grew quiet and no longer wanted to go out with Bradley or the other friends to movies in Bosuns Harbor. She lost interest in everything except writing in a book. Donna would come over, trudge up the two flights of stairs to the third floor, and there would be Norma Ann, sitting on the porch writing in a school scribbler. As soon as she saw Donna, she would slap the book closed and sit on it.

Now Donna sat on her bed, watching the sky lighten through the rain and wiping the edges of her eyes with her quilt. Donna had spent a lot of years berating herself for not doing something on that day. But the dark thing was already in motion and she was powerless to stop it.

A few minutes later the bus had pulled up and the chattering students had clambered out and walked through the mist to the open doors. The American flag hung limply from the flagpole.

"Norma Ann, wait up," called Donna. "What's the matter with you, anyway?"

It was early. Usually when the bus got them here this early, the cousins would hang around the cafeteria or fix each other's hair in the girls' room. But on this morning Norma Ann kept on walking. Donna followed her past clumps of friends who stood beside their lockers and called after them, past Bella, who was already taking her makeup out of her bookbag and heading for the girls' room.

Donna followed her cousin, who was walking very determinedly toward the west wing. Finally, at the end of the hall, Norma Ann turned into Miss Parker's classroom. Donna stood outside the door. She wouldn't go in. That teacher made her jumpy with her talk of God and prayer. She watched Norma Ann approach the teacher's desk.

She watched the teacher rise from behind her desk and give Norma Ann a hug. They talked in low tones, and Donna couldn't make out the words. Maybe five minutes later she heard Miss Parker say, "I'll be here right after school and we'll talk about what it is that's bothering you. We'll get it straightened out. We'll get to the bottom of this."

"You were listening," Norma Ann accused when she walked out of the classroom and saw her cousin.

"I didn't hear anything. What's wrong? Are you okay?"

234

"I will be once I talk to Miss Parker after school."

"Can't you tell me what it is? I'm your best friend."

"I will, after I tell Miss Parker."

"Tell me now. Why do you have that little statue?"

"It's Uncle Clark's."

"Did he give it to you?"

"I took it."

"Why?"

But Norma Ann was already walking down the hall and into her homeroom, her long hair hiding any expression her face showed.

Donna never saw her again. She wasn't at lunch. And because Norma Ann was going to see Miss Parker, Donna didn't see her on the bus ride home.

It wasn't until six months later that she understood Norma Ann's secret. Understood it fully.

Donna rose now, threw off the hot bedcovers, and gazed at her face in the full-length mirror. Her eyes were dark and baggy, and her hair was falling out. Every time she brushed it, more came out. She had read somewhere that nerves will do that, make your hair fall out.

Downstairs she heard her mother and Dolly and Pat talking cheerfully about who wanted coffee and who wanted toast and how many pieces and did anyone want eggs and would anyone like to try the new marmalade that Dolly brought up from Portsmouth. Donna stumbled into her bathroom and vomited into the toilet.

FORTY-NINE

It didn't take Chris long to install new locks front and back on her home. He looked at her, said he'd love to stay with her all day, make sure she was okay, but he had business in Bangor. Margaret said she'd be fine, really. She'd be all right. She smiled at him.

After Chris drove away, Margaret sat at her kitchen table doodling on one of the scraps of paper he had left. The doodling in front of her soon became the face of Anna Coffin. She looked at it again. From the dining room she took the newspaper she'd found in the cellar and stared down at the brittle, yellowed photo of her sister. Yes, the likeness was there. Subconsciously she was drawing her sister, had been drawing her sister all along.

Was this a part of the curse? Her subconscious sketching of her long-dead sister? As if to answer, the wind blew a gust against her kitchen door and the outside screen door clattered open. She shoved the inside bolt aside, opened the door, and pulled the screen door closed, getting wet in the process. It wasn't until both doors were closed and locked again that she felt safe. Was she being warned off, as Chris had suggested? Who wanted her to leave?

She decided to call Mavis.

"Margaret, dear," said Mavis when she answered.

"Mavis, I'd like to talk to you about this offer on my house."

"Well, I knew you'd come to your senses. This is just too good to pass up, true?"

"Who wants to buy my house?"

Margaret could hear the shuffling of papers. "They wish to remain anonymous until after the closing."

"Why?"

"Sometimes that is the case, and it's really nothing to concern yourself over. Sometimes this happens in the case of celebrities, to cite just one example. As it happens, I don't even know the names of the parties wishing to purchase your house."

"Celebrities want my house?"

"I didn't say that, dear."

"Then who?"

"They wish their names to remain confidential."

"But they haven't even *seen* my house."

"Not so, dear. My understanding is that they viewed it before you came down to fix it up in preparation to sell, or so I'm told."

"But my house wasn't being shown then. It has never been for sale."

"Well, as it happens, I wasn't the agent who showed it. I don't know who did. It's not listed here. But they did see it and they do want it. And that's good enough for me."

"Tell these people that wish to remain anonymous that I'll accept their offer under one condition."

"What's that, dear?"

"I get to meet them first."

"Well, I'll try to get them to agree to that, but they're from outside the country."

"Well, those are my conditions."

Mavis sighed.

Next she would call Margaret Mahone. She picked up the receiver and then put it down again. What would she say to an aunt she hadn't bothered to write to or call, not even a Christmas card, in twenty-five years? The last time she had seen her aunt was at her mother's gravesite, where her aunt stood veiled in black. She barely acknowledged the Ochs clan, who had arrived an hour before the funeral in their fleet of Mercedes cars.

During her mother's illness, her Aunt Meg had taken a leave of absence from her teaching job and moved into her mother's bedroom on a folding cot. Margaret herself was twelve, entering junior high school in Bangor and trying to cope with changes. Her body was changing, her school had changed, her family had changed. Her mother had changed from the energetic young woman who threw bread crumbs to the seagulls, cotton housedress swishing around her slender legs, to this frail woman who never left her darkened room. Her father had changed from the strong young man who taught his girls how to bait a hook as good as any boy to this person who sat hunched in a chair in the living room, watching television. Her parents didn't share a bedroom during the Bangor years. Her father had his own, a small, sparsely furnished square room that looked out onto the tiny fenced backyard. Margaret seldom went in there.

Every once in a while her mother would invite Margaret into her bedroom. The dark room always smelled bad, as if death had already invaded. There were plastic pill jars on her mother's bedside table, plus a water pitcher and glass, sometimes a half-eaten egg salad sandwich on a plate, its edges dried and curled up. A paper bag taped to the bed contained used Kleenexes. Margaret tried not to look in there. On these occasional visits, Hannah would reach her thin arm out and attempt a smile. "My little girl," she would say, patting the bed. "Come over here and tell your old mother all about your day."

Old mother. At that time Margaret thought her mother

was ancient, an elderly lady, although now she understood that her mother was only in her thirties. Margaret's age. So young. Margaret would walk obediently to the bed and look down into the hollow eyes of the woman there, hoping to find some resemblance to the mother she once knew.

In a school binder Margaret had drawn a picture of a spaceship. In the cutaway view was a mother, father, and two little girls, smiling, their arms entwined. Margaret liked to think that the aliens had come and taken her real family away and replaced it with these strange, sullen people. Somewhere out there her real family still lived, captured on some faraway planet, awaiting the time when they could all be together again.

She sat as close to the edge of the bed as she could, not touching this alien woman. She would tell her about school, leaving out the important parts. This alien need not know everything.

During these visits her aunt would sit in the shadows beside the drawn drapes. Margaret understood now that her aunt was already grieving, wrapping her sorrows around her like the baggy gray sweater she wore day and night.

Even in better times her Aunt Meg was never flamboyant like the aunts on her father's side. When the Ochs aunts kissed her with their perfumy lipsticked mouths, talking loudly about how big she'd grown, Aunt Meg would shake her hand and comment on one of her latest drawings. "That's a good likeness, Margaret, but are you absolutely positive you have the perspective on the sky correct?" Aunt Meg seemed to possess an inner wisdom that Margaret was drawn to. She was secretly pleased to be named after this proud, smart woman.

But now, sitting in her rain-splashed house by the sea, she wondered — would her aunt even remember who she was?

She picked up the phone.

A woman's voice answered.

"I'm looking for Meg Mahone."

"This is Meg Mahone."

"Hello, this is Margaret Collinwood. I used to be Margaret Ochs. I'm your niece, Hannah's daughter."

"Yes?"

Margaret hesitated. "I've moved back to Maine, to Coffins Reach, and I'm living in my parents' house now, the old one on the waterfront? And I guess I have some questions about my sister's death. Norma Ann?"

"I remember Norma Ann."

Margaret had a vision of her aunt calling to her from the shadows by the drawn drapes, "It's time you went, Margaret. Your mother needs her rest."

"I guess what I'm calling for is I want to come to some understanding of her death. I've inherited the house now, and I've come back here to live." Margaret wished she wasn't stammering. "I thought that by talking with some of my relatives, I could understand her more, my mother, I mean. And my sister."

"You are brave to call."

Brave? What an odd thing to say. Margaret tried to think of something more to say, could think of nothing. Her aunt filled the silence. "There are many things that have been left for too long."

"I'd like to make sense of some of these things." Margaret paused. "Why did my mother die?"

"Your mother died of a broken heart."

"I remember those scarves she wore on her head. Did she have cancer?"

"Yes, that was the official diagnosis. But she had nothing within her, no inner resource to fight the disease after your sister died, no will to live. She wanted to die, and conveniently, cancer came along and provided her the way out."

"I didn't know that. No one told me."

Silence again. "Someone should have."

"I'm also interested in my sister. I have suspicions that she was suffering from some sort of a mental breakdown when she died."

"Mental breakdown? Who told you that bit of rubbish?"

"No one told me. I figured it out myself."

More silence then, which grew uncomfortably long. Margaret tried to think of questions, but said nothing. After a while, just to make sure her aunt was still on the line, she said quietly, "Aunt Meg?"

Meg's voice was barely audible. "Margaret, I would like it if you came to see me. I would like it very much. There are some things you should know."

Before they hung up, they made arrangements for Margaret to drive there on the weekend.

Through the window she could see Ruth Godwish, who, despite the rain, was digging in the soft sand around her house with a long stick. Margaret never saw Bradley, she reflected, never saw him outside at all.

FIFTY

After calling all of the Simon Schultzes in New England and discovering that none had ever worked for the *Bangor Daily News*, Chris decided to take a run into Bangor and pay a little visit to the newspaper office. If he was clever he might find out Mr. Schultz's Social Security number, which would open up a world of possibilities.

Large droplets spattered against his windshield, and his wipers had to do double time to keep up. He turned on the radio. More rain was forecast; odd, said the weatherman, for this time of year.

Normally, this would be a good day to sit in his cabin and read a book or do inside boat repairs, but he was worried about Margaret. A knife through a painting is not just an act of vandalism. But why was she being threatened? Since she came back here, she had been gently probing into her sister's death, uncovering diaries and incriminating bank statements. Who wanted to stop her?

A car swerved behind him, passing him at breakneck speed on the highway, and splashed the side of Chris's Chevette with a waterfall of road grime.

It was still raining when Chris pulled in at the *Bangor Daily News*. When he asked to see someone in personnel, the woman behind the reception desk, who looked no more than eighteen, said, "You can leave your résumé here. They'll be interviewing for the advertising manager's job next week as far as I know." She was a bouncy, flirty little thing, and Chris laughed.

"I'm not here about a job. What I'd like —" and he leaned forward and spoke conspiratorially — "is to get some information on a former employee of yours. I'm a private investigator," he said, winking at her, "on a life and death mission."

"Like on the *X-Files*?"

"Sort of. Yeah."

She grinned, showing a full set of straight white teeth. "Okay." She leaned forward on the counter and looked him straight in the eyes. "What's this mysterious woman's name?"

"It's a him. His name is Simon Schultz and he would have worked here in 1973, thereabouts."

"Simon Schultz? You wait here. Don't you go anywhere, and I'll be right back."

"I'm here, I'm not going anywhere."

He admired the back of her short skirt wiggling away from him as she walked into an office. From over her shoulder she grinned saucily at him. She was back within ten minutes with a file folder, which she laid on the counter. "I got a whole file on Simon Schultz. But I can't let you see it. No can do."

"Why not?" He raised his eyebrows.

"Well . . ." She leaned across the counter, putting her head in her hands. "Why don't you tell me the *real* reason you want to see his file."

"I told you, I'm a detective on a life and death case."

"Yeah, and I'm Madonna."

He put his hands up. "Okay, you caught me. I'm not a detective. Simon Schultz was an old buddy of mine from high school. I'm just passing through town and I thought I'd look him up. You know, renew old acquaintances and all that. Trouble is, I don't know where he got to after he worked here."

"That's better. I had to steal this out of personnel as it was."

"You didn't steal it, you borrowed it."

"Borrowed, right. I'll remember that." She paused. "I don't think this'll be much help, though. We have no forwarding address for him."

"Well, maybe something in the file will help."

"I doubt it." The file was still sitting there, closed. Any minute now her superior or someone was going to come out demanding to know why she wasn't typing out ad copy or something. He had to bring this little game to a close.

"Can I just have a look, pretty please?" He winked at her.

She made a face and opened the file. There it was, right on top, Simon Schultz's Social Security number. He quickly memorized it.

"Well, by george, you're right," he said. "There's nothing in here that can help me. Sorry to have bothered you."

"It's no bother. I love stealing files from personnel." She was still looking at him. "So, what do you do?"

"I told you, I'm a private investigator."

"No, really, what do you do?"

"Okay, I'm an engineer."

"That's better." She looked at him. "Something I've always wondered, what does an engineer do?"

"We engineer things."

"Oh yeah? Is that sort of like invent things?"

"Sort of like."

Closing the file she said, "It's too bad you and Simon didn't keep in touch. I vowed that I would keep in touch with my friends from high school. We made a vow."

"Yeah, sounds like something Simon and I should have done."

As soon as Chris was back in his car he jotted down the Social Security number in his notebook.

FIFTY-ONE

It paid to keep those police contacts current, thought Chris as he sat in the coffee shop, a printout of Simon Schultz's entire work history plus his current address and phone number in an envelope in front of him. All that with just one little Social Security number.

"Thanks, Bill," Chris said.

"You owe me."

"I always owe you. So, what else is new?"

"One of these days I'm gonna come collecting," said the police officer who was also his friend.

Chris said, grinning, "Yeah, yeah, so who bought the coffee?"

"Last of the big spenders here."

A few minutes later, Chris was on his way through town. He passed a Mr. Bubbles Car Wash, and despite the rain, decided on the full meal deal. He ran his Chevy through the car wash, cleaned out empty juice boxes, and plunked in quarter after quarter until the interior was vacuumed to his satisfaction. He also stopped in at First Avenue Cafe and made dinner reservations for seven-thirty.

Simon Schultz was living in Orlando, Florida, and his occupation was listed as retired. From his cellular, Chris dialed the Schultz residence. Good thing Clark was paying his expenses. His phone was answered by a woman who said that Simon was out golfing. Oh wait, here he was coming in the back door now, would he like to hold? It'll be just a minute before he got his clubs put away. Sure, said Chris.

"Yeah?" said Simon when he picked up the receiver.

"Mr. Schultz, my name is Chris Rikken. I'm a private investigator hired to verify certain facts concerning the death of Norma Ann Ochs in 1973. You were the reporter covering it for the *Bangor Daily News*, is that right?"

"Rikken. Rikken. That name sounds familiar."

"I was one of the investigating police officers at the scene."

"Oh yeah? Small world."

"What I'm calling you about is the last sentence of your article. I have it here: 'The police have not ruled out foul play.' "

"I remember. That little line cost me my job."

"Your job?"

"It didn't fit with what the Ochs family wanted. They had the money, they called the shots. So I got fired."

"Really?"

"Yeah. Listen, you were a police officer, did you think everything was on the up-and-up?"

"I'm not sure what you mean."

"What I mean is this, I spoke at length with, what was that guy's name? Jon somebody, the detective on the scene there."

"Yes?"

"He had reservations. But I guess he couldn't voice them. He's dead now, I understand. I can tell you all this now 'cause I don't care who gets hurt. I know what I know. I know what was said to me by what's-his-face, Jon Smith. He told me all this before the Ochses had a chance to give him a talking-to about what should be said and what shouldn't."

Chris leaned into the phone, rapidly taking notes with his right hand. "Detective Smith definitely said 'foul play'?"

"That was the gist of it, yeah."

"Did he say anything else? Did he mention suicide?"

"No, let me think. I think his exact words were, 'This accident,' and he said *accident* in that sarcastic tone of his. He says, 'This accident looks awfully fishy.' That's what he said, swear on my mother's grave."

"Is that all he said?"

"Yeah, pretty much. But I could tell by his body language — you can tell a lot by body language — I could tell he didn't think it was a straightforward accident."

"What was his body language?"

"Well, you knew him, right? The way he'd sneer and stuff, roll his eyes, that sort of thing."

"So that was all?"

"Yeah, that and the fact that he says it was 'fishy.' Those were the two things. So I wrote that into my story, and next thing I know the editor-in-chief is handing me two cardboard boxes and telling me to start packing."

"No kidding?"

"Yeah, no kidding."

When Chris hung up he said aloud, "Alice, it's becoming curiouser and curiouser." At the nearest convenience store, he borrowed the phone book and looked up the number for Jonathan Smith's widow.

She was living in a nursing home just this side of Bar Harbor. He looked at his watch. Midafternoon. He could make the hour trip in forty minutes if he hauled, and he'd be back in plenty of time to shave, shower, and pick up Margaret.

The second retirement home he had visited along the Maine coast in as many days was not nearly as plush as the one in Portland. It sat short and squat, resembling a run-down hospital more than a retirement home for seniors. A cement wart on the skin of the street. He hadn't called first. He hoped Mrs. Smith was in.

The individual apartments weren't accessible from the

outside, so he went to the reception desk at the front. He was told that Phoebe Smith was in room 112. He signed in as an old friend of her late husband's and made his way down the hall to room 112.

His knock was answered by a tired looking nurse in a wrinkled white pantsuit, who told him Mrs. Smith was resting.

"I've driven from Bangor to see her. Any possible way to talk with her for a few minutes?"

The nurse looked at him. "Are you aware of Mrs. Smith's condition?"

"No, not really. I worked with her late husband."

"She has Alzheimer's."

From the inside of the room came a loud voice. "Let him in. Don't keep my Jonny away from me anymore. You're just trying to keep me from him."

The nurse looked helplessly at Chris and opened the door wide.

She said, "I've got other patients that need looking after. If you need something just press Mrs. Smith's buzzer. There's usually someone around." Then she left.

Mrs. Smith lay on the bed, face shrunken, white wisps of hair around her gray scalp. Her skeletal body was encased in a fluffy pink bathrobe that looked new and ten sizes too big for her. He tried to remember Mrs. Smith from twenty years ago, a large woman with a gracious smile who made them sandwiches and iced tea when they came to visit.

Her eyes brightened when she saw him. "Jonny!" she said.

"Hello, Mrs. Smith."

She waved a hand. "Why the missus, Jon? No need to call me missus."

"Okay . . . Phoebe."

"That's better, Jonny. I knew you'd come back. They said you wouldn't, but I knew you would."

"Mrs., ah, Phoebe, uh . . . can we talk about Norma Ann Ochs?"

"Norma Ann Ochs? Who the blazes is Norma Ann Ochs?"

"It was an accident, Phoebe, that's what the police reports said. They said it was an accident, but Jonny didn't believe it was. Do you remember?"

Chris had heard that short-term memory was the first to go in Alzheimer's patients. He hoped Mrs. Smith's long-term memory was still lurking there somewhere behind those vacant eyes.

She raised a bony finger at him. "They said it was an accident, but my Jonny knew better, didn't you?"

He nodded dumbly. She began to wail — great deep, dry groans. It was an unnerving sound, and he looked around half expecting the nurse to walk in at any moment. But no one did. "They chased down his car and killed him. No one could prove it, but I know."

"Who, Phoebe? Who killed Jonny?"

"Knowledge."

"Knowledge?"

"Knowledge killed my Jonny. Knowledge. Knowledge. Knowledge."

"What knowledge? Knowledge about what?"

"I need to get up now. We can go home now."

"Phoebe?"

But the rest of her talk was ramblings in which she mistook him for Jonny, for her nephew, for the doctor who promised she could get out next week, for the nurse in the white pantsuit who promised her apple juice and didn't deliver. No matter how he tried to move the subject back to Norma Ann, it was as if that part of her brain had been stopped up for the evening. He had no choice but to say good-bye.

FIFTY-TWO

After talking to her aunt, Margaret decided to begin a new Anna Coffin sketch. But she soon put it away. She couldn't concentrate. The conversation with her aunt had left her with a lingering curiosity. What would her aunt tell her about her mother? She wandered listlessly through the house. A fire in the fireplace would be nice on a rainy day like this, but she didn't have any firewood, plus she didn't know the condition of the chimney. All she needed right about now was a chimney fire. Maybe next week she'd get someone in to look at it.

Early in the afternoon she drove into Bosuns Harbor in the rain, picked up a hamburger at a fast food drive-through, and, tired of the stillness of her house, bought a television set and a VCR. She made sure she got a small TV, small enough that she could carry it in by herself. She listened as the salesman told what wires went where on the back of the VCR. She also bought a set of rabbit ears when he told her that if she wasn't hooked up to cable she'd get nothing but snow without them. She decided to set it up in her bedroom. It was the nights that were too quiet. It was the nights when she needed voices.

By the time she got home, she had forgotten what the salesman had said about hooking up the VCR and could make little sense of the instruction booklet, which had been badly translated from Japanese. But the TV worked, and for the rest of the afternoon she sat on her bed, finishing the book of short stories, the television on to keep her company until it was time to get ready for dinner.

She chose a casual navy wool dress topped with a silk jacket. She didn't know the kind of place Chris had lined up, but this way she wasn't too casual if the place was fancy, and she wasn't too fancy if the place was casual.

Promptly at 6:30 he was at her door with an opened umbrella.

"Some rain, eh?" she said as they made their way to the waiting car.

"There'll be flooding if this keeps up," he said.

In the car she said, "Is this usual for this time of year?"

He put it in gear and headed up the driveway. "Not really. It's been a strange fall. Really strange. Locals are saying it's the weirdest weather we've had in twenty-five years."

"No kidding?"

"So, you work on your painting today?"

She looked at him sideways. "If you're asking me if I locked my doors, yes, I made sure my new locks were locked at all times. Then I started another painting of Anna Coffin, but got depressed. So many hours had gone into that first one. So I drove into Bosuns Harbor and bought myself a television set and a VCR. But then I couldn't get the VCR hooked up. I'm a complete Luddite when it comes to technical things. How about you? Get your business done in Bangor?"

"Yeah, met a cute little girl at the Bangor paper who gave me Simon Schultz's Social Security number. From there I got his phone number and called him in Florida. He said there was definitely something fishy about the police investigation."

"Really?"

"Didn't get a lot of stuff from him, though. He apparently lost his job over the last sentence in that article you read."

"No kidding?"

"Yeah."

On the way into Bangor, he told her about his quick trip to the nursing home in Bar Harbor and about the incoherent replies of Phoebe Smith.

Margaret's eyes widened. "Do you think Jon Smith was killed to cover up what he knew?"

"Could be, but what did he know?"

She shrugged her shoulders.

Later she said, "On the weekend I'm taking a trip to upstate New York."

"New York?"

"To visit my mother's sister, my Aunt Meg. She wants to talk to me about my mother." She paused. "I think it'll do me good to get away from this place by myself. Maybe I need this."

"You needed to get away from Canada so you came here, and now you need to get away from here, so you go to New York state."

She looked at him sharply and then out the window. They were passing a large, several-storied barn that had been painted slick red and transformed into a gift and antique shop. The rain and ensuing mud weren't keeping the antique hunters away, however, and cars lined the parking lot.

"I'm sorry," he said.

They had dinner in an out-of-the-way, quiet French restaurant that majored in a lot of cream-sauced entrées and baskets of fresh baguettes. Their waiter carried a white cloth over his forearm and wished them dining pleasure. A thick white candle on the table provided the majority of light. During dinner, by mutual unspoken agreement, they did not talk about Norma Ann, about the Ochses, about anybody being paid off, or any painting being stabbed. Instead Chris asked her about her work, and she told him about her painting and her art shows. She told him about Andre and about her friend

Joyce. He told her about his two girls and about the time they sailed down to Chesapeake Bay.

They stretched dinner out as long as possible with two cups of coffee each and cheesecake with raspberry sauce. He told her about his years on the force and why he left to work for himself. She told him about a grant she had received once to do a series of watercolor postcards of New Brunswick scenery. He told her about the new GPS he had just added to his boat, and she told him about teaching watercolor painting down in St. Andrews, New Brunswick. They laughed a lot, and a few times he looked across the table at her in a way that made her feel shy and unsure of herself.

They said little on the way home, just listened to the rain, the radio, and the windshield wipers slapping back and forth across the glass. When they arrived at her house, he offered to hook up her VCR for her. She gratefully accepted.

It felt odd for him to be in her bedroom, and she stood in the doorway, aware of her robe flung across the hastily made bed, slippers to the side, clothes scattered on chair backs, an empty wine glass on the bedside table. Within minutes the machine was wired and working and he was explaining to her how to record, how to play tapes, and how to set the timer. His talk was technical, like the salesman's, and she nodded and swallowed and tried to appear the sophisticated person that she wasn't feeling right now with him in her bedroom, tall and lean and very male.

He stood and said, "There you go. Now you can rent movies and watch TV all night long if you want."

"Thank you," she said, moving toward the stairs.

Downstairs in the kitchen he seemed to hesitate. Was he waiting for her to offer him a drink, a cup of decaf, perhaps? What did people do in this situation? Was it proper protocol to extend this evening further?

"Margaret," he said, extending his hand, "I had a nice time."

She took his hand. He clasped it in both of his and moved toward her, backing her gently against the wall, a slow-motion dance.

"Margaret . . ." His hands were on her face, stroking it, looking into her eyes. Closer. She could feel his warm breath on her face, his fingers in her hair. He leaned toward her. She closed her eyes and felt his mouth on hers. She could hear his sigh, feel his heart beat. So close. There was a part of her that wanted to stay that way forever, stirred, protected. But another part held to a memory.

She turned away and said, "Chris, I'm married."

He backed away from her. "You're married." It was a statement.

"Yes." She looked at him helplessly.

"So if you're married, where's your husband? How come your quite wonderful husband isn't here?"

"Chris . . ."

He began wandering about her house, calling in a loud voice, "Husband, O quite-wonderful husband, where are you?"

"Chris," she said again.

He reentered the kitchen. "Well, that settles it. Your quite-wonderful husband doesn't seem to be here."

She said nothing, just looked down in front of her at the lines in the floorboards where the tongue and groove seamed.

A few minutes later he grabbed his jacket, looked at her sadly. "I'm sorry, Margaret. I misunderstood things. I'm sorry."

She could think of nothing to say.

She watched him go, wet gravel spurting up underneath

the tires of his little Chevy.

For a long time she stood there, leaning against the wall, unable to move, her mouth still warm from his kiss.

The wind was picking up, the rain was ruthless, and suddenly she felt absolutely and terrifyingly alone. She realized she could easily call Chris back. Call him now, leave a message on his answering machine to come back. He would. She knew he would. And no one would really say much. After all, Robin had left her.

But was that what she wanted? To share a bed with Chris, waking up in the V-berth of his boat every morning, leaving Maine every fall for warm southern islands, setting up her easel on white beaches to paint palm trees and coconuts and dark-haired children?

She thought about Robin then, and wondered how it was that she still loved him. He was the only man she had ever loved, the only man she had ever made love to. He had brought light and love into the lonely existence she had led with her silent father. A spiritual breath in her parched desert, he had carried her off to a magical land where she got to know Robin and God at the same time, the two entwined in her thinking.

She had learned about faith as she sat in church every Sunday with Robin and Aislin and all of the other Collinwood children, nieces and nephews. Rows and rows of them filling the sanctuary. A long history they had in New Brunswick, and she had been a part of it for a time.

As she began her nightly chore of locking all the doors and windows, she began to understand that it was only through Robin that she had come to know God. Maybe she had never known him for herself.

In her bed that night, wrapped tightly in the blue bedspread that had covered her parents' bed, she prayed that if

God was a knowable God, if he could be known by her, that she would find him.

And that her loneliness would end.

FIFTY-THREE

For the next two days Margaret worked on her sketches in the daytime and during the evenings she watched television, sitcom after sitcom, where major problems are resolved within half-hour segments, time out for commercials. The rain had not let up; its force had only increased, and the evening news showed pictures of high tides and rivers flooding their banks. She felt detached from it all, passing her days in a kind of apathy. Chris hadn't called. He hadn't come with muffins to her door. Robin hadn't called either.

She phoned Roland's number a few times — coffee at Wellingtons sounded awfully good — but hung up before she got his machine. He was down in Freeport. She should have remembered that. The thought of going to the coffee shop alone didn't interest her.

One night she stayed awake until three in the morning, weeping into a handful of Kleenexes as she watched a late-night movie. Sylvia called her a couple of times wanting to know if the police had any new leads on the random burglary of her home — that's what she called it, "random burglary of her home." Margaret said no.

"Well, I hope they're not just giving up on this one," said Sylvia.

The police never even called her.

On Thursday night Margaret packed. She was leaving tomorrow for New York state. It was good to have something concrete to do, to fill her mind.

The next morning early, with her map of the Northeastern

257

states and provinces laid out on the passenger seat, she carefully locked her house and left. She soon picked up I-95 and
headed south toward New Hampshire and Massachusetts,
where she'd head across to New York state. She felt better
than she had for a long time. Driving sometimes did that.
Once you got to the place you were driving to, the old feelings
came back, but driving itself was a promise, the journey filled
with more hope than the destination. Once she crossed over
the border into New Hampshire the rain stopped. Perhaps it
was only raining in Maine, only raining on her sad, cursed little house.

Halfway to New York it occurred to her that no one but
Chris knew where she was. She felt curiously buoyed by that
fact.

By evening she reached her destination, a white farmhouse
just outside of Albany. She read the directions Aunt Meg had
dictated over the phone. This must be the place, she thought,
this sprawling house with the wide glassed-in front porch, the
path to the front lined with shrubbery, a big elm in the yard.
She pulled her car into the driveway and parked beside a silver Towncar.

Her aunt and uncle had moved to this place after Norma
Ann had died, but Margaret had never visited here. She
walked to the back and knocked on a wooden screen door
that was badly warped. Sheets and towels were pegged to a
metal clothesline, and on a small wooden table beside the
door was a bucket of wooden clothespins. She heard move-
ment from within, and a few moments later her knock was answered.

"Aunt Meg?" Even though she hadn't seen her aunt in
many, many years, her Aunt Meg seemed virtually un-
changed. Her hair was still mostly brown, cut short and
brushed back off her face.

"Margaret! It's been so long." The two women hugged each other. Meg said, "I've made up the front bedroom for you and I've kept supper warm."

"Thank you. I'll just go get my bag from the car. I left it there, wanted to make sure this was the right place."

"This is the right place."

A few moments later, Margaret was scrubbing her face in the downstairs bathroom with its tiny porcelain sink on stilt legs in which the hot and cold water came from separate silver faucets, one on either side. The tub was also like that, she noticed. And no shower. She'd have to figure out a way to wash her hair under those taps.

When Margaret came out into the kitchen, the table was set with a blue woven placemat and soup bowl. Her aunt was dishing a meaty broth into the bowl.

"I hope you'll forgive me," said her aunt. "I've already eaten."

"It's late. I didn't expect you to wait. You didn't have to save anything. I'm fine, really."

Meg's kitchen was small and a wood table was pushed under the window. The appliances were old, but serviceable and clean. The place had a comfortable feel with deep, open cupboards and an antique chest of drawers. A vase of fresh carnations sat on a doily on top of it. On the window ledge were several library books: *Jane Eyre*, *The English Patient*, *Till We Have Faces*. When her aunt noticed Margaret looking at them she said, "I'm in a book discussion group."

"Must be interesting," said Margaret, meaning it.

"Oh, it is quite. I'm enjoying this phase of my life. To be retired, to have nothing to do but to get up and watch the birds, sit in my seat by the window and read, or dabble at my art. Yes, I'm quite enjoying this. It's nice to have visitors every so often as well."

They talked while Margaret ate. Margaret learned that her Uncle Peter had died a dozen years ago, and that Meg had moved here after his death. Margaret told her that she had inherited the old house on the waterfront.

Tea in the front room was next, a comfortable room with needlepoint chair-arm covers and footstools, white lace curtains and a grandfather clock. A large loom took up most of the room, and on it was an unfinished weaving in shades of pale yellow and green. An old-fashioned spinning wheel sat on the glassed-in front porch.

"Aunt Meg, I didn't know you were a weaver."

"I've always loved working with textiles. When Peter died I traded my small loom for this larger one. I spend my days in the quiet pursuit of color and yarn."

"And I suppose that's a working spinning wheel out there."

"It is, yes, but I must admit I don't spin all my own yarns. That can get tedious."

"And you're not teaching anymore?"

"Oh no. I retired from the high school three years ago when I was fifty-five. Come sit down. You didn't come here to find out about my weavings. I know you want to learn about your mother. She wasn't much older than you when she died. I still miss her. She never should have died so young."

"My sister shouldn't have died either."

"Both of us have lost sisters. When I heard that you were in Coffins Reach, when you phoned, I wanted to tell you to get out immediately, go home or to some other place. I am glad you've come here."

Margaret blinked at her. "Why?"

"I'm going to tell you something that you probably don't know, something that I've kept within my soul all of these years."

Margaret leaned forward.

"It's because of Leo Ochs that your sister died."

"Leo Ochs? My uncle?"

"I'm going to tell you the story. Even Peter didn't know this. But Hannah knew and the knowledge killed her. Your father moved you to safety. But Bangor wasn't far enough away. The terror still followed your parents, and they both died. And the money wasn't worth it in the long run. It never is."

"What are you talking about?"

"I have prayed to my God about this. I have even made an attempt to forgive Leo in my heart for what he did . . ." She pulled her cardigan sweater tightly around her. "But he has gone unpunished."

Margaret waited.

"Your Uncle Leo, to put it succinctly, could not keep his hands off pretty young teenage girls. Your sister Norma Ann was one of those pretty young girls. I suspect Donna was also abused, but I don't know that for sure."

Margaret's hand flew to her mouth.

"But it gets worse. Norma Ann was pregnant with his child at the time of her death."

"No!"

"It's true. That's why when you told me the theory about mental illness, well, I knew where that thought came from, right from the Ochses themselves. Still trying to cover up after all these years."

"No, it came from me. I'd been reading through my sister's diary. I brought it with me. It seems she changed in the space of one summer from a cheerful teenager to a very disturbed little girl. I put two and two together, and guessed mental illness." She paused. "I can hardly believe what you're saying, Aunt Meg."

"Well, believe it."

"Why didn't somebody do something?"

261

"Leo wielded a lot of power. In actual fact he is the one who basically owns that hardware business. Even Monty has little say when Leo's around. And that poor Clark. Such a talented young man. So much waste."

Margaret looked at her. "This is *my* Uncle Clark you're talking about here?"

"*Your* Uncle Clark, yes. A great artist. He could have gone on in that career had not his family been so opposed to it. The way they ridiculed him was astonishing. He used to carve soldiers, each one different, each one unique."

"I found a little bagpiper among my parents' things."

"That may have been Clark's."

Margaret shook her head. "I never knew that. He was always so quiet. Still is. He seems so morose. And Leo. All of this is just too astonishing!"

"Leo controlled him, just like he controls him now, just like he controls Monty, and Mitch before him. It's what killed your parents. Mitch and Hannah were paid by Leo to leave Coffins Reach and not come back. They were given a large sum of money, and then monthly installments. Your education fund came from that. The bulk of the money you inherited came from Leo originally."

Margaret sat there stunned. The thirty pieces of silver had paid her education, had set her up with enough money upon her father's death to go out and buy TVs and VCRs and phones with Caller ID and answering machines. She had enough money now that she would never have to work again. And for the first time in her life she had felt truly independent.

"This is true?" Her voice was almost a whisper.

A small bird had lighted on her aunt's front porch railing. Margaret watched it for a minute, sitting there, and then it flew away.

"How did my sister die?" Her voice sounded far away, as though it didn't belong to her. She was afraid of the answer.

Her aunt poured more tea into her china cup. "I have no other explanation than suicide. She was thirteen, pregnant with her uncle's child. I was so glad when I heard you had moved to Canada. I thought, give her some happiness, Lord. Give that child some peace. Part of the reason your parents moved to Bangor was to keep you away from Leo. Your mother loved you very much."

The autumn night was darkening around them, but Meg did not turn on any lights. They sat in the shadows, Margaret scarcely able to breathe, holding on to the brocade arms of the chair for support. "Why didn't my father sell the house?" she asked finally.

"Leo wanted him to. That was part of the bargain. But your father vowed that he would not sell that house until justice had been done."

"Now I live there."

"Now you live there."

"It's so strange to be sitting here listening to you tell me these things. How can you be so sure about Leo?"

"Hannah and Mitch verified it."

"Why couldn't they stop him? Press charges?"

"I know you don't mean them to be, but those are simplistic questions when you're embroiled in a situation. It's like asking an abused wife, 'Why don't you just leave?' Your Uncle Leo held that family together with an iron grip. He still does."

Margaret thought of her Uncle Leo, so concerned when her house was broken into, talking with the police in serious tones, telling Margaret that she must stay with Sylvia and Monty that night. Was that all an act?

That night Margaret lay on the small single bed in the

263

front bedroom underneath the log cabin quilt and thought about her sister. In her mind she was the ten-year-old girl again and it was the morning of the last day of her sister's life. On that morning Norma Ann was already downstairs when Margaret came bounding down, grabbing the cornflakes and milk, late as usual.

"Where's Mom?" Margaret asked.

Norma Ann just shook her head and said nothing. She wasn't eating, just staring at the cereal bowl in front of her. She was holding something very tightly in her fingers.

"What's that?" Margaret asked.

Silence.

"Norma Ann? Where's Mom, I asked you."

Her sister ignored her. Usually both girls chattered constantly, competing for time and space in the Ochs house. Today Norma Ann was completely still.

"Norma Ann, we're supposed to go to Aunt Sylvia's and Uncle Monty's after school 'cause Mom and Dad are going to Bangor. Did you know that?"

Her sister nodded.

"You ready to go?"

Norma Ann nodded. Every day the two of them would walk up the path to catch the bus to Bosuns Harbor. Margaret got off first at the elementary school and then Norma Ann and Donna got off at the junior high school. The girls left without saying good-bye to their mother, without even seeing her. On the walk up to the bus stop Norma Ann said not one word to her sister, even though Margaret kept up a steady chatter.

Once she was on the bus, Margaret sat with her friends and forgot all about Norma Ann.

After school she walked the few blocks from the elementary school to her aunt and uncle's home. Aunt Sylvia

264

brought her cookies and milk and sat her down at the kitchen table to work on her homework. Her aunt wandered through her house that day, frowning, jittery, straightening china figurines, folding dish towels, gazing through the window to the mist on the lawn. Donna was there in the other room, watching one of her soap operas.

Partway through her arithmetic problems, Sylvia walked over to her. "Your sister was supposed to be here. Do you know where she is?"

"Ask Donna."

"I did. Donna said she was supposed to meet a teacher. But I didn't know that. Nobody told me. And it's late now. She should be here by now." Her words trailed off, and Margaret went back to her homework.

Two hours later the phone rang, and the world as Margaret knew it ended.

The front bedroom in her Aunt Meg's house was cold. Fingers of chill were seeping in, finding their way around the edges of the large windowpanes. Margaret sat up in bed and looked out the window. The night was windy and clear. The earth was very light for the middle of the night, the moon and stars whitening the earth, filling her room with a pale translucence. She thought about Leo and Clark and realized she hardly knew them. Her Uncle Leo a child molester? Her Uncle Clark an artist?

In the corner of the room on the floor were a bunch of teddy bears. She chose one. She also found a wool blanket in the closet. She wrapped herself in the blanket and hugged the bear until she fell asleep.

FIFTY-FOUR

Clark watched the rain wander in uneven rivulets down the windowpane next to the back booth in the Bulldog Café, where he sat and waited for the private investigator. Clark looked at his watch. He was already twenty minutes late. What was he paying this guy for anyway, he grumbled.

He had spent the entire day in his shed uncovering shoe box after shoe box of wooden soldiers, each individually wrapped in tissue paper, brittle now from the years. Pat had gone into Bangor, so she wasn't out there every ten minutes bugging him about what he was doing in this old shed and didn't he have anything better to do and if he didn't have anything better to do, she could easily find something. It took some time, and when he had found all of his soldiers he was smeared in dirt, muck, and old machine oil.

There was a time after Norma Ann had died and his art show hopes had been dashed that he had contemplated burning them all. He was glad now that he hadn't. So glad. He carried the boxes inside and took them to the downstairs guest bedroom. Pat seldom went down there. He could clean them off and set them up and no one would be the wiser. He unwrapped each one and set it up on the table. Soon entire armies stood at attention. These soldiers represented a part of his life he thought had been stolen forever, but he had news for Leo and Monty. He had hired a detective, something he should have done a long time ago, and it wouldn't be long before he would be calling the shots. He'd had to put up with all their crap all these years, it was soon going to be his turn. He was only fifty-eight. He had a whole lot of good years ahead of him to work on his miniatures.

From underneath the bed he pulled out a locked trunk. He opened it with the key he kept in the top drawer of the desk and looked through his books. This was the one thing he had kept all of these years, the one thing Pat knew nothing about. He collected books about wars. He preferred the kind with glossy full-color photos; they were better for copying his miniatures. Whenever he was in Bangor by himself he'd stop in at the Barnes & Noble and look at their latest collection of war books. He'd buy them, take them home, read them, and then hide them in the trunk. His newest purchase was a pictorial history of war machinery starting with the medieval battering rams and going right up to the Stealth Bomber. As he looked at the black wings of the Bomber, a strong excitement gripped him. As soon as he got the goods on Leo and Monty he would quit the store and begin his Gulf War collection.

He was nursing his second Coke when Chris Rikken finally showed up and slid onto the bench across from him.

"So, where you been?" asked Clark, making an elaborate show of looking at his watch.

"When you hear what I have you won't be bothered that I'm a few minutes late."

"Yeah? So? What do you have?"

"I've been working my tail off the past three days; I've done nothing else. You should be grateful. It's all here in this report." Chris tapped a thick manila folder. "I don't have everything quite figured out, but I'm getting there. And I've got enough here to make you happy, I think."

"Yeah? So tell me the gist of it."

"Okay. Well, it turns out Leo had been paying Mitch a monthly sum of ten thousand dollars. That doesn't include the original money he paid him to leave Coffins Reach."

"Why'd he pay him to leave Coffins Reach?"

"That," said Chris, "I'm still working on. My theory is that Leo wanted total control of the assets, which include, by the way, all of the hardware stores, which are worth much more than I originally figured. Apparently he owns a whole string of other stores in Vermont. He's known as the hardware king over there, a regular Tim the Toolman. Monty doesn't even know this. But, you ask, since when is the hardware business all that lucrative? And my answer is never. Our Leo is involved in a bit of racketeering on the side."

"What?"

"Leo is involved in blackmail big time."

"Blackmail! To who?"

"Anyone with a secret. His favorite targets are police officers and politicians. It pays to have police officers in your pocket. Next come politicians."

Clark's jaw had dropped. "What's he blackmailing all these people about?"

"Everyone has secrets — you, me — all of us have things we'd prefer the general public not know about. He'd hire his thugs to find out those secrets and threaten to expose them if he wasn't paid off. Now if his target had no secrets, he'd find something. Prostitutes were his favorite."

Clark stared across at the private investigator, whose eyes were bright.

"How'd you find out all this?"

"It's my job, remember? I've been traveling all over Maine, working overtime. There's a list of expenses in that envelope as well."

Clark took the envelope, opened it, drew out the pages. Then he looked up. "You said you weren't quite finished. What else is there?"

"For all intents and purposes it looks like Mitch was, per-

268

haps, blackmailing Leo. From the dates there, it looks as if all of Leo's blackmailing activities started soon after he began paying Mitch off. My guess is that it so enraged Leo to have to pay off Mitch for something that he decided to go into business himself."

Clark put down the envelope and took another swig of his Coke. "But you still don't know why he was paying Mitch off?"

"Not yet, no, but I'm working on it."

"How does Monty fit into all of this?"

"Monty's bank records show a withdrawal on the fifteenth of each month. I'm assuming he was paying Leo off, too, but I can't get anything else on him."

After Chris left, Clark went through the papers, one at a time, a catalog of the misdeeds of his eldest brother. He grinned to himself and placed the papers back in the envelope.

Leo, dear brother, it's time you got a taste of your own medicine.

FIFTY-FIVE

The following morning Margaret and her aunt sat in the small kitchen at the table next to the window that faced the side yard and the elm tree. They drank tea and ate English muffins with homemade strawberry freezer jam.

"I was remembering something," said Margaret. "I was remembering that when I first came to Coffins Reach, my neighbor Ruth Godwish hinted to me that Norma Ann was pregnant when she died and that people were saying that her son Bradley was the father."

Her aunt, who was standing at the counter pouring tea, said, "Why would people say such a thing? That poor boy. There were rumors then that your sister was pregnant — certainly Hannah knew it, and Mitch, too. Leo had arranged for an abortion, but Norma Ann died before she ever got it. In the end the pregnancy was covered up."

"Wasn't there an autopsy?"

"No, there wasn't. Your uncles wouldn't allow it. Even though there should have been." Meg was spreading jam on a toasted English muffin. "I have cereal and milk, Margaret, if you'd like something more."

"This is fine."

"Margaret, I have to show you something. I was going to show this to you last night, but I must make it priority this morning."

Meg left the kitchen and went upstairs. She came back with a hardcover, marble-colored school binder and laid it on the table. "This is Norma Ann's diary. Hannah gave it to me before she died. I'm fairly sure something like this would stand up in court."

Margaret opened the book. The inside front cover read, "The Secret Writings of Norma Ann Ochs, 1973." It began precisely where her other diary had left off, the spring of 1973.

The first entry was the poem Margaret had seen in her father's files. The rest of the book were poems and diary writings beginning in April. Norma Ann wrote candidly about the baby inside of her, about how "they" wanted her to have an abortion, but that she had decided to keep the baby, whom she named Rebecca. "Is it Rebecca's fault that her father is who he is?" She also wrote about being very, very afraid. In the last entry before her death she wrote:

I am going to see them tomorrow. I will tell them that I don't want an abortion. I have proof. I'm going to talk to Miss Parker, too.

"This is so . . . so horrifying," Margaret said. "But what does she mean that she has proof?"

Meg shook her head. "I don't know. This is only the second time I've read through this book. The first time was the day after your mother's funeral. The presence of this book, however, is a constant reminder of my failure." Meg sat down, her muffin and tea forgotten.

"What do you mean, your failure?"

"Before she died, your mother asked me to make sure Leo went to jail. It's been all these years and I've done nothing."

"You're afraid of him."

She wrapped her sweater around her and said, "He is a ruthless, cunning man. Yes, I am afraid of him. Of what new thing he could do to me. I am afraid, God help me."

271

Morning turned into lunchtime while the two Margarets sat and talked and read the diary together, comparing it to the one Margaret had brought. Midafternoon Meg made more tea, and they went into the front room and continued their talk.

"You were talking about a husband," Meg said. "Have you been separated long?"

Margaret looked at her. But of course, her aunt had no way of knowing about Robin and Aislin or even about her move to Canada.

"You talk about losing Norma Ann and Hannah because of what Leo did," Margaret said. "I also lost a child. But I can't blame someone else; I can only blame God. Both my husband and I blamed God. We're separated now because we couldn't get past blaming God."

"I didn't know that. I'm so sorry. I had no idea. When was this?"

"A couple of years ago."

"Tell me about her."

"My daughter?"

"Yes, tell me all about her. What did she look like? What was she like? Did she look like you? I want to know all about my little grandniece, every detail."

Margaret talked about Aislin then, beginning with her birth after so many years of trying, and ending with the midnight ride to the hospital. It felt good to talk about her with someone who genuinely wanted to know. Her aunt nodded every so often and smiled on occasion. Normally when people heard she had lost a child, they quickly changed the subject. No one ever asked her *about* Aislin, about what she was like. Telling the story of her daughter made her relive the good parts as well as the bad. In the end there were tears on both of their faces.

Her aunt said, "Your mother couldn't get past her own daughter's death. It killed her. This shouldn't happen to you, Margaret, not to you and Robin."

Margaret swallowed and nodded. "I've tried. Robin and I tried counseling. We met with the minister of our church, but all I could think, every time I walked into that building, was that this is God's house, the house of someone who killed my child. You wouldn't walk into a murderer's house, would you, and sit down for tea? That's the thought that came to my mind every time I walked through those doors. I quit going to church. Robin kept going. In his family it's sort of expected. But I wouldn't. So that became another black mark against me, another wall. We had everything. Meg, why did God do this to me?"

"These are hard questions, Margaret, and the answers are equally difficult."

"And I suppose you, like everyone else, are going to talk to me about the *sovereignty* of God — whatever that word means, as if saying that word exonerates him for all the evil in the world — and how her death was all for the best and how everything works together for good. And here's another one — my struggles make me learn something so that I can help other people who are going through the same thing. My question is, why do all those *other* people have to go through it in the first place?"

Meg shook her head. "No, I wasn't going to say that. I've been through too much to glibly give the easy answers. Losing Peter was a great sorrow to me." She hugged her arms around her. The midafternoon sun was struggling to filter through the clouds. "All of us are going to die. I will die, you will die, Robin will die. A hundred years from now none of us presently living on this planet will be here. This whole community will be populated by different people in different

273

houses with different families all facing different concerns. Death pervades every cell of our being, Margaret. It's with us from the moment we are born, hanging over us like a cloud. Death is what keeps us fearful and afraid to love — a young wife waiting for her husband to get home through a snow-storm, the call from the hospital that a child has been in an accident, a lump found on the body, a cough that cannot be explained. It's everywhere, and it's so much a part of our thinking and our being that we've no conception of a world without death. We cannot even imagine it."

Margaret stared past her aunt and through the window at the gray autumn earth, dying now, as it did every fall, red and yellow leaves clinging to branches, a last desperate grasp at color before they fell to their deaths. Even now there were leaves on the ground, mingled with brown grass and gathered in muddy clumps along the fence.

Meg said, "Every once in a while we can see God's creative power — a mountain meadow, the smile on a baby's face, the look between two lovers, the sun through stained glass. These are the things of God; these are the things that shine through the evil. God is not the author of death." She spoke slowly and Margaret listened. She was the child again, sitting in the front room at Coffins Reach so wanting to understand the deep, profound sayings of her aunt. "There are two realities: the reality of a creative God and the reality of a death-filled world. There are two forces at work in this fallen world. The remarkable truth is that the reality of God shines through the reality of death and darkness. On the other side of the stained-glass window there is light. On the other side of death there is life, an existence beyond the grave for God's people." She paused. "You had some happy times, didn't you? There was a glow in your eyes when you talked about Aislin; there is a glow in your eyes still when you speak of Robin."

"Yes, he's quite . . ." She didn't say it.

"You love him very much, but death has separated you. Death keeps some people from loving, the fear of it. You've had happiness with Aislin and Robin. You know what happiness is like, but I fear you're going to be afraid to love again, like your mother. She was afraid to love you too much after Norma Ann died. Did you know that? And the sad irony is that in the end she lost you anyway. Don't be afraid to love Robin again."

Margaret rose and stood by the window, her back to her aunt, and said, "There's another person now, a man I'm attracted to. He's funny and smart. Maybe the part of my life with Robin is over. Maybe it's time for me to move on."

"I'm not going to tell you what to do, but I would not turn to this new person before seeing if there is anything salvageable between you and Robin. You love him still very much, and I'd hate to see you throw that away. And you need to be careful to make peace with your past, or you'll take all of those problems with you."

Margaret faced her aunt and put her hands on her hips and smiled. "How did you get to be so wise?"

Meg shook her head. "I'm not wise. I still struggle with what happened to Norma Ann, to your mother. I suppose I will until I can stand in heaven and ask why. And then, maybe then it won't matter. A little girl . . ." Her voice faltered and she looked away. "A little girl who prayed that God would end her pain, make her abuser stop. How could a kind, loving God ignore that? You or I would go out of our way to see that that doesn't happen to any child." Meg stopped, her voice caught. When she was ready to go on she said, "I live my days reading, attending church, having lunch with friends, discussing books, working on my weavings. I have a good life here. But that part of it, the Ochs part, is always there in the background. I've never told any of my new friends here about it. I haven't gone to my minister about it, partly because I know what he would tell me, that Leo must be stopped — no telling how many other young girls he has molested. He would say that I must do this, not for the sake of revenge, but to protect the innocent. He would also tell me that I must make peace with what has happened to my family. There are times when I feel that I am over this, and then there are times when I'm filled with a rage still. I lost my sister Hannah because of him."

"I remember when you stayed with us when my mother was dying."

"I was so angry then. I must have come across as very stern."

Margaret smiled. "Sometimes."

"When Peter died I had to come to some peace in my soul or I would be destroyed, like Hannah, like Mitch. I began seeking God, wondering if there was some power outside of myself. I did find that God, but not in the way I expected. I expected a great thunderous, miraculous acknowledging that he was in control. I think I expected some voice from heaven, I'm not sure. Instead, I learned who he is by sitting quietly beside a stained-glass window."

Margaret looked at her. "You talked about a window."

"The stained glass, no matter how magnificent the artist, would be empty without the light shining through it. It's as if God the Light shines through all the fumbling beauty we try to create. Your artwork, Margaret — I trust you're still painting?"

Margaret nodded.

Her aunt continued, "When we paint our scenes with watercolors and oils, when we arrange colored glass in frames, when we carve little soldiers in minute detail, when we weave

276

our fabrics from yarns and threads, we are participating in the creative act of the Almighty, we're partnering with him in creation. Did you know that?"

Margaret nodded, yet not entirely understanding.

"God is a creative God," Meg said. "He's not the author of the evil that denies life. Death and rape and suicide and sickness and famine and all of the unspeakably evil things that go on in our world are an affront to God's beauty and creativity. I realized all of this when I sat beside the church window." She took another sip of her tea.

It was quiet for a moment. Then Margaret said, "Tell me about my Uncle Clark."

"He was the youngest of the boys. Did you know we went to art school together?"

Margaret shook her head. The whole thing was just too unbelievable.

"He was very talented, a kind, gentle, trusting soul; perhaps that's where his problem stemmed. He was too trusting, too naive. He and I used to have long talks. When he started dating Pat, I thought to myself, this is the beginning of the end for him. She was one of those self-absorbed society women. For the life of me I don't know how they got together. Monty knew Pat. I think he arranged it somehow. We talked about her, too, he and I. I think he was overwhelmed with that Hollywood type of blond beauty."

"I can't believe this about Clark. This is so strange."

"Would you like more tea, Margaret? I could put on another pot." Her aunt rose.

"Do you have coffee?"

"I might have some instant in a cupboard somewhere; let me look."

Margaret followed her into the kitchen, where Meg put on the kettle and found a small bottle of very unpromising looking instant coffee granules. "I was like the sister Clark never had, and he was like my brother. It was through our friendship that your father met my sister. I knew all of the Ochses back then. Even Leo."

"What was Leo like?"

She paused, hesitated. "Your Uncle Leo has always been a driven individual, a perfectionist. And I believe your grandfather had a lot to do with turning him into the manipulative, controlling, unhappy man that he is today. I told you I used to feel sorry for Clark, but I think the person I felt the most sorry for in those early days was Leo. Nothing he ever did was good enough for his father." Meg poured the boiling water over the coffee granules. It had that instant coffee smell that Margaret detested, but she'd drink it anyway. "But I firmly believe this gives him no excuse for what he did. He has made his own choices and he made bad ones."

Margaret looked down into the dark liquid in her cup, a new thought entering her mind. Quietly she said, "Robin and I have never had a lot of money. It's always been a struggle. And then suddenly I have all of this money. All to myself. I'm an independent woman. When I found out I had inherited this house, I came down here and opened a bank account with this huge inheritance. I keep buying things. Now I find it has all come from Leo." She put her hand to her mouth.

"I have money, Margaret. It's just me. I have my teacher's pension, and this place is paid for. None of it, thankfully, has come from Leo Ochs. I could help you."

"I couldn't take your money."

"Consider it a loan, then."

Twilight was descending. The two Margarets had spent the entire day in conversation. "He should be stopped," Margaret said. "Maybe together we could do something." She hesitated. "I have a friend, a detective, who might be able to help."

FIFTY-SIX

Donna was sitting very still in a straight-back chair against the door of her father's study. No one knew she was there. She was supposed to be at the store, but had left work early because of a migraine and had come into this room because the lights were dim and the leather furniture soothed her. When she had heard her father and her uncles enter the dining room just beyond, she had taken a seat beside the door.

She had been doing this all her life, sitting quietly, listening, learning. It's how she learned about Bradley; it's how she learned about what really happened to Norma Ann.

She could hear her Uncle Clark's voice. That she was sure of, but he sounded different today. Usually he never said much of anything, just kind of stood around the store, getting out of her way when she passed. Now he was in there talking loudly, sounding confident and in control of himself.

"It's my turn now, O elder brother," she could hear him say.

Her Uncle Leo said, "Your turn for what?"

"My turn to get my fair share that I've been cheated out of all these years."

Leo grunted, laughed. "And what makes you think you've been cheated for all these years?"

She could hear the stomping of feet. "Oh, don't give me that! I wasn't born yesterday."

"We bought out your shares fair and square, Clark." Her father was talking now. "There was even a lawyer there if you'll remember."

Clark spat, "Yeah, one in your pocket, no doubt. And Monty, don't think I don't know about you and Pat carrying on all these years."

"What 'all these years'? Your wife's a fat cow."

Donna could hear the sounds of a scuffle. Don't tell me Clark is standing up for his wife's honor, she thought, smirking.

She heard nothing for a while, and she wondered if they had gone. She was about to get up and walk through the door when she heard the shuffling of papers and Clark's voice. "It's my turn," he was saying. "I've got stuff here a mile high. So you've been blackmailing people? I can do the same. And you're first on my list."

"Blackmail is a dangerous game, little brother of mine," Leo said.

"Nevertheless, I have documents here that I'm sure you'll pay a pretty penny for once you see them. And these, my friend, are photocopies. You can be sure the originals are somewhere safely stashed away. I'm not that stupid."

"What have you got?" This came from Monty.

"Just proof that our Leo has been blackmailing just about anyone who wields any power. You think this little empire was built on business skills and hard work? Forget it."

"How'd you get this stuff?" asked Monty.

"I have my ways."

"The mysterious detective," Leo said. "So what fly-by-night detective agency did you hire for this, Clark?"

"You and Margaret are in on this," Monty added.

"Me and Margaret?" Clark sounded genuinely surprised.

"Don't play with us, Clark," Leo said. "She's all the time been seen with that — what's-his-face guy — Christian Rikken, the cop turned detective who was there when the little girl went head-over-teakettle off the porch."

"She has? Well, he wasn't the one I hired. I had a different guy."

"Yeah, right." Leo was still talking. "My sources tell me the two of them, him and Margaret, are really tight these days."

Margaret and a detective? Donna thought. Whoa, didn't take her long to get over loverboy from Canada.

Clark's voice had taken on a whiny tone, and Donna could barely hear what he was saying. "You want to see what I got or not? And this isn't all. He's getting more stuff, too. He's not finished."

Leo said, "I might as well take a look at the pack of lies that detective dug up for you." Donna heard papers shuffling. "Oh lookee here, the mayor. Oh my, you've been a busy bee, little Clark."

Donna put her hand over her mouth. She was going to sneeze. Please, don't sneeze, she told herself. Not now.

"Oh, this is rich; ain't this rich, Monty? Blackmail the mayor of Bosuns Harbor, the police commissioner. Oh, I'm shaking in my boots over this one. Can't you see me shaking in my boots? Besides being a pack of lies you and Margaret dug up, these things'll never fly."

Donna sneezed. She couldn't help it.

A minute later, her father and her two uncles were standing over her, staring down to where she sat small and scrunched-up in the chair. Even though the three of them were there, the only face she saw was Leo's looking down at her, leering. The way he used to.

"You heard all of that, I suppose," he said. She stared into his broad red face.

He waggled his finger at her. "Let me tell you something, girlie, any word of what you heard and you'll end up just like that cousin of yours."

He bent down until his red, bulbous face was inches from hers, his breath on her face. She stared hard at him, right into those small, phlegmy eyes. Then she pursed her lips and spat square into his face.

FIFTY-SEVEN

When Chris got back to his boat late that night there was a strange, cryptic message from Margaret on his machine. "Chris? This is Margaret. I don't want to leave the number here, but we need your advice and help on a very important matter. I feel funny calling you after our last time together, but this is so urgent I have to put all that aside and tell you that we really need you. Remember I told you where I was? Well, that's where I am. And we'd like you to come here as soon as you can if you're not busy. It's an urgent matter. I don't know if I should keep calling. So I'll just leave this message once and pray you get it. We have a room made up for you here. Please come."

He left the following morning at seven. It didn't take him long to throw a few clothes into a duffel bag, unplug and pack up his computer and modem, and lock up his boat. On the way out of town he deposited the check Clark had given him in the bank machine — that would keep him in groceries for the next little while — and took out a hundred in cash. He also stopped at a convenience store, bought about a dozen juice boxes of varying flavors, and then stopped at a Dunkin' Donuts for half a dozen muffins.

He had to admit the thought of seeing Margaret was brightening this somewhat gray day. He headed out Route 3 to Augusta and switched on the radio. For about an hour he hummed along to his favorite oldies station, but as he passed though Augusta and beyond, the music crackled and faded. He eventually found a talk show where three individuals were hotly debating gun control. After a few moments of that, he turned to a light rock FM station that was featuring five-in-a-row love songs. Great, thought Chris, just what I need. He thought about Margaret. It wasn't the first time in his life he had misread the signals. He'd had a whole marriage of misreading the signals.

Halfway through a Rod Stewart tune, he decided he really didn't need a marathon of love songs to remind him of what he didn't have. He moved back to the radio debate.

The trees lining the highway were fully clothed in their fall garb of red and yellow. At least it was a pretty drive. That he had packed up so quickly and left surprised even him. Why Margaret wanted him there was unimportant. That she wanted him there would be enough for now.

The day passed in a driving haze, stopping at roadside turnoffs for greasy burgers and fries and gassing up at expensive highway stations.

Early evening he arrived in New York, and called the Mahone number from his cellular and got directions. Not long after, he pulled up behind Margaret's car.

She met him at the door, worry furrowing her brow. "I'm so glad you could come," she said.

Margaret's aunt stood behind her, a pretty woman in her late fifties with soft brown hair, flecked with light gray. The introductions were made, and Margaret's aunt, who asked him to please call her Meg, led him to a bedroom on the main floor, where a single quilt-covered bed lay beneath a large window that opened into the front yard. A family of teddy bears sat on the floor in the corner.

"There's a small bathroom just to the right. Margaret was in this room, but she and I have moved upstairs. The whole downstairs is yours. Fresh towels are in the bathroom closet."

"Thank you."

He unpacked quickly and washed up in the postage-stamp-sized bathroom. He looked at the old-fashioned claw-footed bathtub and decided it looked shorter than a regular tub. As if the single bed wasn't bad enough for his large frame.

Margaret's aunt insisted that he eat something before they talked, and so he ate — roast chicken, mashed potatoes, peas and salad, a dinner fit for a king. And he still didn't know why he was here.

Finally, the dishes cleared and washed, and cups of coffee or tea in hand, the three of them made their way to the living room.

"The reason we wanted you to come here," Meg began, "is that we need someone we can trust. My niece said we can trust you. We must move carefully in this; we don't want one slip-up."

"The thing is," Margaret said, "we have to get Leo Ochs put behind bars."

"Leo Ochs?"

Meg opened up an old-fashioned school binder that had been sitting on the coffee table and explained that this was Norma Ann's diary. She told him about Leo Ochs's penchant for young teen girls, about Norma Ann's pregnancy, and about Margaret's mother's death. He skimmed through the book, and Meg pointed out more salient passages. In the end she said, "What we want to know is, will this book stand up in court?"

"I would say so," he said, rubbing his chin. This guy was a worse sleazebag than he had first thought. "Leo Ochs is as slick as anyone I've seen." He told them what he had uncovered about Leo's various blackmailing schemes, ending with, "What would help is testimony, people to come forward and testify that he has abused them." He turned to Meg. "You say you think Donna was abused. Do you know this for sure? Do you think she might testify against her uncle?"

"First of all," Margaret said, "we're only guessing that she was abused. And secondly, she's a total basket case."

"I wonder why?" Meg said sarcastically.

Chris said, "And then there's that little matter of the break-in at your house."

Meg looked up in alarm. "What break-in?"

"I didn't tell you about that, but someone came in and walked up to my studio and placed a butcher knife through a portrait I was working on."

"How horrible!"

"To me that's a warning," Chris said. "Someone's trying to warn her away, and then that outlandish offer on her house . . ."

The older woman looked at them both again. "What outlandish offer?"

"Someone offered Margaret an unbelievable sum of money for that old house."

Margaret said, "I called the realtors and found out that the buyers wish to remain anonymous until the closing."

"I'll just bet they do," Chris said.

"Hey, it's not that bad. It's waterfront property with historical significance," she said, grinning.

"If I were back in Bangor I could find out who these mysterious buyers are," he said.

They talked together for most of the evening, and a few hours later, they had a plan pretty much worked out.

"Do you think Monty's involved, or do you think it's just Leo?" Margaret asked.

Chris shook his head. "I'm not sure. So far I only have stuff on Leo, but my intuition tells me that Monty's involved somehow. Or else why would he stay so close all these years? I just haven't figured that angle out yet."

Later Meg went upstairs to bed, and Chris and Margaret were alone in the living room. She was sitting on the couch across from him, and between them was the coffee table with the remains of their tea. The only sound in the room was time moving ahead, as the grandfather clock ticked out the moments. She looked down at her hands in her lap.

"Margaret, about the other night . . ."

"It's all right. I'm kind of skittish these days."

"I understand." He looked at her, sitting small and vulnerable on the couch, one leg pulled up underneath her, running a hand now through her hair. The clock bonged eleven times.

After it quieted she said, "I have to work things through with my past. I've been thinking about that. I have to come to some sort of terms with it before I can move on."

"I've had the skin ripped off me too, Margaret. I know these things take time."

She looked up at him. "You've lived alone all these years?"

"More or less. In the summer my girls come out, but mostly it's just me and the boat and the sky and the sea."

"You must like solitude."

"I pray for solitude."

"Do you ever get lonely?"

He looked at her, a child's innocent face asking those questions. More than anything else in the world right now he wanted to go over there and hold her, bury his face in her hair, kiss her.

He put his hands on his knees. "I've got friends in Maine. Some of the lobstermen. We play cards. I've got my work. Every winter I sail down to the Bahamas and beyond. I'll be leaving soon. I've got friends there too, part of the whole community of sailors."

She shifted her legs and studied him again. "I feel like I'm at some sort of a crossroads. I've lost my daughter. I'm no

287

longer living in Canada. I have a house down here. I could just stay here, maybe teach art, start over, start right over here. That's one choice. The other is to go back and try again with Robin. He's called me several times. My aunt says I shouldn't think about starting over with someone else." She paused and looked at him shyly. "Until I go back to Fredericton and talk everything through with Robin. Make some peace with the ghosts of my past."

"Your aunt's a very wise woman." It killed him to say it.

"That's what I told her." She paused. "What I was wondering is this." She spread her fingers out, folded her hands. "If I go home to Fredericton and find there is nothing more there between Robin and me, if that part of my life is over, well, if I came back here would you . . ." She looked at him. "Would you still be here?"

"I'd be here." He said it suddenly. "I wouldn't want it any other way."

"When this whole thing with Leo is over, I'll have to think about what to do."

"When this whole thing is over. Until then —" he put out his hand, tentatively she took it — "friends."

"Friends." She smiled at him, and her smile lit through the murky depths of his mind, his heart, through to his very soul.

FIFTY-EIGHT

At eight the following morning the three of them were in the office of Meg's church making four copies of Norma Ann's diary. The previous evening Meg had called her minister and gotten permission to use the copier. Chris kept two of the copies plus the original, one copy they left in Meg's house, and Margaret and Meg took one with them in Margaret's car. Chris left for Bangor about an hour before Margaret and her aunt were on the road.

The day-long trip gave the two women more time to talk. They talked about Leo. They talked about Hannah and about Mitch and Monty. They talked about Aislin, Meg still wanting to hear everything about her.

"You're sure I'm not boring you?" said Margaret. "I told you about her the other night. I might be repeating myself."

"Not at all," said her aunt, looking up at her from the passenger seat. "Peter and I never had any children of our own. I love listening to the antics of my nieces' and nephews' children now."

Margaret told her aunt about the time Aislin had worn her best yellow dress to school and came home with it ripped after she had gone down the playground slide numerous times. "She always wore dresses, that girl," said Margaret. "She was lucky that her aunt, Robin's sister, loved to sew for her. I couldn't get her in pants, so she would play in the sand, play in the dirt with dresses, always in dresses."

She told her aunt about the time Aislin was the angel Gabriel in the Christmas concert and wore a costume that was hopelessly too big for her. "Her arm ended before the costume did. When she stuck out her hand and said, 'Fear not,' she looked like the ghost of Christmas past."

She told her aunt about the time Aislin had picked boxes and boxes of apples at Robin's cousin's orchard in Keswick Ridge and then went around presenting gifts of apples to everyone in the neighborhood. "She was very outgoing, that girl," said Margaret. "She was so healthy and full of life . . . that's what I don't understand. She was never sick a day in her life."

They talked about Leo again, and what it might take to topple him. "I just hope we're doing the right thing," said Meg, nervously fiddling with her glasses.

"I think if anyone can pull this off it's Chris."

"You trust him, that has to be good enough for me."

Over lunch at Denny's, Meg turned to her niece and said, "He's the one, isn't he?"

"He's the one, who?"

"Chris? He's the one you were talking about, the man you're attracted to."

Margaret spread a packet of Italian dressing on her salad and looked up. "It showed?"

"Only to another woman. He's quite charming."

Margaret paused. "Right now I don't need this confusion. I came down here to escape confusion, and I've been plunged into even more confusion. I was hoping the sea would give me peace."

"The sea won't give you peace. No outside thing can give you peace, Margaret. Not pills, not sitting by the sea. Peace has to come from someplace inside of you, a place that has accepted all of the ghosts and made peace with God."

"But I'm still angry. I'm still hurt."

"I know. It's the human condition to be hurt. Some more than others."

Margaret sighed and looked at her salad. "I know you've been hurt, too." She looked up at her aunt. "Did you and Uncle Peter want children?"

Meg folded her arms on the table and looked across at her niece. "Desperately. There was a time I couldn't even talk about it. But I was chosen not to have children."

"Chosen? An odd word."

"It took me a long time to accept it. Sometimes I still don't."

"I know how you feel."

Meg reached her hand across the table and found Margaret's. "We women of the Whyte clan, we're not a very fertile bunch, are we?"

"Anna Coffin didn't have children either. Maybe that's part of the curse."

Meg leaned back. "I've heard the Anna Coffin story, but what's this about a curse?"

"Anna Coffin cursed my house just before she committed suicide. Her body washed up on shore, and then it was lost. No one has ever found where she's buried."

"So now she's an unburied ghost that goes around cursing inanimate objects like houses."

"Exactly. You sound skeptical. Like Roland."

"Who's Roland?"

"A friend of mine. He doesn't believe in anything."

"Everybody believes in something," Meg said.

After lunch they drove, and in an hour her aunt was reading, absorbed in the book of short stories Margaret had brought, proclaiming some of them very good. "I'm going to have to bring this one up at my book discussion group," she said at one point.

While Meg continued to read, Margaret turned on the radio and listened to quiet music. The trees along the highway blazed with color, as if the entire hillside were in flames. It made her think of Robin. Every fall she and Robin would drive up the St. John River to take pictures of the fall leaves. She would always bring along her sketch pad and often her paints. They would make a day of it, packing ham sandwiches on crusty buns, granola bars, and slices of apple pie that Robin's mother made. Sometimes they would stay overnight, stopping at bed-and-breakfasts along the way. The first time they did this, they had only been married a year. It was an extraordinarily warm day in late September when Robin came home from work on a Friday and said, "Let's go."

A few hours later they stopped at Woolastook Provincial Park and watched two sailboats on the Headpond, a place where the river widened above the dam. They sat at a picnic table in the deserted campgrounds and ate their picnic supper, the sun on their backs.

The trees along the bank were a conflagration of color that striated the blue water with lines of red and gold, orange and brown. The sailboats took on these hues as they glided in and out of the fiery ribbons.

She said, "Sometimes reality is stranger than fiction. We only have an illusion of what is real, when in actual fact what is really there often cannot be believed. If I were to paint that picture exactly as it is, no one would believe that it was real. They would all think I was doing an abstract, a representation of something real." She paused. "Maybe nothing is real. Maybe everything is just a representation."

Robin took a whole roll of film of the boats, the lake, the trees, and soaked his feet as he stood at the edge of the lake. They held hands as they walked along the water's edge. They swam naked in the river and dried off later in the sun.

When evening came they drove north and stayed in a bed-and-breakfast in Hartland. They spent the evening in the living room of the old house with the proprietors, a retired couple named Jed and Irna O'Malley, who sat on the couch across from them. A wood fire crackled, and Jed told them that "he and the missus" had moved here from Nova Scotia seven years ago "to be near the kids." Jed's hobby was model boats, especially tall ships. His masterpiece, a wooden replica of the *Bluenose*, stood proudly on the mantel. It took him three years to make that one, he said. Irna, his wife, served them fresh apple crisp with cream on white-and-blue china plates.

That Margaret would think of that time, that time before Aislin, surprised her. Because Aislin had been a part of every memory that she and Robin clung to, it seemed wrong somehow to think of a time without her.

"Are you afraid?" Margaret asked when she and her aunt stopped for coffee.

"I wouldn't be honest if I said I wasn't."

Margaret knew that her aunt had called her minister to pray for them. She had heard her the previous evening on the phone. "The details are very confidential at the moment, but it concerns a very grave family matter, a criminal matter."

Margaret said, "I just wish we could do something. We should be doing something rather than just sitting still and letting Chris do everything."

"Chris said to keep still," Meg reminded her. "We're not to raise suspicions."

As they passed through Bangor, Margaret said, "When this thing is over we must keep in touch."

"It would disappoint me if we just kept in touch," Meg said. "I would like us to be friends. I'd love to come to Fredericton in the summer. I've heard it's very beautiful there."

"You're so sure I'm going to go back there?"

"I think that place is in your blood."

They arrived at Margaret's house in Coffins Reach early that evening. When they got out, even before Margaret unlocked the door of the house, Meg walked down toward the gray sea and spread her arms wide. "Oh, this is glorious, this smell. How could I have left it!"

Fog obscured the view to Dragon Back Island. The water was a dark gelatinous mass wrinkled with ripples.

"Christ walked on the water," said her aunt. "It almost looks as if it would be firm enough to walk across tonight, doesn't it?"

It began to rain softly.

"Do you remember the storm?" said Meg, making no move to go inside. "You must have been around eight at the time, Margaret. It was a hurricane; I can't remember which one, wish I could. But I do remember standing right here on this spot while the winds blew mercilessly. The waves were as high and as forceful as I've ever seen them. But I felt rooted to this spot. It was so majestic. Your Uncle Peter had to literally carry me inside. And then all of us — you, your sister, me, Peter, your mother and your father — stood in the bay window and watched."

"I don't remember that."

When they finally went to unload the car, Ruth Godwish, her yellow slicker flying out behind her, rushed toward them, hands waving wildly.

"Bradley went missing!" she yelled.

"Bradley?" Margaret asked.

"He's gone. I don't know where he is!"

Her little face was screwed into determination and her eyes were glistening and wet.

"Mrs. Godwish, when was the last time you saw him?"

"Did you take him? I wouldn't put it past you and that detective."

"No, of course not."

"Then where is he?"

"I don't know. Why don't you come in out of the rain? This is my Aunt Meg from New York state. Come in, I'll make a nice pot of coffee and we'll try to figure this out. When was the last time you saw him?"

Ruth, sniveling and small, rushed into Margaret's kitchen, talking and sobbing into the Kleenex Margaret handed her. The bright yellow child's raincoat made her face look sallow and gray. Her matted hair was caught back loosely in a red rubber band.

"Ruth," said Meg, "Margaret and I will help you find Bradley. So, now when was the last time you saw him?"

"This morning. This morning when he boarded the bus for the ceramics workshop."

"Did you call Arnie?" Margaret said.

"Yes. He said Bradley never arrived at the workshop. And those idiots over there never even called me to tell me. I didn't know he was gone until he didn't arrive home this evening. When I called those people they said he never showed up! And they never called me!"

"Did they say why they didn't call you?"

"Arnie said it was because Bradley misses so much they figured he was just missing again."

"But he got on the bus to go in the morning?" asked Meg.

"Yes, he did. I saw him off myself. I watched him get on."

"Did you call the police?"

"The police cannot be trusted. They have proved that to me."

"Have you called anyone?" Margaret asked. "Does anyone else know he's missing?"

295

"You are the only ones."

"But you definitely saw him get on the bus?" Meg said.

"Are you accusing me of lying?"

"Did you call the bus driver? Did he see Bradley get off at any stops?"

"Arnie said he called the bus driver. The bus driver let him off at the ceramic factory."

Meg shook her head. "Now that is odd. So he must've gone somewhere after he got off at the ceramic factory. What do you make of that, Margaret?"

Ruth looked at Margaret and with real pleading in her eyes, said, "Can you please help me find my son? There are people who have wanted to take him from me from the moment he was born to me."

Margaret looked at the curious little woman, crouched small and fearful in her kitchen chair, her yellow slicker still on, the metal catches fastened at her neck.

"We will help you, Ruth," said Meg softly.

The two men, Chris and his friend Bill, were seated in a back booth of a coffee shop about half a mile from the Bangor police station. On the table in front of them was Norma Ann's diary, the original, plus all of the things he had unearthed for Clark.

"There's a lot here," said Bill, leafing through the stack of papers.

"I'd like you to set in motion the process that would arrest this sack of horse manure."

"We need people who will testify against him. Have you talked to any of these people he's blackmailed?"

Chris shook his head. "Blackmail victims don't often like to come forward, that's why they're so easy to blackmail."

Bill leafed through the collection of papers and bank statements and letters. "We'll have to find someone."

"I'll find them. I'll work around the clock on this. If I get them, can you get this dirtbag?"

Bill took all of the files, folding them and placing them back inside the manila envelope. "Consider it done," he said.

FIFTY-NINE

It had been relatively easy, reflected Donna, to get Bradley to come with her. He just got off the bus at the ceramic factory, walked in, walked through to the back where Donna was outside motioning. He walked right through the back door and into Donna's car, which was idling quietly. No one saw them. She made sure of that. Arnie and the other workers were still out front helping the wheelchair patrons from the bus, while Donna waited along the side. When everyone was safely inside, she sped out the front way.

Donna had packed a duffel bag for herself and had brought along a few things for Bradley — toothpaste, tooth-brush, comb. She had withdrawn all of her money out of her account. When they got to where they were going, Donna would buy him all new things.

She felt stronger now. She had felt strong ever since the night she'd spat into the face of her abuser. But when she had seen her spittle dripping down his nose, seen the surprised eyes, she knew she couldn't stay. She had heard too much. She knew too much. Leo would find some way to punish her, and she wouldn't stick around to find out what he planned to do. Leaving, driving on unfamiliar highways, risking the de-bilitating migraines, the fearful fluttering of her heart, would be better than staying. She knew he wouldn't rape her any-more; that much she knew. He only liked "sweet young things." And Donna was neither sweet nor young. Leo had seen to that. After being repeatedly raped in junior high school, something in her had snapped. In high school she had the reputation of being fast and easy, and many a teen boy had his first experience with Donna Ochs. After high school she prostituted herself for countless men in bars and in hotels until she didn't know herself anymore, and ran screaming down the beach, ending up on Rusty MacGregor's back step. She was hospitalized for a long time with "depression and anxiety." Years of therapy had not gotten rid of the hard, black part of herself that she kept hidden and tightly clenched.

But now she was going to do one good thing. She was going to leave. But leaving without Bradley was incomprehensible. She'd head west, away from the ocean, get as far away from the ocean as possible. For Bradley's sake.

They had spent that first day in the airport, a familiar place where she could gather her strength for the trip. "Did we come to watch the planes?" said Bradley at one point. Donna nodded. "Watching the planes," she said. They spent their first night at the Scotsman Inn in two rooms side by side.

The following morning she knew they would have to leave today. It wouldn't be too long before someone would come looking. She had driven through Bangor and was on the outskirts of the city when fear overcame her. She had no maps with her, and no understanding of what lay beyond the city limits. When she came to an intersection she slowed the car and pulled over.

"Where are we going?" Bradley asked.

"Somewhere far away from the ocean."

"Why, Donna?"

"No one's going to hurt us anymore, Bradley." She paused. "But I don't know where to go. I don't know what to do now." She was practically in tears.

He pointed to a highway sign. I-95 North, it read. "Why don't we go that way?"

Donna steered the car slowly onto the on-ramp. "This will be fine, Bradley. I'll follow your lead. You just tell me the roads to take and we'll take them."

He smiled, in his round doughboy face. "An adventure," he said.

"Yes, an adventure."

But as Donna drove north on the strange highway, she could hardly keep her hands from shaking as she held the steering wheel. She could feel her heart beating wildly in her chest. She could die here. Die right here on the highway, killing both of them as the car swerved out of control. Be strong, she told herself, clinging to the steering wheel as if it might fly away under its own power. Be strong for Bradley's sake. You're finally doing one good thing for you and for him. After all these years of pain. You're going to make things right for you and for him. Be strong, Donna. Be strong.

SIXTY

"I can make your life exceedingly miserable," Leo said to Clark that afternoon in the store. Clark was in the coffee room heating up a fast-food burrito in the microwave when Leo walked over to him and said that.

Clark just shrugged. He had been so confident before, as if he were going to finally get things to go his way. Clark never did figure out how Leo turned that around. But Leo had a way of turning everything around to his advantage.

"I just want to know one thing before I leave. Who was the detective you and Margaret hired for this?"

Clark shrugged his shoulders and said nothing. Leo grabbed him fiercely and spun him around, causing Clark to drop his burrito. It splattered all over the floor.

"Now look what you made me do," Clark said.

"It was that guy on the boat? Right? It was him? Right? That what you're going to tell me? Well, we went over that boat, every inch of it, and I never found anything pertaining to these crazy things you're accusing me of. He's not there, by the way, and, oh yeah, Margaret's gone, too. Away, no doubt, for some tryst."

Clark could not look his brother in the eye. "Maybe that wasn't the guy I used," he said, wetting some paper towels underneath the tap.

"If you don't tell me who it was, I can cut your measly pay-check in half, and don't think I won't."

A niggling worry began as a small pain in Clark's stomach. Leo was wrong about one thing. It was Pat who could make his life exceedingly miserable, not Leo. Clark still had the papers the detective had given him, but he had lied when he said he had made copies. They were folded in a box in his shed behind the lawn mower, underneath a whole bunch of tools. He hadn't decided what he was going to do with them. Go to the police? But who there? Half of the force was being blackmailed by Leo, the other half was on his payroll.

"Anyone who tries to cross me," Leo said, "anyone who accuses me of the stuff you're accusing me of — and that includes Margaret and her detective friend — anyone who tries to cross me gets put out of the picture permanently."

Clark said nothing, just wiped up the spilled burrito.

SIXTY-ONE

An hour north of Bangor Donna was calming down. Slowly the panicky feeling was leaving, giving way to a steadiness that surprised her. Bradley was singing Beatles songs to her that he'd memorized. His voice was clear and on key.

"We all live in a yellow submarine, a yellow submarine, a yellow submarine . . ."

He stopped at one point and she said, "Keep singing, Bradley, please keep singing. It makes me feel better."

Then he smiled at her and sang his way through all of the Beatles songs he knew, then went on to other melodies.

"I'll give you a daisy a day, dear, I'll give you a daisy a day. I'll love you until the rivers run still. And the four winds we know blow away . . ."

"Will I see you in September or lose you to a summer love . . ."

He sang for her until his voice grew hoarse and Donna felt more steady at the wheel. North of Bangor the traffic thinned; only the occasional car passed her in the double lane. They took the exit to Howland and stopped at a roadside truck stop. She and Bradley sat in a booth by the window and ordered coffees. She bought a hamburger for Bradley and ordered a salad for herself. Their waitress was a short, round woman wearing a stained, white apron, who wrote their orders down on a little pad. They were the only ones in the restaurant. Donna didn't even know what time it was.

"Excuse me," said Donna as their waitress began to walk away.

"Yes?"

"Are we in Maine? Is this Maine?"

The woman looked at her, surprised. "Yes, this is Maine."

"Well, where does the road go?"

"North on I-95?"

"Yeah, this road."

"Clear up to Houlton and then on into Canada. Where are you headed?"

"The end of the road," said Donna.

The woman looked at her curiously and then took their orders into the kitchen.

Canada! They could go to Canada! She wondered how far it was, and what it was like there. They would keep driving.

"We got to get you some clothes, Bradley."

He looked at her surprised. "I have clothes, Donna."

"You need clothes here. I'll have to buy them for you. You need clean clothes; you can't keep wearing the same clothes every day."

"I could go home and get them. We could go home and get them. I have clothes at home, Donna."

"We'll get new clothes. Maybe we'll get you some clothes in Canada. Canadian clothes."

"Canadian clothes?"

"Yeah. But I don't know how far Canada is. Maybe we better get them here . . . and a razor, too. You can pick that out. Unless you want to grow a beard."

"I have a razor at home, Donna."

"I know, Bradley, but we'll get you a new one."

When the waitress came with their plates of food, Donna asked her if there was a place in town where they could buy some men's clothes. The waitress wrote down on a piece of paper the name and address of a shop and handed it to her. "That's the best place. Not much to say for the outside of it, but you can really get some bargains in there."

After lunch, they parked in front of Apex Clothiers. Like the waitress said, it didn't look like much. Stacks of shirts and boxes of shoes and boots lined the walls. Bins of underwear and socks sat edge to edge in the middle, and everywhere were jammed racks of shirts, pants, jeans, and work clothes. It looked as though it had been lifted from the 1940s and placed here in this little Maine town. Orders were rung up on an old-fashioned cash register at the wooden counter.

An man about Donna's age approached them. "What can I help you with today?"

"My, uh, my friend needs some clothes."

He sized Bradley up. "What kind of clothes?"

"Maybe a couple shirts, pants. Everything."

"Probably an extra-large then. Well, let's get you outfitted."

Half an hour later Bradley and Donna left with three new shirts, two pairs of jeans, socks, underwear, boots, a jacket, gloves, a scarf, and earmuffs. Donna thought it might be cold in Canada.

Their next stop was a drugstore, where they bought a brand-new rechargeable electric razor, toothpaste, shampoo, and assorted items of makeup for Donna, plus cans of pop, bags of chips, and chocolate bars.

Back in the car, Donna placed her head on the steering wheel. She felt shaky and uncertain, exhausted from the shopping. Her heart was pounding in her chest. She said, "Bradley, when we get back on the highway, will you sing to me like before?"

"You're my friend, Donna," he said, but he didn't sing. Instead he fell into a comfortable snoring afternoon nap in the passenger seat. She panicked momentarily. What if she had a heart attack? What if something happened to the car?

She learned in the next few minutes that if you kept your eyes on the road, and your thoughts only on the destination, mile after mile, it became easier.

SIXTY-TWO

It had been a day and a half since Bradley was last seen. When Margaret had called Arnie yesterday, he told her he had not seen Bradley, nor had any of the volunteers and staff. And since Ruth absolutely refused police involvement, Margaret and her aunt were at a standstill. In the morning they had driven very slowly through the streets of Coffins Reach and Bosuns Harbor, but they did not see him. Ruth gave them a photo of Bradley, and they showed it around, but no one had seen the man in the red sweatshirt, blue jeans and red, velcro-fastened sneakers.

Partway through the afternoon, Arnie called Margaret.

He said, "I was getting a little concerned here, so I put in a few more calls to some of the clients. One of the clients said she saw Bradley walk through the back door and get into a car with Donna."

"So he's with Donna."

"It looks that way."

"Thanks, Arnie. I'll tell Ruth."

When Margaret and Meg took that news to Ruth's back door, the woman screwed up her face and pointed her finger at the sky. "He can't be with Donna. She will ruin him! She will fill his mind with all sorts of unspeakable lies."

"Maybe, Ruth, it's time we called the police," said Meg gently.

"Never! Never, never, never, never." Ruth shut the door, shutting them out. They looked at each other and went back to Margaret's house.

Back in her kitchen, Margaret said, "Boy, is she a strange one."

Meg shook her head. "She's had a lot of pain in her life."

"How do you know that?"

"Her face. What is her story?"

"I don't know that she has a story. It's always been just her and Bradley living there for as far back as I can remember." Margaret stopped and said, "I have an idea. I'm going to call my Aunt Sylvia. If he's with Donna, maybe Sylvia might know something."

Sylvia told her she had no idea where Bradley was, and what in the world would give Margaret the impression that she would know anything about the whereabouts of Bradley in the first place?

"He got in Donna's car yesterday. Someone saw that."

"Then as soon as Donna gets home, I will ask her if she knows where Bradley is."

"Do you know where Donna is?"

"Of course I know where Donna is," she snapped.

After she hung up, Margaret turned to her aunt. "She acted real strange. I'd like to go over there and talk to her in person, face-to-face. See what she knows."

On the way to Bosuns Harbor, Meg said, "What do we do if Leo's there?"

Margaret turned the windshield wipers on high as they sped through the rain. "We act as nice as pie. Remember, you're just here for a nice little auntly visit. Nothing more."

"He's going to see me and know something's up."

"No, he won't. Before I knew this about him, he was charming and friendly. That night that I was broken into, he played the part of the concerned uncle, making sure the locks were fixed and bolted, making sure everything was all right. He and Monty stayed for an hour after the police left, cleaning up, checking all of the windows, telling me to bolt everything twice from the inside."

"How nice of them, since he was probably the one who did it."

Margaret turned to her aunt. "You think Leo ruined my painting?"

Meg shrugged. "Who else?"

"That thought hadn't occurred to me."

"Think about it. You said he removed the knife, right? Got his prints all over it so it would confuse the police?"

Margaret shook her head. "This is becoming so bizarre. But what if I had called the police before Leo had a chance to put his hands on the knife?"

"I'm sure he would've found a way to get there first. He's a dangerous man. You said your aunt called, right? At the precise moment that you found the knife? Maybe that was a little too convenient."

"That's what Chris said."

Halfway to Bosuns Harbor, Meg whispered, "Maybe you'd better drive me back to your house."

"Aunt Meg, you're shivering. Are you okay?"

"There something I didn't tell you."

"I don't know if I want to hear this."

"I need to tell you why I'm afraid to see Leo Ochs. I need to tell you about the last time I saw him. At Hannah's funeral."

As she listened to her aunt's story, Margaret's mind went back to the day of her mother's funeral. She had been twelve at the time, scared and uncertain of life with this stranger who was her father. What would the years be like without her mother in the bedroom, without her Aunt Meg making meals and doing the laundry?

Following the service, a reception had been held in the

309

basement room of the church that Hannah was a part of. It surprised Margaret to hear from Meg that her mother was a part of a church. At the time of the funeral, she hadn't paid much attention to where it was held and why. As far as she could remember, her mother never went to church in those days, just stuck to her bed most of the time. But here was her aunt telling her that a pastor visited regularly, read Scriptures to her, and that the pastor's wife gave her a Bible. She would make Meg read parts to her, especially the Psalms.

Meg, however, had wanted nothing to do with her sister's newfound religion and told her so. How could she love a God who took her daughter and who created monsters like Leo Ochs?

"I found those answers later," Meg said, "but too late to pass them on to my sister. Hannah was one of those precious, sensitive people. She felt things. I always had to think everything through before I allowed myself to feel. Still do. She felt first and then thought about it later."

During the funeral Meg could barely hold her anger in; it swelled in her soul and body like a malignant sore. She could eat nothing at the reception, but stood against the back wall, dressed head to foot in black. She spoke to no one, accepted no one's comfort. She was especially enraged at the Ochs brothers and their wives and children, who seemed to take over the place with their boisterous prattle and laughter. Their children chased after each other in and out of the Sunday school classrooms, while their parents filled their plates with cheese buns and bread-and-butter pickles, and chatted about the weather.

Even Peter could not get through to his grieving wife that day, and his offers of tea or punch were met with silent shakes of her head. The only Ochs to appear confused was Mitch, who sat on a chair, large square hands folded in his lap. Perhaps Mitch realized now that he was the sole parent for this motherless child. Eventually the guests began to depart, leaving their paper plates of food crumbs here and there on the tables and chairs. Leo was beginning to say his good-byes. If Meg was going to confront him, the time was now. She left her place beside the wall and walked determinedly toward him.

"Leo Ochs!" she called in a voice uncharacteristically loud. The people who were still there — the ladies in the kitchen, the minister and his wife — stopped when she called out. They watched her walk toward Leo until she stood square in front of him.

"Leo," she said, "I know what you have done to my family. I know what you did to Norma Ann. I hold you solely responsible for her death. I hold you solely responsible for the death of my sister. I will leave this place never, ever to see you again. But be warned, the next time I set eyes on you, the next time I see your face, it will be to put you in prison!"

The room was hushed. The ladies in the kitchen held their dish towels and looked at each other. The minister, after a moment's hesitation, cleared his throat and started to step forward. Leo looked at Meg, smiled, bowed slightly and said, "Madam, may God forgive you for your anger."

A few months later, Meg and Peter moved to New York state. Meg kept her promise. She never saw Leo again.

"Until now," said Meg, turning to Margaret. "When he sees me he will know what I'm here for."

"We're not even sure Leo and Dolly are still here," said Margaret, making a left turn into Bosuns Harbor. "They could've gone back to Portsmouth for all I know. And if they're still here, well, we're just going to have to be great actors. You ever take drama in school?"

"Never."

"Me neither. I guess we're going to have to fake it. But we're not going there to confront Leo Ochs. Hopefully we won't even see him. We're going to see Sylvia about Donna and Bradley as a favor to my neighbor."

Sylvia answered the doorbell. She looked at Meg, and a look of amazement filled her face. She put her glasses on.

"Sylvia, Aunt Meg is visiting for a few days and she decided to come with me tonight. We're looking for Donna."

The woman's eyes went from Meg to Margaret and back again. "Meg, my goodness."

"Hello, Sylvia. It's nice to see you again."

"We're really here to see Donna," Margaret said.

"I told you on the phone, Donna isn't here." Sylvia didn't invite them in, but left them standing on the porch in the dark.

"And you don't know where she is."

"Of course I know where she is."

"Then where is she?"

Sylvia's eyes would not meet Margaret's.

Margaret said, "You don't know where she is."

"She's in Bangor."

"Well, that's nice, because she has Bradley with her. We're here because Ruth is beside herself with worry."

Sylvia put a trembling hand to her cheek. There was a moment's pause before she said, "I don't know where she is. Exactly."

"Could he be in Bangor with her?"

"Perhaps. I doubt it."

"But she stayed overnight last night."

"I don't know . . ."

Lights came on in the back of the house, and Leo's booming voice was unmistakable. Sylvia, her hands visibly shaking, whispered to them, "You'd better go."

Margaret stood her ground. Remembering something Donna had said to her on their ill-fated trip to Bangor, she said, "Sylvia, has Donna ever gone overnight to Bangor before?"

Sylvia shook her head and looked toward the ground.

"You're worried about her, aren't you?" Meg asked.

"She's a grown woman. There wasn't a day went by she didn't threaten to leave. But she never left in the morning when she wasn't back that same evening."

"Why did she never leave home after all these years?" Margaret asked.

"She had problems. Numerous breakdowns. She's had to be hospitalized." Her voice was quiet, seemed to trail off at the end.

"Why?" Meg said. "What caused those breakdowns?"

Margaret was surprised at the force her aunt's voice had taken on, and she cautioned her with her eyes.

"Do you have any idea where she might be in Bangor?" Margaret asked.

"She would never go beyond the city limits. I'm worried something happened. She would never stay overnight."

"Does Monty know?" asked Margaret.

She nodded. "He says she's a grown woman, able to make up her own mind, that's what he says."

"But she's taken a disabled man along with her," Meg said.

"He's a grown man, too," said Sylvia very quietly. The voices from the back grew louder. Leo and Monty were walking toward the door. "You'd better go. Now."

But they were not quick enough. Margaret heard Leo's booming voice. "Sylvia, you didn't tell me we had company." Leo was walking toward them down the dimly lit hallway. "And why's it so dark in this place, you forget to pay the elec-

313

tric bill this month?" He flicked the switch as he passed it, sending brightness into the foyer. "Well, well," he said, looking at the two women on the porch. "If it isn't my lovely niece Margaret, and oh ho, who do we have here? Who do we have here?"

"Hello, Leo," said Meg calmly.

"Come for a tea party, have we, ladies?"

"They came to visit me, Leo," Sylvia said. "They're looking for Bradley. He seems to be missing."

"And you thought he was here?" said Monty.

"He's with Donna," Margaret said.

Leo's eyes rested on Meg, stayed there. "Meg, Meg, Meg, and you're just here for a casual visit, too, I suppose."

"Yes."

"Well, well, now isn't that interesting. Isn't that something, Sylvia? The widow Mahone all the way from Albany, New York, just come over for a casual visit. That's a drive of, let me see, how many hours? Just to casually visit her niece."

"I'm retired, Leo," said Meg. "I have all the time in the world."

Margaret noticed Clark staring at her open-mouthed. He had been standing behind the two brothers. Now he moved forward.

"Hello, Clark," Meg said.

"Meg," he said.

Leo was talking again. "Oh, Margaret, before you leave, before you go back to your house for your casual visit with your aunt, there's something I need to tell you about sailboats." She looked at him sharply. "Now, if there's one unsafe boat out there, it's got to be a sailboat. They've been known to sink. Right at the dock, Margaret, did you know that? I've heard of it happening. With people in them, even." He snapped his fingers. "Just like that, no warning, and they're down. Let me give you an example. Oh, let's say a thirty-three-foot boat can sink in maybe three minutes. Now, that's hardly enough time for the person sleeping in there to get out. Especially if that person's been foolish enough to lock himself in."

A look of horror crossed Margaret's face, a look no amount of drama school preparation could have disguised. She stared at her uncle. Meg put her arm around her niece. "Let's go," she said quietly to Margaret. She led her away.

"What's the matter with everyone? I'm just giving Margaret a friendly warning about sailboats."

SIXTY-THREE

"Calm down," Meg said to Margaret as they pulled out onto the highway. "Chris isn't even there. He's in Bangor. We know that."

"But what if he came home? What if he's there right now? What if he's on his boat this very minute?"

"But what if he's *not* there, Margaret?"

"I'm so scared." She paused. "And how did Leo know about Chris? I don't understand any of this."

"Margaret, do you know which marina his boat is moored at?"

"No, I don't. I just know it's in Belfast. I've never been there."

"When we get home, we can phone all the marinas in Belfast. There can't be too many. Maybe someone can tell us if he's there or if he's still in Bangor."

Margaret let out her breath and drove home through the rain.

Back home Meg said, "You sit. I'm going to make the call. Then I'm going to fix us some nice tea."

She made Margaret sit at the table while she looked up the marinas in Belfast. A few moments later, Meg hung up. "He's not there. He told the office that he'll be away at least a week. I told them that if he arrives home or calls, to get in touch with us immediately before he goes to his boat."

"Thank you, Meg."

Meg put her hand on Margaret's shoulder. "Margaret, everything is going to be all right."

"You don't know that for sure. I hate it when people say that to me."

"You're right, it was a stupid thing to say. What I meant to say is, I have a good feeling about this. I saw something in Leo's face tonight. Fear. He's running, Margaret, and he's getting tired of running. I think if we're careful, he may run out of steam very soon." She sat down and put her hand on Margaret's arm. "Margaret, it's early. I think the two of us have to get out, not sit in this house like a couple of scared old spinsters. I'm here for a casual visit. It should be like a casual visit. I was going to make you some tea, but I think we should go out and have tea instead."

"That's the last thing I feel like right at the moment."

"And that's just what Leo wants, to keep us captive in this old house with its gazillion locks."

Reluctantly Margaret rose. "But we're supposed to be helping to find Bradley."

"We'll discuss it over supper. Sylvia thinks they're in Bangor. We'll come up with a plan. But in the meantime, we have to have that casual visit. You're too shaky to think about Bradley. I'll drive. You just tell me where."

A few minutes later, Margaret had splashed cold water on her face, combed her hair, and stuck a couple of hoops into her ears. Before they left she checked her phone messages. There were two: Roland calling from Freeport with some information about Anna Coffin, and Robin, wanting her to please call. Meg descended the stairs while Margaret rewound the tape. Both of them could wait.

The downpour had downgraded itself into an uncomfortable cold mist, and on the way Margaret said, "You were the one who was so nervous before. Now you seem quite calm."

Meg smiled. "It was seeing Leo, after all these years, realizing that he's just a man, a frightened little man running from his own shadow, making threats. I realize he has no power over me at all. What he has done must have eaten away at him all these years. Didn't he look terrible to you? What filled his mind with so much hate? I'd like to ask him that sometime."

"I hope when you get to ask him he's sitting behind a Plexiglas screen and you're talking to him on a two-way phone."

Meg smiled and glanced at her niece. "Now, be sure to tell me where to turn here."

"It's a great place, best coffee in town. And they have tea, too."

Wellingtons was packed as Margaret poured herself a coffee and found Earl Grey tea for Meg. Margaret had a veggie sandwich on a toasted bagel and Meg had a slice of spinach quiche. There were no empty tables in the room, but Lorne, Stu, and Vivian invited the women to join them at theirs, moving chairs and tables to make room. Lorne wanted to know who Margaret's attractive friend was, and Vivian said Roland had found some more information about Anna Coffin.

Under the lights, the warmth, the fire in the woodstove, the boots lined up beside it, the happy chatter, Margaret felt she could almost relax. She would almost call these people friends, and none of them knew the real reason why her attractive aunt, who was chatting books with Lorne, was visiting. Margaret felt she had been living on the underside of the world for so long that she had forgotten what the good side felt like, the side where people talked and took care of each other, where uncles didn't abuse nieces and children didn't die and good husbands didn't leave.

"I hope his trip to Freeport was worthwhile," said Margaret to Vivian.

"He said he tried to call you. He has some new leads on Anna Coffin's grave."

"How neat," said Margaret. "That must make him feel quite good."

"I know I'm speaking out of turn — I know Roland wanted to tell you this himself — but he wants to do a whole book on Anna Coffin, and he wants you to illustrate it for him."

Margaret took a bite of her toasted veggie bagel. "You heard about my break-in? It may be a while before I get to these pictures of Anna Coffin."

"Break-in!" said Lorne, looking at her.

"Yes." She would remain casual. If the police thought it was random vandalism, well, she'd go along with it. Casual, casual. "Some kids, or at least the police think they were kids, broke into my house and destroyed my newest — actually, my only, so far — painting of Anna."

"You weren't hurt?" Stu said. "Was anything of value taken?"

"Nothing, just a whole lot of headache, believe me!"

"Kids!" said Vivian, shaking her head. "We're so afraid of that at the museum. The board decided to install a security system. We have so many valuable things that could be vandalized. Why do kids these days do this?"

Dr. Stoniard, who had been stoking the fire, sat down heavily and said that in his opinion, the best, most effective security system was a good dog.

"But if the dog attacks, then the vandals will sue," said Vivian. "I've heard cases of that happening. A crazy world we live in when the criminals get to sue the people they're criminalizing."

"And win," added Stu.

Margaret and her aunt stayed for another hour, drinking more coffee and tea and sampling the fig squares Isabelle

Stoniard said were "to die for." They talked about books, vandalism, which dogs made the best watchdogs, and what could really be done to keep one's house safe in this day and age.

SIXTY-FOUR

Meg was back. Clark let his mind move around that thought for a while. There was something different about Meg now. She seemed more like the old Meg, the knowledgeable, purposeful Meg he knew from college days, rather than the enraged Meg of Hannah's sickness days. The last time he had seen Meg had been at Hannah's funeral, and she had been completely unapproachable, even to him.

He rubbed his hands back across his balding head. Seldom did he allow himself to think about Meg, the memories filling him with a kind of pain that would not go away. They were both art students at the University of Maine, the same age and in many of the same classes. Clark could see her even now, long hair flying under her red beret, her black art portfolio under her arm, striding purposefully across the campus. She always had that air of someone who knew exactly where she was going and what she wanted out of life. In a time when women went to college to find husbands, Meg let it be known that she never planned on getting married. Her dream was to teach art in high school, denouncing most public school art programs as "dismal." At a time when other women students were teasing their hair into beehives and lining their eyes with black, Meg's light brown hair was perfectly straight and hung to her waist. She wore a lot of red in those days: a small red beret cocked to one side of her head, red tights, penny loafers, and a red wool car coat. And at a time when most young people were jiving to the music of Elvis and Chuck Berry, Meg would take the Greyhound to New York City to listen to

Thelonious Monk and Miles Davis.

Clark was shy, uncertain of his artistic talents in those days, having grown up in a household where playing football and getting what you wanted, which usually meant the captain of the cheerleading squad, was revered foremost. Clark didn't particularly like sports, which proved to be a constant sore spot between him and his father. The domineering Ernie Ochs told Clark that pursuing a career in the arts was a sissy occupation, and would get him nowhere fast. Ernie Ochs vowed not to put even a dime toward his son's education. As a result, Clark worked hard to support himself through school. On weekends he waited tables at a local pizza place that was one of the university hangouts. For weeks he would see Meg come in, surrounded by her group of eclectic friends. They would sit at one of the larger tables, eat pizza, drink beer, and spend the evening solving the world's problems. He knew who she was, of course. Everyone did. But to her, Clark was just the pizza waiter.

That all changed one evening in late fall. He was carrying a tray of half a dozen beers when she looked up at him. "Aren't you Clark Ochs?"

He nodded.

"You," she said in a loud voice and pointing her finger, "are a wonder and a treasure."

He smiled awkwardly.

"No, I mean it. Your life drawings are absolutely exquisite."

Shy, he smiled.

"You possess a gift that is remarkable."

He felt his face turning red, especially when others in the packed establishment were now turning their heads in his direction. He excused himself and fled to the kitchen.

When he got off work at two that morning, she was sitting

on the cement ledge outside the restaurant waiting for him. She apologized for embarrassing him. He said that was okay. She said that that was her biggest problem, just blurting out what was on her mind. He said that was okay. She said it was one thing to know your own mind and not be afraid to say it, it was quite another when you embarrassed people in the process. He said that was okay. They walked, talked, and ended up going to a coffee house she knew, where they listened to a local jazz group until almost dawn.

This became the pattern of their lives, meeting after his work, walking and talking art and jazz. She seemed to know an awful lot about a lot of things, and he felt totally unsophisticated in her presence. He knew, and it was well understood, that Meg wasn't looking for a husband or any kind of relationship; she said it often enough — "nothing other than platonic." Like a fool he believed her. She became a sister to him and he her brother. Their relationship was clearly defined, by her, and if he wanted to be with her, he had no choice but to go along. When he wasn't working they visited art galleries and went to New York to attend concerts in the Village. She once told him, "If I were going to think about getting married — I'm not, of course, but if I were — you would be the sort of person I would marry." That gave him hope.

Their friendship lasted four years. When they graduated, she went on to teach school and he moved back to Bosuns Harbor. They kept in touch by letter. Her resolve not to marry didn't last very long, however, and a year later she wrote that she was engaged to Peter Mahone, a grad student in philosophy. "You should meet him, dear brother Clark. I'm sure you'd approve." Clark ripped the letter into little pieces and threw it away.

When Monty dropped his current girlfriend, Pat, for the richer and better-heeled Sylvia, she went to Clark on the rebound. On the rebound himself, the two of them married before the year was out. Meg still wanted to keep in touch, however, even after Clark was married. She addressed her many letters to him as "My favorite brother Clark." He wrote to her for a time, "My sister Meg," until even this hurt too much.

And now she was back. It was funny seeing her after all these years. It was as if she hadn't changed at all. She was just as pretty as in the olden days, still the same soft brown hair, the color of elm mixed with maple, with only a bit of gray flecked here and there now.

While Clark had been reveling in his remembrances, Leo had been storming around the house in a foul mood. "What's *she* doing here?" he yelled. Sylvia, the only female in that company of men, stood in the dining room, her hands clasped together in front of her, trembling, frowning.

Monty was talking now. "Leo, Leo, calm down, get ahold of yourself."

"I just want to know what she's doing here!" he bellowed. A spot of spittle formed at the corner of his mouth.

"She's just here for a visit, that's all," Monty protested.

Leo pointed a finger at him. "Yeah, and what do you know about it? What about you and your dirty little secret? Do you want the whole world to know about *that?*"

Sylvia uttered a small gasp, covered her mouth with her hand, and fled to the kitchen.

SIXTY-FIVE

In Bangor, Chris and Bill were working round the clock, rounding up women who'd been abused by Leo when they were younger, rounding up those who'd been blackmailed by Leo, persuading them to testify. He was sure that very soon they would have enough to make the charges stick.

"He's slick," Bill said.

"That's why all this evidence has to be absolutely impeccable."

There was one bit of evidence Chris needed. He hadn't shared his suspicions with Margaret, but in reviewing the twenty-five-year-old file on Norma Ann's accidental death, a few things didn't add up. He remembered how distraught young Bradley was, and how at the time his mother refused to let him talk. But when he did talk it was about the "bad people" on the beach. And now Bradley was missing. He found that bit of information by calling Arnie at the ceramic factory. He spent a lot of time talking to Arnie. He was hoping Arnie would be the link that would get Bradley to talk. Certainly not his mother. Arnie said that Bradley had taken off with Donna. Chris had met Donna briefly, only seen her from a distance, really, but that relationship was one that made him shake his head. From what he saw, Donna didn't seem the type to want to care for a retarded man. Chris needed Donna as well. He had no idea where they'd gone, but he discovered that they stayed at the Scotsman Inn in Bangor the first night, and he had spoken to the proprietor there. But after that, where?

By this time Chris was working on coffee and adrenaline and had called in favors from practically every friend he'd ever known.

SIXTY-SIX

In less than two hours Donna and Bradley were in Houlton, Maine, and there were signs pointing to the Canadian border. Donna was surprised at this. She figured that Canada, being another country, had to be very, very far away. She hadn't been outside Maine since she was a small child, when her family would drive down to Boston and Martha's Vineyard. But that was a long time ago. Her hands tensed on the wheel. She could scarcely believe she had come this far. She allowed herself to think ahead, just a little bit. She had money. She and Bradley could live in Canada. Maybe when her money ran out she could work. She would get Bradley enrolled in a better school than that stupid ceramic factory. But first, she had to tell Bradley why he was with her.

"Bradley." She turned to him, but he was sleeping, his head back against the seat, drooling slightly. That would be the first thing she would do, make sure he got some exercise. Walking, they would walk together. Not by the ocean, but down paths and roads near their new house. Maybe they would get horses. Maybe they would both learn to ride horses. Or bicycles.

She didn't know what to expect at the crossing into Canada, and her hands shook as she neared the booth. When it was her turn she pulled forward.

"Citizens of what country?" asked the lady at the booth.

"What?"

"What country are you citizens of?"

"Maine."

"Both of you? American citizens?"

"Yes."

"Where are you going?"

"To Canada."

"Where in Canada?"

"Do you have to know that? We're not sure. We're just going for a visit. To see the fall trees," she added as an afterthought.

The woman stopped suddenly, looked at the two in the car, looked across to Bradley, shuffled some papers and said, "Are you Donna Ochs?"

"Me?" Did they really know the name of everyone who crossed into Canada?

The lady came out of her booth and checked the license plate of Donna's car and then looked at a piece of paper that she held. She came to Donna's car window.

"Is that Bradley Godwish?"

When Donna nodded, the lady said, "Could you just pull in here for a minute?"

"Yes, this is Bradley, but I've every right to travel with him."

"Can you just park up there for a minute?"

"Why?"

"I've got a notice here that you're wanted in some sort of police investigation."

"Me? I didn't do anything." Kidnapping! Could she be in trouble because she wanted a better life for Bradley?

"The information I have here is about a police investigation. Can you come in for a minute? Just pull up over there. You're supposed to call a police officer in Bangor."

Donna thought momentarily about driving away and hiding from Ruth, who was obviously behind all of this. Nervous, shaking uncontrollably, she parked her little car in the indicated space. Somehow she managed to get out of the driver's seat. Bradley slept on.

When she walked into the office the woman handed her a phone. The man on the other end identified himself as a detective named Chris Rikken. What did he have to do with Ruth Godwish, she wanted to ask, but didn't. It was all about Leo, he told her. Donna said nothing. He begged her not to hang up and not to be afraid, either, that he understood why she was running, but that they had come up with a lot of people who were willing to testify against Leo Ochs, that they were building a case against him one block at a time. They had other women, women who worked for him when they were younger. He used to hire young teen girls in his hardware stores, and he had a lot who were willing to testify. Would Donna be willing to?

"I don't know what you're talking about," she said.

"I think you do. I know you've been hurt. We have a journal of Norma Ann's; that journal alone would be enough to lay charges, but we're looking for real people here. We've got a number who are willing to testify to blackmail, too. Please don't hang up, Donna. There's another reason why I need to talk to you. I need to see Bradley."

"What does Bradley have to do with it?"

"I was there when he found your cousin's body. At the time he kept talking about the bad people. I believe Leo may have been responsible for Norma Ann's death. A charge of murder would get him put away for a long, long time. But I need to talk to Bradley."

"Bradley's sleeping now."

"Could you wake him?"

"No, he needs his rest."

"Donna, this is important."

"I'm going to take care of him now. I'm going to take

care of my brother."

Silence. Chris said, "What?"

"My brother. Did you know that? We have the same father. I'm a good detective, too, Mr. Rikken. That's why I took him with me. My mother wouldn't hear of letting this out, that my father had an affair with Ruth Godwish and that his son was a retard. That's what Sylvia says: 'Do you want everyone to know that your only son is a retard?' I've heard her talk like that. So, all he does is give money for Bradley's school each month. But I'm taking care of him now."

"Well . . . this is news, isn't it? But could I talk to him? Could I talk to both of you?"

"I don't think so. We're on our way to Canada."

"What will you do there?"

"Live in a house. Get Bradley into a better school. Maybe work."

"You need landed-immigrant status to work there."

"I'll get it."

"It's not that easy. Donna, can I meet you and Bradley in Houlton? I can be there in a couple hours. Can you wait? This is vitally important. I'd like you to wait for us at the police station."

Donna was quiet for a minute. The man really sounded sincere. Could he really put Leo away? But what if this was a great big trick of Leo's? Could she trust him?

"Okay, but not the police station. How about Pizza Hut? My brother and I can have something to eat while we wait."

"I'll be bringing Arnie with me. He knows Bradley."

"He's pond scum."

"Donna, I've talked to Arnie about this. He feels that in the right setting, Bradley might talk. He talks to Bradley a lot. If anyone can get through to him, I believe Arnie can. If you don't permit it, you will be just like Ruth, trying to protect him, not letting people talk to him. Getting this out, seeing Leo arrested, may be a healing thing for him. Did you ever think of that? Bradley's a grown man; he can make up his mind. Part of his problem is that everyone around him has over-protected him. Donna, don't be another Ruth. Don't mother him. If you are his sister, be a sister, not a mother."

Donna held the receiver tightly. "Okay," she said quietly. "Pizza Hut in two and a half hours."

"We'll be there."

SIXTY-SEVEN

"It's the waiting that's the most difficult," said Margaret to her aunt as the two of them walked along the beach in the morning mist. Meg had found a piece of driftwood she was using as a walking stick. They were heading toward the point.

"Chris has done this thing before, Margaret. We just have to trust and pray that things will work out."

The bay had a glassy sheen to it; it was misty, and the rocks they walked upon were wet with it. Margaret could feel the wetness seeping through her canvas shoes. In the distance a foghorn sliced through the thick salt air with its mournful warning.

"It's lovely here," Meg said. "That Peter and I moved inland is still a mystery to me. I should have never left this shore."

"You could buy my house," Margaret said.

"Nonsense. You'll be back. You and Robin will be back. You've got to come back to illustrate that book now."

"Ah yes, Anna Coffin. This is where I saw her," said Margaret, pointing. "Both times. The ghost of Anna Coffin."

Meg smiled. "It's kind of neat to own a house with a ghost attached. If it were mine, I'd never let it go."

"Now there's a place for you," said Margaret, pointing towards Rusty MacGregor's abandoned cabin.

"Is it for sale?"

"I was just kidding. The place is a wreck. Look at it — boarded-up windows, it needs paint, porch sagging into the dunes, plus it's way too small for you."

"I'm a small person."

"Do you remember the old guy who lived here?"

"A picture comes to mind of a gray-haired woolly old salt who caught his own fish and set his own lobster traps."

"He died some years back," Margaret said. "The place has been abandoned since then."

"But is it for sale?"

"I have no idea."

"Why don't we go have a look?" Meg was already heading up toward the structure. Sand grasses and rocks around the front gave the place a sorrowful, neglected look. It was small and square, a cabin, really, and not a house at all, certainly a far cry from the grand mansions down the waterfront.

"This place has possibilities," Meg said.

"If you're thinking of kindling, maybe."

"Look." Meg was standing next to the structure, her arms spread across the boards. "It's beautiful. You should paint this."

"It needs paint, that's for sure."

"No, I mean as a painting. A watercolor. It's exquisite."

"This place?"

"This place."

"Why don't *you* paint it, then?"

"Maybe I will. After I buy it. I could set up my loom in the front room."

"Your loom would take up the whole room."

"This could be the beginnings of a nice little home, a little addition here and there, of course, trying never to alter the basic design of the place."

Margaret looked sideways at her aunt. "I hate to break it to you, Meg, but this place doesn't have any design."

"Yes, it does. Rustic. Can we get inside, do you suppose?"

"Meg, you're not serious."

"You don't expect such daring from an old widow lady, do

333

you? Let's see if we can get in."

The two women walked around to the back. Margaret saw fresh tire tracks. "Someone's been here."

"Probably the place for some lovers' secret rendezvous."

"Always the romantic," Margaret said. "Here I'm thinking about a pirate's secret drug stash and you're thinking lovers. And speaking of lovers' secret rendezvous, how come you never got married again after Peter died?"

She laughed lightly. "I'm far too eccentric for any male on this planet."

"Peter married you."

"He was an exception."

Margaret turned back to the house. On tiptoe she peered into the bottom part of the window. "It has furniture," she said. "I can see furniture."

"Maybe it's occupied."

"Not that I know of," said Margaret, who knocked loudly on the door anyway. "I've never seen anyone here."

Meg ran her hands over the door ledge and all around. Finally she produced a key from underneath a rock near the door. "Ta da. The old key under the rock trick."

"You're not really going to go in?"

"Why not? I'm a potential customer."

"I don't believe it."

"Are you coming with me or not?"

"You're crazy," said Margaret, shaking her head but following her anyway.

Inside was one room, with a woodstove on the north wall, and on the woodstove a large rusty kettle. To the right was a single bed covered with a gray wool blanket. There was a rocking chair, too, an old broken-down cane one, and along the front window was a couch, which was leaking stuffing. Margaret thought of mice. Cupboards on one wall contained a few dishes, along with a few packages of dried soup and tea bags. Meg was running the water in the tiny bathroom. "I can't believe the plumbing still works. And look, hardwood floors."

"Aunt Meg, you can't put old logs on the ground and call it a hardwood floor."

"A little buffing, a little sanding is all it needs."

"A lot of buffing and a lot of sanding. I can't believe Rusty MacGregor actually lived here all those years."

At the foot of the bed was a large rectangular box made of wood. At one time it probably held logs for the woodstove. Today it was filled with fabric scraps. Meg was kneeling and examining its contents. "Look," she said, lifting out a piece of cloth. "This place even comes with curtains!"

Margaret walked toward her. "Let me see."

As Margaret laid out the white fabric on the bed, she stopped, stunned. "These aren't curtains. These are the clothes of Anna Coffin! Of the ghost of Anna Coffin!" Excitedly she reached into the box for more — a pale dress and a long white shawl. Underneath and wrapped in a piece of cloth was a flute, and then a long wig. Underneath she found more clothes, clothes resembling the ones Margaret had found in the boxes Chris brought.

"It couldn't be her white shawl preserved like this after all these years," said Meg.

At the bottom of the pile Margaret found the answer. She held up a yellow wig, black leather pants, leather gloves. "Donna," she said. "Donna is Anna Coffin." She sat down on the bed. "Donna. I should have known."

"Donna who has taken Bradley?"

"The same," said Margaret, holding up a set of black driving gloves. "The very same. She must come in here and get dressed and then wander around the beach. That's why I couldn't catch up to her that time."

"But why?" asked her aunt.

"I have no idea." Margaret was sitting on the lumpy bed, the white shawl on her knees. She examined it in her fingers. It was just a white bedsheet, not a piece of embroidered cloth from India. And the flute was a child's toy. "I should have known. She loves dressing up. She was always telling me that. She is a lady with problems."

"Makes you wonder what kind of person she would've turned out to be if Leo hadn't abused her," Meg said.

SIXTY-EIGHT

Clark was arranging a display of floor tiles when the police came. From where he stood he could see three patrol cars pull up quietly at the front of the store. Leo had been in a bad temper all morning. Monty had to physically restrain him from firing one of the stock boys who mistakenly unloaded a box in the wrong receiving bay. Later Monty apologized to the young man.

All morning Leo had been talking about leaving. The sooner the better, he kept saying, get out of this one-horse town. At noon he was going to pick up Dolly and head down to Portsmouth. "Gotta see what kind of state they left *that* store in," he grumbled. "I come up here and the place is falling apart around me. I put a lot of my own money into this business, and all I've got is a bunch of incompetents running it for me."

Leo was in Monty's office with the door closed when the officers came into the store and asked for Leo Ochs.

"Right back there. No problem," said Clark cheerfully. "Knock twice. If no one answers just walk in. That's what I do. That's the code."

Clark felt in good spirits, and it was with a bit of amusement that he watched the cops walk with purposeful steps toward Monty's office. He had already decided that this was his last day on the job. He hadn't told Leo and Monty yet. Actually, he was waiting for Leo to leave. Then he'd tell Monty.

Seeing Meg had done one thing for him, and that was to get him to rethink the direction of his life. He was fifty-eight

337

years old, but he could still carve. He could still set up that studio and war museum in Bosuns Harbor. And this time, he wasn't going to let Monty, Leo, or Pat get in the way. Not this time. Not ever again.

The cops walked into Monty's office without knocking. Clark smiled a little. Income tax evasion? Some sort of bankruptcy thing? He wouldn't put it past his eldest brother. Clark didn't figure Leo made all his money by being an honest hardworking joe.

But when he listened to the list of charges being read to his eldest brother, he stood fixed to the spot, unable to move. Murder? Two counts? Norma Ann Ochs? (Murder?) And Jon Smith. (Who was Jon Smith?) Sexual assault, rape, blackmail. A hint of a smile formed on Clark's lips. There was a part of him, a deep-down part that was not surprised. Clark regained enough of his composure to usher the few stunned customers out the door and put up the closed sign. Already TV news vans were pulling up.

Clark locked the door and walked toward Monty's office in time to hear the police officers say, "You have the right to remain silent . . ." Clark looked toward Monty. A handcuffed Leo was being led away, and he was yelling loudly, "You'll hear from my lawyers on this one. I'll turn around and sue you for false arrest so fast your head will spin. Monty, call the lawyer, will ya? Don't just stand there, get me out of this!"

But Monty just stood there.

After Leo had been taken away and Clark relocked the door, he walked back to Monty's office. "Are you going to call a lawyer?"

There was an odd tone in Monty's voice when he answered. "He's got one phone call. Let *him* call his own lawyer."

Then Monty sat down behind his desk, put his head in his

hands, and began to sob. For a while Clark stood there, then he said, "Monty, you want to tell me what's going on here?"

"There's so much you don't know, little brother."

"Apparently."

"It'll all come out now. There's no stopping it now."

"What will all come out now?"

"It's about time he got what's coming to him. For all these years I've let him control my life. Mine and Sylvia's. I'd do any little thing he said. If I didn't follow his every whim he'd threaten me with the one thing he held over my head. All these years. All these many long years."

Clark was silent. He pulled up a chair and sat down across from his brother. He felt that Monty wanted him to stay there and hear him out.

Monty said, "I knew all these years that Leo murdered Norma Ann. I came to the house, Mitch and Hannah's, to try to persuade him to just let her be. She was pregnant, you know. By Leo. He demanded that she have an abortion."

Clark raised his eyebrows, staring open-mouthed at his brother.

"Norma Ann was a feisty little thing. The night before she had come to Leo's house. I was there at the time — he didn't know it, I had come on store business — and I heard their whole conversation. He demanded that she get an abortion, and she said no, that she was afraid. She went running out past me, holding one of your little carved figures. 'This will prove that I was here today,' she was saying. 'It'll prove that I was here.'

"And she left. I could hear Leo grousing around, you know the way he does. He was miserable the next day at the store, and I followed him out to Mitch and Hannah's that evening. I followed him up to the third floor, and as God is my witness, I saw him shove Norma Ann off the balcony.

339

When he turned and saw me, just about the first thing he said was that if I told anyone about what I'd seen, that he'd tell everyone my secret."

Clark looked steadily at him, waited.

"But now it'll come out. And if Sylvia leaves me, she leaves me. But I love her. What will I do if she leaves me?"

Clark said nothing, could think of nothing to say, and Monty's next few words shocked him to the core.

"Bradley Godwish is my son." He said it simply, plainly. "It was many, many years ago." Monty was wiping his face now with a white handkerchief. He was still crying. "It was before Sylvia and I were married. Ruth Godwish and I had an affair. I was still going with Pat at the time, but it was a confused time for me, for everyone. I thought I loved Ruth then."

Clark continued to stare. The idea of his brother and Ruth Godwish, the idea of *anyone* and Ruth Godwish.

"Strange how life goes sometimes," Monty said. "I was already engaged to Sylvia when Ruth came to me and said she was pregnant. Well, there was nothing I could do. She was just a poor girl from the wrong side of the tracks. There was no way I could break with Sylvia and marry Ruth. No way at all. Dad just hit the roof. There was nothing I could do. I bought that house next to Mitch and Hannah's for them, and I've provided for Bradley and his mother down through the years. I haven't shirked my responsibility. Not one little bit. Not ever. Sylvia found out about Bradley when he was about two. She was furious, hurt. She demanded that no one ever find out about this, and that if it ever became public, she would leave me. I've kept my promise to her all these years. That's what Leo's held over my head, over both our heads all this time."

He put his head on the desk and wept.

SIXTY-NINE

"He did it," Margaret said to her aunt that evening. They were sitting on Margaret's bed, eating sandwiches and watching the six o'clock news. "Chris really did it. I was worried that he wouldn't be able to pull it off, but he did."

Earlier that day Chris had called with the news that he had found Donna and Bradley. Arnie had gone with Chris and had gotten Bradley to admit that he saw Leo and Monty drive away from Norma Ann's house at the time of her death. "We brought Monty in for questioning shortly after we arrested Leo. Man, you should hear his story. Monty's testimony will be the one that puts Leo away for good."

"Monty testified?"

"Monty saw Leo push your sister through the railing."

"Why didn't he ever say anything?"

When Chris told Margaret about Bradley and Monty she said, "So that's why Donna took off with Bradley. He's her brother." She paused. "She's the ghost, you know."

"The ghost?"

"She's the one who dresses up as Anna Coffin and goes roaming the beach."

"That makes sense, sort of. Arnie's been talking to her. Seems she really identified with your sister . . . I guess they were pretty close. I kind of got the whole story from the investigator. After Norma Ann died, Leo went on to abuse Donna. Apparently Monty and Sylvia knew about it but didn't do anything. This whole Bradley thing was hanging over their heads big time."

341

"Why would any parent, a mother especially, not intervene when a daughter is being abused? I'd have moved heaven and earth if something like that were happening to Aislin."

"There was a whole lot of denial going on. Plus, this was twenty-five years ago, and things like this didn't happen to nice families. I think Sylvia knew but didn't quite believe. She never really questioned the whole thing too deeply. I think she thought all the therapy Donna was getting would somehow fix it. That's the sense my cop friend Bill had."

Margaret shook her head. There were no words to say.

"Donna identified with Norma Ann, and since Norma Ann identified with Anna Coffin . . . maybe that's why Donna dressed up as Anna. She said she would think about walking into the sea and not coming back."

"Just like Anna Coffin."

"The thought of Bradley kept her from killing herself. He was her brother and seemed to be her only link with reality. And oh, by the way, it *was* Leo who destroyed your picture and made that offer on your house. He wanted you out of the picture, felt you were finding too much out. And Ruth Godwish is a part of this mix, too. She, like Bradley, saw Leo and Monty leave on the day of Norma Ann's death, but was afraid her monthly payment for Bradley would dry up if she told anyone."

"This is so unbelievable."

"Just watch the news tonight. I called all the media. Get as much public humiliation for Leo as possible."

It was strange now for Margaret to be watching her Uncle Leo on TV. She could see him spitting and cursing as he was led handcuffed into the police car. A reporter was standing in front of Bosuns Harbor Building Supplies speaking into a microphone. "It may be a long time before all the pieces to this

342

bizarre case are put into place."

Meg folded her hands in front of her, almost in an attitude of prayer. Her eyes were glistening. She sat very still. "It's over," she whispered. "I have finally kept my promise to my sister." She paused. "But I wish it felt better. Somehow I thought it would."

SEVENTY

On the day two weeks later when Chris left, the sky was a peculiar mass of color: ash yellow, dun brown, pale pink. It was as if someone had taken handfuls of beach sand and flung them into the sky. Margaret had driven down to the marina in the sunshine to see Chris off. He was tightening something on the side of the boat and smiled when he saw her.

She sensed an ambivalence in him, a sadness when he saw her, but there was a smile on his face nonetheless. She wondered at his smile until the sea wind touched her face. Then she knew. He was leaving. Soon it would be him alone with the salt swells, the wind in the sails, flying fish, the whales, the Sargasso Sea, and the Trades.

I pray for solitude.

"Thank you, Chris," she said. "None of this could have happened without you."

"The great PI saves the day, unties the fair damsel from the railroad tracks just in the nick of time." He was grinning, and she thought of the first time he had brought muffins to her door. That same grin. "Come on aboard. I'll show you around."

She was surprised at how nicely outfitted it was. "You even have a TV. And look at all your books."

"I stock up on paperbacks before I go."

"You have so much room here."

"Well, it is my home, so it's got to have some creature comforts."

"You're leaving soon," she said. "I don't want to keep you."

344

"There's a good offshore breeze out there. I want to take advantage of it."

"I'm glad I didn't miss you."

"I'm glad, too," he said.

Out in the cockpit of the boat and under the warm sun, he hugged her for a long time. "I'll never forget you, Margaret."

Then he helped her back up on the dock, where he began loosening the mooring lines. She watched his lean body perform these ministrations with ease. He got in and started the motor.

"Find God," she said to him as he undid the last mooring line and cast off.

"I will," he called back. She watched him steer the craft expertly through the maze of buoys and fishing boats. Just before he left the harbor, he turned and waved. She waved back. She watched him, a tiny figure now, scramble on deck, and then a majestic unfurling of white. When the sails caught the wind, the boat heeled slightly and headed away from her. She stood and watched and watched until the boat was just a speck of white on a blue horizon.

Then she turned and walked up to her car.

EPILOGUE

Three weeks after Leo was arrested, Margaret was sitting on her front porch, her hands on her knees, watching the sun glint off the water. Meg was inside finishing up the last of her packing. They would be leaving in about an hour. Margaret's eventual destination was Fredericton, but she planned to spend a few days with her aunt in New York. Robin was taking the bus down from Fredericton to meet her there, then they would drive home together the long way.

"You'll love my aunt," she had said to her husband the previous night when they talked on the phone. "She's really special."

"I can't wait to meet her then."

It was late when she had lain in bed, the blue spread to her chin, the phone cradled beside her, talking to Robin. The night and its stars illuminated her darkened room.

He said, "On the way home we can look at the trees. We can stop if you want. We're in no rush."

"I'd like that."

"Do you remember the man who made those model ships?"

"The *Bluenose*. I remember."

"I remember those apple fritters his wife made."

"It was apple crisp. Apple crisp and cream."

"Those were favorite times for me. Especially when we stopped so you could sketch. I'd be sitting there at a picnic table pretending to be reading my book, but I'd be watching you and the very intense expression you get on your face. And

346

I would think to myself that you were the smartest and most beautiful person on the face of the earth. And that I was the luckiest guy alive."

"Maybe we can go back there," she said.

"To the place with the model ships or to that time?"

"Both."

"I think we should make it a priority. To go back there."

"I want to start over again," she said. "I want to see if we can. But I have to start from the very beginning. I'm figuring out who God is for myself, Robin. Not the God of your family or the God of your family's church, not even the God of you. I need to know God for myself."

A pause. "I understand that. I do. For all of my life I've gone to church, sang in the choir, done the right 'churchy' things. I knew the routine. I knew the dance. But when the hard times came, the church wasn't enough. I realized then that my faith was in the culture of my church. When you believe in church, when that's all you have, you really have nothing. It may be enough to get you through the good times, but not the bad. It wasn't enough for me. I have to find God for myself, too."

A round white moon shone in her window and covered everything with iridescence. It was almost as if the bedspread were liquid.

"I never knew that about you," she said.

"It was hard for me to tell you those things. I felt it was my responsibility to be the strong one, the whole 'head of the house' thing, but I got too tired and too scared, and I just couldn't do it anymore. In some ways I envied you. You at least could be honest about your feelings and quit church if you felt like it. I couldn't — or at least I felt I couldn't — not with my family, not with my father the chairman of the church board, not with the reputation of the famous

347

Collinwood name. My anger against God finally came out in another way — as anger against you. It was wrong and cowardly of me to leave." He paused. She said nothing, just held the receiver with both hands and stared out at the moon. Then he said, "There's a beautiful moon here."

"A full moon," she said quietly.

"I love you, Margaret."

She thought about Robin as she sat on the weathered porch with its bleached boards and watched the water gently lap the rocky shore. Maybe there was a place for them to start over. Maybe she and Robin would come back in the summer. Maybe they would make it a yearly thing. Maybe Meg would buy the cabin on the point. Maybe Bradley would once again join them for walks on the beach. Maybe Donna would start to laugh again.

Yesterday, with Meg's help, she had taken her VCR, TV, her answering machine, and the telephones back to Radio Shack. She got a full refund when she explained her story, which by now was all over the news. She was donating the money she had inherited, all of Leo's money, to victims of abuse. It would go to women's shelters, halfway houses, and education and counseling programs for women. Donna would be the first to receive help. She had changed her bank account into a fund where donations could be made in the name of her sister, Norma Ann Ochs. That had been Meg's idea.

On the water in front of her now, way down by Dragon Back Island, she saw someone frantically rowing toward her in a wide wooden boat. Margaret stood and shaded her eyes. As the figure drew closer she could hear the rhythmic slapping of the oars against the metal oarlocks.

"Margaret!" The person in the boat took off his white safari hat and was waving it wildly. "Margaret!" he called.

Roland? She hurried down toward the beach. It was Roland.

"Roland!" she called, cupping her hands around her mouth. "I haven't seen you in ages!"

"I've got great news," he said. "Something to show you." He had reached the shore now. She pulled up on the bow and he scrambled out, talking all the time. "I've got pictures! Everything!"

Together they pulled the boat above the tide line. "I should have known," he said. "You'd think with all the research I've done that I would know."

She laughed, caught up in the excitement. "You'll have to slow down and tell me what this is all about."

"I've found them. The final chapter can be written now."

"The final chapter of what?"

"I've found the bones of Anna Coffin!"

Out of his jacket pocket he pulled half a dozen Polaroids. "Here it is, her gravesite!"

The years and the wind and the vegetation on the island had all but hidden the little tombstone. But Roland had cleaned aside the vegetation and dirt and had taken a clear shot of the grave marker.

The name on the stone was barely legible, but Margaret read *Anna Coffin 1828-1855*. "Her gravesite!" Margaret said. "But what does it say underneath? I can't make it out."

" 'Woman of the sea, the flute, and the shawl, may she finally find rest with God.' "

"Rest with God, I like that," Margaret said.

"This will be a marvelous book. Your drawings and now this, this final chapter. And to think I was looking in all the wrong places. I just assumed she would be buried on the mainland. I mean, I even wondered if she was buried in your basement, perish the thought. But if I'd given it even a moment's thought, I would've realized she was right there in front of me. Right there all the time."

"Yes," said Margaret, smiling. "Right there all the time."